Ink Wreathcraft

Gadhio Lathcutt

Eterna Rinebow

Flum Apricot

Ottilie Fohkelpi

Milkit

"Th-that's right! I just didn't know what to say after being put into such an awkward position!!"

Sheitoom

Tsyon

"H-hey, we're the ones who should be annoyed here!"

ROLL OVER AND DIE

NOVEL 2

I Will Fight for an Ordinary Life with My Love and Cursed Sword!

STORY BY
kiki

ILLUSTRATED BY
kinta

Airship

Seven Seas Entertainment

ROLL OVER AND DIE: I WILL FIGHT FOR AN ORDINARY LIFE
WITH MY LOVE AND CURSED SWORD! VOL. 2

©kiki 2018
Illustrations by kinta

This edition originally published in Japan in 2018 by
MICRO MAGAZINE, INC., Tokyo.
English translation rights arranged with
MICRO MAGAZINE, INC., Tokyo.

Seven Seas press and purchase enquiries can be sent to
Marketing Manager Lianne Sentar at press@gomanga.com.
Information regarding the distribution and purchase of
digital editions is available from Digital Manager CK Russell
at digital@gomanga.com.

Follow Seven Seas Entertainment online at
sevenseasentertainment.com.

TRANSLATION: Jason Muell
ADAPTATION: Brock Wassman
COVER DESIGN: Nicky Lim
LOGO DESIGN: George Panella
INTERIOR LAYOUT & DESIGN: Clay Gardner
PROOFREADER: Jade Gardner, Stephanie Cohen
LIGHT NOVEL EDITOR: Nibedita Sen
PREPRESS TECHNICIAN: Rhiannon Rasmussen-Silverstein
PRODUCTION MANAGER: Lissa Pattillo
MANAGING EDITOR: Julie Davis
ASSOCIATE PUBLISHER: Adam Arnold
PUBLISHER: Jason DeAngelis

ISBN: 978-1-64505-939-4
Printed in Canada
First Printing: March 2021
10 9 8 7 6 5 4 3 2 1

CONTENTS

3 · The Spiral Children and Their Proliferation of Hate

EPISODE 3

The Spiral Children and Their Proliferation of Hate

ROLL
OVER
AND
DIE

Making Sense of the Nonsensical

SELAYDE, the land of the demons, stretched across the northern reach of the great continent.

The spell-wrought stone buildings were a far cry from the architecture of the human capital as a matter of necessity. Except for the brief respite provided by summer, the lands were constantly blanketed in a fresh dusting of newly fallen snow. Due to the demons' strong magical affinity, there was little in their daily lives that wasn't touched by the power of magic.

The immense, imposing outline of the Demon Lord's castle loomed off in the distance. Its walls were black as pitch and covered in strange engravings. The watchtowers shooting up from the ominous form rose so high that you had to crane your neck just to see their peaks. Just standing before it was enough to fill one with a sense of dread.

In reality, however, the occupants were nowhere near as terrifying as the building's exterior implied.

Three demons sat in the dining room on the first floor, knives and forks in hand, bathed in the gentle glow of candles placed strategically around the room. A roaring fireplace made the room quite comfortable in spite of the bitter cold outside.

One of the room's occupants was Neigass, the hematophage who encountered Flum and Sara back in Anichidey. The weather did little to inspire her to cover up her largely exposed body. Sitting across from her was her fellow Demon Chief Tsyon, the will-o'-the-wisp. The collar of his shirt stood straight up, as if locked in place.

Next to Tsyon sat a young girl dressed in a white gown, her chair so tall that her white heels dangled freely in the air. This was Sheitoom, the Demon Lord. To human eyes, she looked no more than twelve years of age.

Sheitoom spoke up just as Neigass was about to tuck a forkful of meat into her mouth. "How did your investigation of the laboratory go?"

Neigass paused, a slight frown on her face.

The night's entrée was a huge goat sauté accompanied by mushroom sauce. The meal was made by the third and final member of the Demon Chiefs, Dhiza, known as "The Fathomless Mire," whose cooking would have been right at home in even the finest restaurants of the human capital. The meat was tender beyond belief and delectably moist. The juices from the meat mixed with the ever-so-slightly acidic sauce to create a symphony of flavor that practically begged to be devoured.

Considering Neigass skipped lunch so she could savor Dhiza's cooking all the more, this interruption felt like a body blow.

"Nng. I found the materials, as expected. They seem to be about thirty years old. Oh, and I found one of those creatures with a core in it."

This was, of course, the spiral ogre that Flum encountered back in the cave complex.

"I see. Thirty years ago... That'd place it around the time of the human-demon war, yes?"

Sheitoom was referring to the time a human army had invaded their lands. It had been a short-lived battle; no matter how many men they had, the humans stood no chance against the demons' powerful magic. The human troops' morale had been at rock-bottom levels even before the first skirmishes began, which begged the question of what their king had ever planned to achieve with such slipshod tactics.

"My best guess is that they were trying to create a new breed of soldier for the next war," Neigass said.

"Do you think they'll try again?"

"Considering they gave their original, stupid plan a go last time, I don't see why they wouldn't try again if they actually manage to bolster their military might."

"I still don't see why they'd even attack us in the first place..." Sheitoom said.

"The humans are a selfish lot. As long as there's land out there to be had, they'll want to take it."

"I just don't understand what their leaders could possibly be thinking."

"I know, right?"

The last war had been brutal. The demons had done everything they could to minimize human casualties, but the human troops took advantage of this and filled their front lines with child soldiers. The normally peaceful demons, enraged at this reckless behavior, had redoubled their attacks on the remaining adults.

Neigass's discovery only confirmed what had long been whispered of in Selayde.

"There were so many bodies, both human and animal alike, that I lost count. Every one of them had this weird spiral formation on its face. It seems the nature of human leaders never changes."

"All that and they couldn't even control these things? More importantly, where did they find the power to do this?"

Tsyon's voice took on a playful, teasing tone. "Perhaps the Demon Lord's seal is weakening?" he said.

Sheitoom puffed out her cheeks. "Not a chance! I've never had a single seal of mine break, not since I first started my studies! Besides, Dhiza was there with me!"

"Whoa, whoa, no need to get so testy, your Lordy-ness."

"Are you trying to get a rise out of me, Tsyon?? 'Demon Lord' this, 'Lordy-ness' that. Just call me by my name, all right??"

"Hey, you're the one calling us Demon Chiefs; I just figured it sounded right."

"Ugh...it's not like I had a choice. The people are growing frustrated; I needed a diversion."

The demons were generally an even-keeled people, but even their patience had its limits under nearly constant assault. The Demon Chiefs were meant to be the answer to that problem. While they'd been appointed and named as such for the ostensible reasons of fighting the heroes, in truth, they generally moved and acted independently.

"I just don't get the point in giving us such a silly name if it's all for show, anyway."

"I'm really not interested in hearing complaints from a jerk with a popped collar!"

As Sheitoom and Tsyon fell into yet another of their infamous shouting matches, Neigass looked over Sheitoom's shoulder and caught Dhiza's gaze. Dhiza, clad in a tailcoat and wearing a monocle, smiled wryly. The gentle demon had been taken in as an orphan by the Demon Lord several generations ago and served as the family butler ever since.

"Whoa, whoa... Now don't go knockin' my style!" Tyson objected. "I'm a total trendsetter, you hear me?"

"Oh, but I am! What is it with you and popping your collars, anyway? Just imagine what it must feel like to walk around town with you! Seriously, you *might* be good-looking if you tried, but that collar just spoils the whole effect."

"Nnnggg—watch yourself, little missy. You've crossed the line! Why don't we go outside and take a look around town then, huh?"

"With pleasure! I'll gladly expose your tackiness for all to see."

Tsyon and Sheitoom were leaning over the table at this point, their voices rising, when they were interrupted by the sound of Dhiza clearing his throat. The dining room instantly fell silent.

"Quiet at the table, please."

"...Sorry."

"Apologies."

The two quickly settled back into their seats, though they couldn't resist the opportunity to shoot dirty looks at one another. Sensing that another shouting match was about to take off, Dhiza locked eyes with Neigass. She gave a firm nod and thrust forth her hand, palm forward, in Sheitoom's direction, causing the Demon Lord to float up into the air just before she had the chance to snatch some meat off of Tsyon's plate in revenge.

"Whaddya think you're doing, Neigass??" Sheitoom swung her arms and feet around with all her might, but her struggles were no match for Neigass's wind magic. Neigass carried the smaller girl through the air and right over Tsyon before dropping her firmly in his lap. Both Demon Chief and Demon Lord immediately turned a bright shade of red.

"Heh. At least that got you two to quiet down."

"I dunno if I should be happy or disturbed that this was so effective."

"H-hey, we're the ones who should be annoyed here!"

"Th-that's right! I just didn't know what to say after being put into such an awkward position!!"

But despite their protestations, Sheitoom made no effort to get off Tsyon's lap, nor did he make any attempt to evict her.

Neigass continued to press the attack. "You two really haven't changed at all, have you?"

"Like you're one to talk," Tsyon shot back.

"I don't know, Tsyon. You seem to be pretty fond of your title as a Demon Chief, don'tcha? Introducing yourself as 'Tsyon of the Great Demon Chiefs' every time we get into a fight..."

"Is that true?" Sheitoom asked.

Tsyon mumbled for a bit, searching for words. "I, uh, well...I just kinda get carried away up in the heat of things, is all."

He couldn't bring himself to lie to Sheitoom. After all, they'd known each other most of their lives, and he thought of her like a little sister. It was clear to Neigass that he did actually love the title of Demon Chief. He and the Demon Lord only locked horns all the time *because* they were close.

"You two never change, do you?" Neigass repeated.

Tsyon stuck out his lower lip and glared at her. "Shut yer trap!"

This only managed to elicit a hearty laugh from Neigass. She continued, "Well, at least the heroes don't seem to have caught on that the Demon Chiefs are just a cool kids' club formed by a bunch of friends."

"It wasn't on purpose," Sheitoom said. "I brought together the most powerful people I knew of, and it just happened to be you guys. Besides, you're getting me results, so who cares?"

"Results, eh? I dunno how I feel about destroying villages, to be honest."

"It is what it is. If we take no action, our people will continue to grow upset. Besides, you're not actually killing anyone...right?"

"Of course not."

Sheitoom was desperately reluctant to invade human lands for fear of setting off another protracted war. But the fact remained that humans were actively raiding demon towns, and her people needed to see her doing something about it.

After wrestling with the problem for some time, she consulted with Dhiza and came up with the idea of destroying villages while sparing the lives of their inhabitants. The Demon Chiefs would warn villages well in advance before they attacked, giving their inhabitants time to flee. If anyone was still around by the time they arrived, Neigass or Tsyon would personally escort them to safety. Bizarre as it sounded, these measures had helped quell the anger of the demon population.

"The heroes' progress into our lands is slowing down. Maybe the humans are slowly coming around to the idea that we don't really want to fight."

Come to think of it, the heroes hadn't made much progress as of late, had they? Also, their party seemed to be shrinking. Neigass knew there were other factors at play here. She'd known that ever since she met with Flum and took possession of the broken core.

◇ ◇ ◇

After dinner and a delicious slice of cake for dessert, Neigass finally retrieved the core and showed it to Sheitoom.

"That's..."

"I got it from this Flum girl, one of the members of the hero party."

Dhiza leaned in close and examined the object with great interest. "Hmm. it appears to be broken."

Tsyon crossed his arms and furrowed his brow. "Despite our best efforts, even we couldn't destroy it. But a little thing like that Flum girl could do this? She's the useless one with the zeroed-out stats, isn't she?"

"That's right. I have no idea how she was able to do it. She has some sort of mysterious power."

"...Reversal?"

The Demon Chiefs had never seen Flum use any magic; she simply didn't have the stats for it. But everything was different, now.

Dhiza mumbled aloud. "The power to reverse the direction of the spinning helix set in motion by Origin..."

"That must be it. After all, she's the only one who's ever been able to break a core."

The sheer degree of force Flum had brought to bear against that bizarre ogre was remarkable. Her physical strength, her prana, that formless power that almost seemed to resemble magic—it had to be due to her Reversal ability.

"Think that's why she was chosen to be a hero?"

"She was just a little kid from somewhere out in the boonies, y'know. If Origin hadn't called upon her to join the heroes, then she'd probably never have uncovered her powers in the first place."

Tsyon let out a sigh. "I get wanting to keep your enemies close, but they must've had *some* reason to go find and recruit her. I just don't get what those people are thinking. I really don't."

A deep silence hung over the room before Sheitoom finally spoke.

"Regardless of their reasoning, we need to ensure neither the heroes nor that Flum girl get anywhere near the seal. This isn't just for our own sakes but for the safety of the entire world."

The conviction was clear in her voice.

"No matter what, we can't let that cunning god Origin have its way."

◇ ◇ ◇

Yet again, the party had failed to reach their intended destination in time. Annoyance was writ large on Jean's face as he stormed out of the teleportation room. The rest of the party shared his sense of anguish, especially having lost Flum and Eterna in rapid succession.

Linus desperately wanted to keep the party from dissolving, but try as he might, no words came to mind. Ultimately, he decided to retire to his room to mull over the problem. Maria watched with great concern before hurrying off after him.

This left Cyrill and Gadhio alone in the teleportation room. The younger woman made for the exit, looking dejected, when suddenly Gadhio called out to her.

"A word, Cyrill?"

She stopped and turned. It was rare for him to initiate a conversation. "What is it, Gadhio?"

"I'm thinking about leaving the party. The next outing will be my last." The words came out easily, as if he were discussing the weather.

"I...see. So even you're leaving us?"

She'd sensed that this might happen. He'd always taken a liking to Flum and was close to Eterna. With them gone and the future of the party growing less clear by the day, it seemed unlikely that a talented adventurer like himself would stick around. After all, neither fame nor fortune had led him to join them in the first place.

"I truly am sorry, but frankly, I don't really see any real need for me to continue to accompany you on this journey."

"No 'real need'? Are you saying that the Demon Lord doesn't need to be stopped?"

"'Demon Lord' has become a catch-all term for all things evil, as of late. The real truth is that the Kingdom is seeking to overpower the demons in armed conflict."

"Demons who have attacked our people and killed scores in the process."

Gadhio shook his head. "The humans started that war."

"What? I was told the demons were the ones who invaded."

"The Kingdom makes sure its history books paint it in the best possible light. The popular conception is that the demons, who were evil, started to crop up around fifty or so years ago. After twenty-odd years of brewing distrust, the Kingdom went to war with them."

"Did something happen to trigger the war?"

"Not particularly, no. The royal family simply came to the conclusion that demons were our enemies. There was little contact between the two peoples at the time, but I can say with certainty that the demons weren't the ones to initiate conflict."

"So, the humans were the invaders... Then why are we trying to destroy the Demon Lord?"

"As the church tells it, the Divine Creator Origin considers demons a plague upon the world. Whether you believe that or not is up to you."

He probably could have left that last part out. He knew that Cyrill felt the weight of the people's expectations on her shoulders; she couldn't give up on their journey that easily. Gadhio couldn't bring himself to encourage her to continue, so he left her an opening to do whatever she saw fit.

"There are many dark forces moving in the background," he said. "Don't be fooled by their pretty packaging. If you're not careful, that darkness will swallow you."

"I don't know if I can do that..."

"Nor can I. That's why I rely not only on what people tell me but also on what I see with my own eyes."

"What I see...?"

Cyrill couldn't help but wonder if her reckless drive had led her here. Her friends were leaving one after the other, and she could no longer control her abilities properly. Maybe this was her chance to start over.

"There's one last thing, and it's important..." Gadhio

glanced to the doorway to make sure no one was around. "Keep a close eye on Maria."

This was unusual coming from Gadhio. He was a strict, stoic man who never spoke ill of someone behind their back.

"Why do you say that?"

"I sense she's hiding something. Besides, she's a member of the church, so it can't hurt to be especially wary of her. I know I just said to trust what your own eyes tell you, but I think this is worth keeping in mind."

With that, he moved toward the door. Cyrill stood with her thoughts for a moment before she remembered something important and quickly called out after her comrade. "Wait! One more thing!"

Gadhio stopped and turned around. "Yes?"

"I was, umm... I was just wondering about Flum's hometown, and..."

Gadhio let out an uncharacteristic sigh. "I've been wondering about her as well. If any of my jobs take me in that direction, I plan on stopping by."

"Thank you, Gadhio."

"Just doing my duty." He waved his hand and started off again down the hall.

Cyrill knew that she had no right to check in on Flum herself, but she had to ask. Ever since Origin chose her to be the hero everyone was waiting for, Flum had been the only person she'd truly considered a friend.

◇ ◇ ◇

Linus and Maria left the castle and walked side by side through the town.

Linus had his own suite back in the castle where people would fix up his gear, prepare his meals, and generally tend to all his needs, but the prospect felt cramped and unwelcoming at the moment. He decided, instead, to stay the night at a hotel off in the East District.

"Don't you need to head back to the cathedral?" he asked Maria.

"Is there something wrong with me worrying about you, Linus?"

"I, uh, no. Of course not. I'm actually quite happy to hear it. But did I look that bad?"

"I mean, it was pretty obvious that something's really bothering you. As a woman of the cloth, I could hardly look the other way."

"Sorry for the hassle..."

"It's nothing, especially considering the circumstances."

He really did have a lot on his mind: Flum and Eterna were gone, and their journey was dragging on far longer than it should. Then there was Jean's constant attitude and Cyrill stuck in a rut. As if that wasn't enough, it looked like Gadhio would be leaving the party any time now.

"Hey, Maria..."

She cocked her head to the side—an adorable gesture. "Yes?"

Linus stopped to look at her, his expression growing dark. "What would you say if...if I told you that I wanted to leave the party and asked you to live with me?"

Maria's eyes went wide at the sudden confession. Her heart began to race, but it wasn't an altogether unpleasant feeling. "The church...they'd come after me."

"I'm pretty good at evading capture."

"And where do you plan on taking me?"

"I don't have a particular place in mind, really. I just want to travel the world. Maybe we'd find some interesting places along the way."

Maria closed her eyes, imagining the scene. "That... that sounds absolutely splendid, Linus." It sounded like heaven, compared to their grueling journey to depose the Demon Lord. But...

"Is something wrong?" Linus asked.

"It's not that I don't want to travel the world with you. Really, I'm overwhelmed that you'd ask me to join you. I think we could be happy together. It's just that..."

"You can't let yourself be happy until all the demons have been scoured from this world?"

Deep frown lines etched Maria's face. "So you picked up on that."

Her hunger for vengeance followed her like a curse. Even if she were to fall in love and find her own chance at happiness, she knew that desire would never leave her in peace until every last demon was dead.

"I'm going to be completely honest here—I did a little research on you, Maria. I'm sorry for prying."

"I don't mind. I'm just flattered you took such interest in me."

"You truly are a saint...or a nun, at least."

"I'm not this kind to everyone. Had anyone else done what you did, I wouldn't be so forgiving. But I have to ask... I guess that means you know about my hometown, yes?"

"I know it was destroyed by demons when you were eight, yes."

Maria gazed off into the distance as she recalled that fateful day ten years ago. "That's right. By the time the sun rose the next morning, I was the only one left alive amidst the ruins."

The memory was seared into her brain. It felt like it had just happened yesterday.

"Everyone I ever loved was cut apart—crushed—impaled—burnt. I remember them all."

"I... I'm sorry."

She clenched her fists as a look of raw hatred washed across her face. "The stories of friendly demons are lies, all lies. Those...things took so much pleasure in killing everyone. That's why they must be destroyed."

Everything she said seemed true. And yet, as far as Linus could tell, the demons weren't lying when they said that they never killed any humans.

"I'm sorry for ruining the mood," he said.

"No, not at all. Besides, I'm the one who brought it up."

Maria's dark history was just another reason why Linus was so smitten with her. He wanted to stay by her side and support her in all she did.

Finally, Maria spoke again, her voice barely above a whisper. "I still believe I should put that above all else, even my own life."

Though he heard her, Linus didn't respond. Hard though it may have been, he knew that this was a line in the sand that he just shouldn't cross. It was a decision that Maria herself would have to make.

The two stood there in silence, Maria staring down at her feet with a forlorn look on her face.

After a few tense moments, Linus finally clapped his hands together and let out an excited yelp. "I just remembered! There's a great ice cream parlor nearby. Just the right kind of place to lift our spirits. Whaddya think?"

Maria grinned. "Sounds good. I confess I have a bit of a sweet tooth, even though they forbid snacks at the cathedral."

She was truly beautiful when she relaxed and let herself smile like that. Linus promised himself that he would stay by her side until the day came when she could let go of all the hatred inside of her and smile easily once again.

◇ ◇ ◇

The sun was setting by the time Jean walked out of the teleportation room, mumbling angrily to himself as he stomped his way out of the darkened palace. "S-Rank adventurer? Yeah, right! I haven't seen those idiots pull off a single thing worthy of that rank. They're nothing more than worthless cowards!"

He continued his tirade all the way back to his room, where he immediately vented his rage on his desk until his fist was bruised and bleeding. He tossed books and papers around the room, then finally tipped the whole bookshelf over with a crash.

His outburst wasn't entirely without reason: Gadhio had just told him that he would be leaving the party. With how little progress they'd made of late, his departure would be the final nail in the coffin of their quest. Making matters worse, this would probably further weaken Cyrill's resolve and threaten the reputation Jean had built for himself.

"What the hell is his problem, anyway?! Once the journey's complete, we can live out the rest of our lives in the lap of luxury, basking in the adoration of the people! We'll have titles bestowed by the royal family! I thought adventurers were all about the money. As long as it pays, who cares about the rest?? And besides, how often does one get the chance to work with a genius of my caliber?"

He clenched his fists tight and heaved in deep breaths as the weeks and months of pent up fury poured forth. Alas, it did little to assuage his anger.

Why was the journey going so poorly with someone of his brilliance to shepherd them?

Jean couldn't recall a single time in his life that he had failed. Even when people tried to trip him up, out of jealousy no doubt, he always managed to maintain a calm demeanor and solve every problem presented to him. He'd always been a loner, never seeing much need for friends. He threw himself fully into his research, and was rewarded in spades, learning to cast magic that was beyond even the Kingdom's best mages. Jean was proud for a *reason*. His achievements spoke for themselves!

And yet here he was, up against a wall that he just couldn't seem to surmount.

"Haah...haaah..."

He slumped down into his chair once he calmed down a bit, reaching for his quill. Dipping the tip into a bottle of ink, Jean grabbed a discarded sheet of paper from the desk and began to write. His face was so close to the paper that his cheek nearly brushed it, and his hand shook from how tightly he was squeezing the pen as he listed magical theorems.

He let loose another angry growl at the futility of it all and crumpled the paper up into a ball before throwing it across the room.

"Why must the world defy me like this?? Even my research isn't going like I planned! The world needs me if we're ever to meld the four affinities together. Once I master that, I can do the rest on my own! I won't need that piece of trash Flum or those other losers!" He ran his hands through his hair as his mind raced in a desperate attempt to find some way to turn his fortunes around.

Jean's thoughts were interrupted by the sound of a loud, crisp knock at his door.

"Whoever it is, get the hell out of here!"

He was in no mood for visitors, but the voice on the other side of the door persisted.

"Jean, it's me...Maria."

She should've been back at the cathedral now that her date with Linus was done, but he wasn't about to turn away a woman of the cloth at this hour. With an annoyed click of his tongue, Jean stood up from his chair and released the lock before swinging the door open to glare out at his unwanted guest. "What?"

"It's the duty of those who follow the holy path to shepherd wayward lambs, you know."

"Don't even pretend that you know how I feel."

"But you have lost your way, no?"

Jean clicked his tongue once again in annoyance. "I think you're the one who's lost, lady."

"And what makes you say that?"

"I dunno. You just seem like you're always wearing some sort of mask. It's revolting, to tell the truth."

Jean leaned in, closely inspecting every feature of Maria's face closely.

"But there's something different about you right now." A sinister grin graced his lips as he spoke. "You aren't some sort of wicked witch pretending to be human, now are you?"

His cold glare caused Maria to shudder internally.

"Aah, so you've found yourself bound to Linus, have you?"

"This has nothing to do with him!"

"My, my. Getting emotional, are we? That's definitely not like you at all."

Maria grimaced in silence.

"I see you don't like me throwing around the name of the man you love? Hah. Commoner or clergy, you're all the same in the end. You're a woman, after all. Gyahahaha!"

"Jean, you pathetic scum!!" Maria raised her hand to slap him right across the cheek...but her arm stayed frozen in place, shaking with barely contained rage. She clenched her jaw and waited for her rational mind to kick back in, and the anger subsided.

"My, my, how commendable of you," Jean sneered. "I'm surprised a holy woman would hold herself back in such a manner."

Maria slowly lowered her hand with a heavy sigh. "As I said, it is our job to assist wayward lambs."

"Yes, you keep saying that. Why don't you just skip the sermon and get to the point? I'm a busy man."

They were finally both calm enough to have a rational conversation. Maria produced a black crystal and showed it to the arrogant man in front of her. Her usual gentle smile eased its way back onto her face.

"I heard that you were seeking more power," she said. "I thought this tool might be of some use to you."

A powerful energy spun deep within the crystal, like a contained storm. Jean stared into it intently as if in a trance.

"My, my," he said. "You've certainly brought me something intriguing."

**ROLL
OVER
AND
DIE**

The Scoundrel Laughs On

MERE DAYS SINCE Flum was first able to look at Milkit face-to-face, the bond between the two girls continued to grow stronger and stronger.

After an evening out shopping, they walked side by side, chatting about their earlier excursion as they made their way through the darkening streets to head home for dinner. Passersby shot scornful glances toward the two slaves, but neither of them cared much about it anymore.

"So Marinn watched Pyle fall into the hole and said 'you know, it serves ya right to dive in a hole like that outta embarrassment.'"

Milkit snickered. "That must have been tough to hear."

"I bet, but to be fair, it was totally Pyle's fault, right? I couldn't help but burst out laughing, too."

"It sounds like you were pretty good friends with Marinn and Pyle, Master."

"You could say that. Like I said, we were pretty much together since birth. One of these days I'd like you to meet them, Milkit. I'm sure you guys would get along great."

"I'm sure any friend of Master's must be a lovely person."

Flum smiled broadly at this. She had been telling Milkit about her hometown of Patolia, getting lost in the excitement of all the stories from her childhood days. "Aaah, sorry, Milkit, I kinda took over the conversation there."

"Not at all, Master. I love hearing about your stories."

"Oh?"

"Of course! I want to know everything I can about you." Milkit's cheeks flushed pink under the amber glow of the setting sun.

Flum's heart skipped a beat at the sight. Milkit was so beautiful, even with the bandages back around her face. She felt her own cheeks begin to burn and quickly averted her gaze. Milkit cocked her head to the side, curious as to why Flum had jerked her head away so suddenly.

"A-anyway, I'm really looking forward to dinner tonight!" Flum stammered.

"I'll work extra hard on it, since Sara's coming over."

"Oh, Milkit, anything you make is absolutely a treat. I'm sure Sara will wolf it right down and love you for it."

Flum meant every word, too. Though Milkit was embarrassed by the praise, she was clearly happy to hear it.

The two girls walked cheerfully down the relatively empty road connecting the Central and West Districts, content to simply enjoy each other's company for now. Alas, their contentment was short-lived, as the loud sounds of argument erupted from around the next corner.

"Hey, lemme go!!"

"You're from the church, aren't ya? Why don't you be a good little girl and come with me!"

Flum's shoulders dropped as she let out a heavy sigh. She'd hoped for at least a brief moment of peace and quiet, despite the West District's relatively dangerous reputation. "Hang on, Milkit. I'll be right back."

"I'll be waiting, Master."

Flum set down her bags and took off after the voices. Just as she suspected, she found two large men closing in on a young girl.

"Why're ya cowering like that, huh? Scared of a couple of big guys like us?" they jeered at the girl. Flum guessed by their vicious demeanors that they were part of Dein Phineas's crew. He was something of an unofficial leader out in these parts.

Flum summoned a glowing black blade nearly as tall as she was—the Epic-class Souleater—from the parallel dimension where it waited to be called upon, and held it at the ready. Under normal circumstances, the curse placed on the sword would drastically reduce the stats of its wielder... and melt their flesh right off their bones. Her "Reversal" ability, however, transformed these curses into boons.

"Hey," she said. "Any chance I can convince you guys to cut it out and leave?"

"Well, I'll be, if it ain't Flum Apricot. What're you doin' here, girly? Coming to stick your nose where it don't belong again?"

"You're the ones who keep showing up uninvited!"

In the short time since Flum became an adventurer based out of the West District, she'd had more than her fair share of Dein and his crew trying to sabotage her—preemptively taking down monsters she'd been hired to hunt, setting traps for her, drawing out monsters to attack her, and more. She'd finally had a day free of them, and now here they were, accusing *her* of butting in? Ridiculous.

"Ugh, talking to guys like you is a waste of time. Listen, just let the girl go if you don't want to get hurt."

"Heh. Have it your way." Much to her surprise, the men let go of the girl and walked away.

"Well, that was weird..."

Though taken aback by how easily the encounter ended, Flum had more important things to think about. She quickly turned her attention to the girl, kneeling to offer her a hand. "Are you okay?"

Only then did she notice that the young girl's face was bandaged up. Not unlike Milkit's, though this girl's bandages completely covered her eyes, almost certainly obscuring her vision as a result. *She must be afflicted by something, too.*

"Thank you, ma'am." The girl reached out, grasping at thin air for a moment before finally catching hold of Flum's hand.

"The West District is pretty dangerous, y'know. You shouldn't walk around alone out here."

"I know."

"Then what're you doing out here?? Anyway, that's beside the point. You probably don't even know where you are right now, with your eyes like that."

The girl responded with a firm nod. Flum had an increasingly bad feeling about this, but she couldn't just leave the poor girl alone to get attacked again, so she gently took her hand and led her back to Milkit.

"Is that the girl they were attacking?" Milkit asked.

"Yup. Hey, uh, what's your name?"

"Ink, Ink Wreathcraft."

Flum immediately followed up by casting Scan on the girl. After her recent encounter with the ogre, she couldn't be too careful.

Ink Wreathcraft
Affinity: Water
Strength: 18
Magic: 43
Endurance: 28
Agility: 23
Perception: 49

Wreathcraft—the name had a dignified ring to it that was at odds with her appearance.

"I... I feel like someone's staring at me. Did you cast Scan on me?" Ink was surprisingly perceptive.

"Sorry. I was just kinda curious." Flum wasn't sure why she was apologizing.

"Why would you do that, you pervert?!" Ink, on the other hand, didn't seem too keen on the idea of people looking at her stats. Her bandaged appearance made it easy to assume the girl was weak, but it was quickly becoming apparent she was anything but.

"You probably already heard my name from Dein's thugs, but I'm Flum. And this here is..."

"My name's Milkit. I'm Master's slave."

"Slave? You mean, like, in the kinky kinda way?"

"Whoa, no, nothing like that!!"

"Master never bought me. Rather, she took me on. I had nowhere else to go."

"Huh, I guess Flum here must be a really nice person."

"She most certainly is."

Flum's cheeks flushed at the sudden praise.

Now that the introductions were out of the way, it was time to get this girl back to wherever she needed to be. Ink looked as young as Sara, and blind to boot. Flum was definitely not about to leave her alone. "Hey, Ink. Where do you live? If you can't make it back on your own, I'm more than happy to take you."

"I... I don't know."

"No, I'm serious."

"Really, I've lost my memory. I don't know."

"Did you run away?"

"I told you, I have amnesia!!"

"Your parents must be worried sick about you."

"I don't have any parents!"

Flum had hit an impasse. Milkit pouted and then asked, "Were you staying with relatives? Or an orphanage?"

Ink shook her head vigorously, sending her ponytail flapping about.

"Then where are you from?"

"Dunno. I don't remember anything."

Flum let out a sigh of exasperation. Either this girl really was a blank slate or she just didn't want to say.

"Why don't we take her back to our place for a bit?" Milkit suggested. "She looks tired."

"Don't exactly have a lotta options. How does that sound, Ink?"

"Great!" The young girl nodded excitedly, almost as if she'd been waiting for them to suggest that. Though slightly annoyed with herself for falling for the girl's ruse, Flum took Ink's hand and led her back to their home.

◇ ◇ ◇

The moment they walked through the door, Ink mumbled something in a deadpan voice about how sleepy she was. To be fair, she *did* look ready to pass out right where she stood. Assuming she'd only run away the day before, it was unlikely she'd had a wink of sleep on the lawless streets of the West District.

"Welcome back. Whoa, who's the kid?"

"Hi, Eterna. We ran across some of Dein's goons trying to rough her up on the way back."

"Then take her back home."

"Apparently, she doesn't know where that is. I decided to bring her back here for now so she could get some rest. I'll put her in our room." Flum took the younger girl's hand, intending to lead her upstairs to her bedroom.

"Hold up," Eterna said. "Let's get her some water before you put her to bed. Oh, and why don't you put her in my room instead?"

"Your bedroom?"

"Yeah, there's something I want to check on."

"Got it."

Flum directed Ink to Eterna's room and sat her on the bed. A moment later, Eterna arrived in the room with a cup of water, which Ink quickly gulped down before curling up on her side. She was asleep in mere minutes.

Milkit looked down at the girl's sleeping form. "She must've been exhausted."

Staying up all night on the run, lost and alone in the West District, was no small feat for a child. The three looked at the snoozing girl for a moment before Eterna finally reached out and began to undo the bandages around Ink's eyes.

"Should you really be doing that?"

"You saved her, didn't you? I figured we can at least do this much. Anyway, take a closer look at this, Flum."

At Eterna's urging, Flum leaned in for a closer look at Ink's face. She saw thread, clear as day, stitching the girl's eyelids shut.

"Wh-whoa! What's that??"

"That looks painful..."

Flum and Milkit were both taken aback at the bizarre sight. Even if she were blind, there was no logical reason to sew her eyes shut.

"Her eyes were probably removed," Eterna said.

"R-removed? Do you think she was sick?"

"Hm...no. There'd be no reason to sew her eyelids shut if she were just sick. Honestly, this looks like the work of a very disturbed individual. If I were to hazard a guess, I'd say there was some sort of ritual involved. At any rate, something's not quite right with this girl."

Flum had already figured Ink was in trouble, but what Eterna was saying was something else entirely. Milkit spoke up next. "Do you think the church has anything to do with this?"

Flum nodded. "That's what I was thinking. A ritual... It has to have some kind of religious significance, right?"

It had been just a few short days ago, on their way to harvest medicinal herbs in the town of Anichidey, that Flum and Sara had battled an ogre with a bizarre spiral carved into its face. The creature had been horrifyingly

faster and stronger than a normal ogre. The girls had also found an abandoned underground facility that had once been operated by the church of Origin—followers of the Divine Creator.

There was still a lot they didn't know about that place, let alone the experiments conducted there. Flum couldn't rule out the possibility that the church was conducting further tests at their cathedral in the capital, too.

Eterna spoke up, breaking the tension. "We don't know that for sure. She may have been held for ransom or something. There's just not enough here to definitely prove that this is the church's doing."

"You're right... I guess for now, we just need to keep her safe, right?"

"I think that's the best approach. But Flum, you should think long and hard before you get yourself involved in yet another problem."

Flum offered up a dry laugh. "Too late for that. My life became one long series of problems the moment Origin called on me to join the other heroes."

And yet, she felt like a heavy weight had settled on her shoulders.

◇ ◇ ◇

"I'm heeeeere!"

Sara showed up for dinner right on schedule. The delicious aroma wafting from the house had clearly put her in high spirits, though her face tensed up the moment she entered the room. "I-Is that Eterna Rinebow? The legendary hero, Eterna Rinebow? What are you doing here?!"

Her shock was understandable. It had to be surprising to see a famous person kicking back at a friend's house, though Flum couldn't help but feel chagrined that she hadn't elicited the same reaction when she first met Sara. Sure, she'd had the mark of a slave on her cheek, but Sara hadn't even recognized her as a member of the same band of heroes.

"What am I doing here? I live here."

Eterna gave Sara a brief overview of how she'd left the party because they weren't getting along and moved into a squat she'd been eyeing for years. Sara didn't look like she was entirely following, but it was enough to sate her curiosity. Her practical outlook made her quick to accept things for what they were.

Taking back control of the conversation, Flum asked Sara to take a look at Ink, hoping to confirm some connection to the church. Unfortunately, it was to no avail.

"Huh. Never seen her before," Sara said.

Ah, well. All Flum could do was sigh as she looked back down at the sleeping girl. Of course, it wasn't going to be that easy. It never was.

◇◇◇

Sara jabbered on cheerfully as Milkit finished laying out the smorgasbord she'd prepared. Flum and Sara's stomachs growled in unison at the delightful aromas mingling in the air. They both looked around nervously, hoping no one heard them, and finally took their seats. Once everyone was seated, they all put their hands together and said a quick blessing.

Sara was the first to dig right in, taking a large helping of harpusy, a cream stew filled with greens grown near the capital. The greens gave it a nice, satisfying crunch before melding together with the smooth white sauce. She mumbled excitedly around a large mouthful of food. Though the words were unintelligible, their meaning was clear: she loved it.

Flum, on the other hand, went right for the main course at the center of the table: sautéed genofish. Milkit had basted it in a rich marinade that shone through the skin along the grill-marks; the steam rose off it in spice-scented plumes. The genofish was a D-Rank fish monster that could grow up to around two meters in length. The one they bought at the market today was a mere 50 centimeters long but still quite a sight to behold.

Using her knife and fork, Flum carved up the fish and passed a plate out to everyone at the table before bringing a forkful of the grilled meat to her mouth.

"Woow! Thish ish great!" she gushed excitedly, if muffledly, around the mouthful of food.

The message got through loud and clear to Milkit. "Thank you, Master."

To be on the safe side, she'd also prepared a meat and vegetable stir-fry, soup made with genofish stock, freshly baked bread—the list went on.

"That was absolutely divine." Even Eterna, a woman of few compliments, had to praise Milkit's efforts after making her way through each delectable course. Milkit beamed at the abundant praise the meal received.

Flum scooted in close and lifted a fork of genofish meat toward Milkit's lips. "Say 'aah.'"

"M-master, I can feed myself. Please don't bother yourself."

"Right, and here you are just smiling away while we eat. Now open wide!"

"Aaaaah..." Never one to disobey the will of her Master, Milkit finally opened her mouth and took a bite of the fish. It was delicious, but the fact of Flum feeding her so occupied her brain that she hardly tasted a thing.

"Well, they sure are friendly," said Sara.

"It's pretty much always like that nowadays," said Eterna.

"Aww, I'm jealous. Hey, Milkit, I've been meaning to ask something. Why do you still wear bandages over your face? Weren't you cured?"

"She said she'll only show her face to Flum."

"They sure are...close."

"Right? Annoyingly so."

Eterna was more than a little exasperated by the billing and cooing she had to witness, but it was worth it to finally see Flum happy. The poor girl had never looked this content on their travels together.

◇ ◇ ◇

After dinner, it was time for Flum and Sara to trade notes. Milkit brought them some tea before heading off to go clear the table and do the dishes. They both offered to help out, but she stubbornly refused, insisting that this was her job.

"I can't be of much help to your investigation," she said, "so at least let me do this."

Flum couldn't say much to that.

Sara went first, looking dejected. "I've been hunting for information on the facility since we got back, but I got nothin'."

"What about those documents you mentioned? The ones that said where we could find the kialahri?"

"I think one of the Central District priests accidentally left those out. The next time I went looking for them, they'd disappeared along with a buncha other stuff in the same vein. I remember a couple of places on the map, but that's about it."

"In other words, the clergy know at least *something* about this."

"I'd say so. Or...at least I think so. I'm just a nun in training, y'know? Don't exactly have free run of the place. There are whole areas of the cathedral I haven't been in, but I was thinking...maybe a hero might be granted access?"

"Even if I were, they'd be keeping a close eye on me. There's gotta be something else we can do. Maybe we have a shot with the churches in the East and West districts?"

"Hmm. I'm pretty tight with two knights stationed in the West District, but I'm pretty sure there's nothing there."

"What makes you say that?"

"There's a big orphanage there. There are a lot of abandoned kids out in the West District; y'know what it's like here. I've been there a few times myself, but kids are curious, and they go everywhere. It'd be hard to keep a big secret facility all hush-hush down there."

That made sense to Flum. Sure, the church could disappear a kid who stumbled on something covert, but that risked drawing attention in its own right. "How about the East District, then?"

"That's the rich side of town. It's even less likely they'd risk bringing danger over there than the West District. Honestly, I figured they'd be set up someplace remote, like what we saw back in Anichidey."

"You're probably right. We could spend forever searching the capital and never find anything. We don't even know if they're still continuing their research at this point…" The facility where they encountered the spiral ogre had been closed for at least a dozen-odd years.

Eterna, however, was unconvinced. "The kingdom has been experimenting on people for far longer than you two know. I think it's likely that the experiments continue somewhere here in the capital."

"Oh?"

"They were already happening when I was born, at least."

No one in the room had any idea how long ago that was. Perhaps Eterna wasn't aware that none of them knew her real age.

"Even if there are no active research labs, there should at least be some defunct ones to find," Eterna said. "I think it makes the most sense to scour the capital before you expand your search."

"Aw'right," said Sara, "I'll check out the churches in the East and West districts, then. I'll ask about Ink at the orphanage while I'm there."

"Sounds good," said Flum. "I'll look into places outside the church. Thanks for your help, Sara. I'm really sorry for asking all these favors of you."

"No problem. Besides, it's my holy duty to expose any corruption in the church!"

Sara didn't want to believe that the church of Origin—the people who'd taken her in and cared for her since she was only two years old—could be committing such heinous acts. But after the horror and death she'd seen at the Anichidey research lab, she had to know the truth. It was the church that had taught her never to turn a blind eye to true evil, after all.

"By the way, Flum, whatever happened with Dein? He's not out for revenge or anything after Anichidey, is he?"

"He probably is."

"I guess he would be, huh? He's too big a hypocrite to consider he brought it on himself."

Besides which, Flum had killed two of his men. She didn't regret it in the slightest, but she knew Dein wasn't going to take their deaths lying down. He and his crew had already redoubled their efforts to make her life difficult.

"I keep telling you to let me help you take those thugs out," said Eterna.

"You're already helping by keeping Milkit safe, Eterna."

"I'm just sitting around the house..."

"That's more than enough."

Flum's greatest fear was that they would take seek revenge by hurting Milkit. Dein almost certainly knew she was the most important thing in the world to Flum, and she had a sickening certainty that, one way or another, he'd try to get his hands on her.

"Well, I wanna help out, too," Sara declared. "Just let me know what I can do, 'kay?"

"Thanks, Sara, I really appreciate it."

With the serious discussion out of the way, the three moved on to lighter topics. Milkit joined them soon after, and they carried on like that for several hours. It was only when Sara began to yawn loudly that they decided to call it a night. She was still a growing preteen girl, even if it was easy to forget that fact.

Flum offered to escort Sara back to her home in the Central District church.

◇ ◇ ◇

Elsewhere in the West District, Dein and his lackeys were tying one on in the guild's bar when a somber-looking man walked up and sat across from a rather tipsy Dein.

"What's with you?" Dein demanded. "Drink up!"

The man offered up his crystal glass and watched as Dein poured a dark liquid into it. "Sorry, Dein."

"Hah? What's gotten into you all of a sudden?"

"Earlier today we grabbed a girl who seemed like she might have something to do with the church. Y'know, to use her like we planned. But then that Flum girl showed up and ruined everything before we could drag her off."

The smile immediately faded from Dein's lips. "I see. That girl really likes to stick her nose where it don't belong, huh?"

He knocked his drink back, draining it in a single gulp, then let out a loud burp and slammed his glass down on the table with such force that the man sitting across from him immediately tensed up. "Ah, sorry 'bout that. Didn't mean to scare you. Now hey, listen, don't let that get you down, huh? It's not like I explicitly asked you to do this for me. No one's gonna get mad at you missing out 'cause of something completely unanticipated."

"...Thanks, Dein."

For all his faults, Dein made sure his men were rewarded as long as they had something to show for their efforts. He mercilessly expelled anyone he deemed useless, but it took a lot for him to reach that point. Those who showed promise, meanwhile, became part of his inner circle.

Though many called Dein a coward, his enemies had a peculiar habit of vanishing for good. He had excellent resources for a man who lived among rogues—probably because he was the first son of the noble Phineas family. Unfortunately for Dein, that family fell to wrack and ruin when he was just a boy. With his parents dead and nowhere left to go, he grew up on the streets, scraping to get by. His parents' failings and the throes of poverty taught Dein a very important lesson: strength wasn't about one's individual might or even financial standing. No, true strength was found in your personal connections.

He would never forget that violence and money were the two levers of power that operated every human being. A person's emotions only mattered insofar as they could be used by someone skillful enough to manipulate them.

"He's one scary guy..." people would say about him, *"but if I could just get into his good graces, there'd be no greater ally."* Cultivating this persona had allowed Dein to

expand his influence until he became a driving force in the West District.

"Still," Dein said to the man sitting across from him, "if you don't fix this little problem soon, it's gonna make me look bad. She killed two of my guys, y'know? I can't have that."

The blood debt Flum owed him for Anichidey wasn't just personal. If he wanted to maintain his hold on the West District, he had to prove he could smack down any who opposed him.

"Why don't we just pull all the lads together and make a night of it?" the man proposed.

"You're getting warmer," Dein said, "but I'm not too keen on just overpowering her. I wanna do this with some *flair*."

"How are we going do that?"

Dein grabbed a stick of jerky and began to wave it around like a conductor's baton. His lips curled up into a sinister smile. "First we go for her heart. Then, when she's at her weakest, bam! In for the kill."

**ROLL
OVER
AND
DIE**

Trapped in the Spider's Web

INK WOKE EARLY the next morning, around the same time as Flum, and emerged into the living room alongside Eterna. It was clear that the young girl still wasn't fully awake by the way her head bobbed from side to side as she walked. Milkit guided the girl to a seat and poured her a glass of warm milk.

Ink wrapped her hands delicately around the glass and sipped at the liquid. After emptying about half of the cup's contents, she seemed to finally rouse completely awake. "Wow, what is this?? I've never tasted something so delicious!"

There was nothing particularly special about warmed milk...unless this was her first time tasting it. Flum had a lot of questions for the newcomer, but her grumbling stomach distracted her before she had a chance to start digging. The women sat down around the dining table and made short work of the scrumptious breakfast Milkit had prepared. Eterna had to help Ink along in the beginning, since she couldn't see where anything was, but she got the hang of it eventually.

"You're quite good at that," Milkit observed.

"I've been like this ever since I was born. You get used to it," Ink responded nonchalantly. She quickly changed the subject back to the meal at hand. "You know, everything here tastes absolutely amazing! I've never had anything like this in my life!"

The spread consisted of relatively common dishes in the kingdom. Milkit was a gifted cook, but this still raised a lot of questions about where Ink came from.

After finishing their breakfast, the group took a short break before finally moving on to the questions at hand. Unfortunately, Ink continued to claim amnesia for anything she didn't want to discuss.

"Listen, Ink, I know you said you didn't live in a normal home. But you weren't from an orphanage either, right?"

"I can't really say for sure, but I'm pretty sure it wasn't an orphanage, yeah."

"Were there other kids there? If so, how many?"

"Dunno."

"Was there anyone that took care of you?"

"Mother...I guess."

"This Mother person, was she some kind of caregiver?"

"I dunno. But she was kinda like a parent to us."

"But not your real parent?"

"Right. As far as I can recall, I don't think I've ever met my real parents. Maybe."

A place where you could leave kids without any relatives. That sounded like...

"Isn't that an orphanage?"

It was the only idea that came to Flum's mind. Ink shook her head emphatically. "Hmm... I really don't think so. I don't know a whole lot about orphanages, but Mother didn't seem too keen on them."

"Why's that?"

"I guess it's because she thought of us as her own children...maybe?"

Eterna smiled gently at the young girl. "There's just one thing I wanted to ask you, Ink. Have you had any problems with your heart, by chance?"

"No... At least not that I've heard of. But..."

"But?"

"Never mind. It's nothing."

She was clearly lying. But no matter how much they pushed, she just wouldn't budge.

"Hmm...were you in a hospital?" Flum tried, approaching the question from a slightly different angle, but Ink once again shook her head. Just where was this girl from?

What answers she did give them were surprisingly detailed for someone with supposed amnesia. Ultimately, they concluded that Ink most likely did live somewhere in the West District. Though she may have spent an entire evening out on her own, it was doubtful she could have made it very far on foot. It was also clear that there had been several other people living with her, wherever that was. The place was apparently kept under wraps, meaning it probably wasn't a public institution, and definitely not one prepared just for Ink's sake.

"Hey, can we stop? All these questions are making my head hurt."

"I'm sorry, Ink," Eterna said. "You're right, you must still be exhausted. But can I ask one last question?"

Ink paused for a moment before nodding.

"From what I'm hearing, it sounds like you lived in this place your whole life. So why did you run away?"

Ink's expression darkened at this. She struggled to answer the question, perhaps not quite certain of the answer herself. "Something...felt strange. Once I noticed it, I couldn't get it off my mind, and the feeling started to grow stronger and stronger, until I couldn't take it anymore."

"What felt strange?"

"My family." Her answer came out in barely above a whisper. "We were all raised together like a big family, and it always seemed so natural to me... Like that was how things were supposed to be. But I started to feel like what Mother called a family wasn't actually what felt like a family to me."

"Well, I think Ink has had enough for now. Why don't we take you back to my room to rest?" Eterna helped Ink to her feet.

"Thanks, I think I'd like that."

Flum felt a little bad for how hard she pushed the young girl, but she couldn't get over the feeling of unease welling up within her. The image of the ogre from back in Anichidey kept springing to mind. Its creators had likely spent the decade since they released that abomination into the world refining their work. Who knew what they could create now?

If Ink's situation had something to do with the church, then the odds of running into another of those monstrous creations were far greater than she liked. Her heart sank just thinking about it.

Flum propped her chin in both of her hands and leaned forward on the table, gently massaging her temples with her thumbs while she let out a heavy sigh.

"...Master?" Milkit gingerly placed her hands on Flum's shirt collar. "This might be a bit presumptuous of me to say, but you really shouldn't carry the world on your shoulders like that."

"Milkit..."

"The same goes for the events back in Anichidey and everything going on with Dein. I... I suspect I weigh heavily on your mind, Master, and that burden is taking a lot out of you. I think it would do you some good to rely more on others and let yourself breathe more freely."

Though Milkit struggled for the right words, it warmed Flum's heart to see her try so hard to cheer her up.

"Thanks Milkit, that really helps." She reached up and ran a hand through Milkit's silver hair, eliciting a smile from her companion.

"Whenever I feel Master's touch, I can feel a warmth building up in my chest. Almost like I'm the one being cheered up instead."

"Not at all, Milkit. Just seeing you smile brings me happiness."

"Even though you're doing all the work?"

Flum laughed. "I'd hardly call rubbing your head work. Honestly, I could do it all day if you'd let me"

"So I guess it's not just me who feels that way, then."

"Nope. So just sit there, enjoy the sensation, and let that warm feeling spread."

Contentment took a different shape for everyone: while some were happy to be doted on, there were others who enjoyed doing the doting. But maybe those weren't quite the right words for it. In their own way, they were giving each other the happiness they needed.

After administering Milkit's dose of love and affection for the day, Flum made her way out into the city in search of answers to her surfeit of questions.

◇◇◇

Though Sara already planned to check out the West District church, it was right on her way to the adventurers' guild, so Flum took a quick detour.

Generally speaking, the farther you traveled into the West District, the more the streets were strewn with garbage, and the more businesses of ill-repute and vagrants you were likely to encounter. The church stood out in stark contrast to the rest of the neighborhood. The tireless efforts of the nuns and knights to keep the area clean made it feel like it was scarcely part of the West District at all.

Today was apparently the knights' turn at cleaning duty, judging by the number of men in plate armor sweeping the streets. It was a bizarre sight. Flum did a quick circuit of the perimeter and spotted a familiar face. "Oh, hey, Sara."

Much like the knights Flum saw earlier, Sara was wielding a broom. "Hiya Flum. What brings you here?"

"I was on my way to the guild and figured I'd just stop by. You?" Sara had her own duties to fulfill as a nun in training, and Flum never expected that she would be out here so quickly. The girl was much more enthusiastic than Flum gave her credit for.

"I already had plans to come out here, actually. If I didn't, those two would get lonely."

"Hey, who are you saying would be lonely?" A blonde knight stepped up behind Sara and ruffled her hair.

"You're...Ed, right?" Flum asked.

"Oh, hey, I remember you. You caught that thief, right?"

"Call me Flum."

"She's my friend!"

Ed put a hand to his chin and looked Flum over. "Ya don't say."

His gaze was locked on the slave brand burned into Flum's cheek, but she didn't get the sense that he was judging her.

"So I guess this little punk finally made a friend outside the church, huh?! That should be cause for celebration, I'd say!" A broad grin broke out on his face.

"Knock! It! Off!" Sara thrashed about to get away from Ed's grasp, but his arms were just too long for her to put up any effective resistance.

"You know that's never gonna happen. How long has he been teasing you, now?" A blue-haired man approached them from the other direction, walking with a relaxed gait.

Flum bowed politely to the newcomer. "Thanks for your help earlier, Jonny." This was the first time they met since he helped out with the whole Leitch snatch-and-grab ordeal.

"It's nothing. You were a huge help, after all."

"Not like we got any extra cash for our efforts, though..."

"Of course you didn't! We don't do this for money, y'know?! Now cut it out and stop mussing up my haaaair!!"

"Aww, c'mon, how can you see a cute li'l head like that and not want to touch it? It's like trying to turn away a puppy in need of a belly rub. Right, Jonny?"

Jonny kept his face expressionless as Ed continued to play around with Sara's hair. "No comment."

"You guys must be close," Flum said.

"Not at all! How could I be friends with jerks like these?!"

Flum couldn't help but laugh.

According to Sara, they'd known each other for eight years. The two older men had basically adopted Sara as their little sister when she was taken in by the church, and they'd only grown closer since. Despite their protestations to the contrary, they were a tight-knit group.

Jonny turned his attention away from his squabbling friends to ask Flum a question. "So, what brings you to our church? It doesn't seem like you're here to worship."

"Well, you see, I found a lost girl yesterday and took her in for the night, but she claims she doesn't know where she's from. You don't happen to know if the orphanage happened to have a runaway, do you?" Flum felt she could probably trust a close friend of Sara's, even if he was a knight of the church. She still kept the details to the absolute minimum.

"I haven't heard of anything like that at the church's orphanage, no."

"Nothing like that from outside the West District, from what I've heard."

"I even asked around the Central District church, but no one seemed to know of anyone that fit the description. Hey, I told you to cut it out, Ed!!"

All three seemed to be in agreement.

"Do you want me to see about having her admitted to the orphanage here?"

"I, uh... No, that's okay. She seems to be doing all right for now."

"Huh, I see..."

Under normal circumstances, it would make a lot more sense to leave her in a place used to dealing with orphans while they continued to look for her family. Alas, Flum just couldn't hand the girl over to the church. Not with the possibility that she could be returned to whatever place—possibly even a research lab—that she'd run away from.

It was quickly becoming apparent she wasn't going to learn anything useful here. Flum decided it was about time to move on. As she scanned ahead, though, she caught sight of someone off in the distance, behind Jonny.

"Huh?"

It was a woman with two red ponytails emerging from the top of her head, dressed in a white military uniform and armed with a long saber that hung from her waist. She was watching Flum intently.

"Is that...Ottilie?"

The three members of the church turned instantly to look in the woman's direction. Once all eyes were on her, she moved in toward the group with confident strides. She never took her gaze off Flum's face.

"So it is you, Ottilie."

"Is that really you, Flum?"

"I can't promise no one's out there pretending to be me, but I *can* say that I am Flum Apricot."

Ottilie's cheek twitched slightly at this. After a tense moment, her shoulders dropped, and she let out a heavy sigh. "What's this all about?"

"Did something happen, Ottilie?"

"You... I mean, just what's going on here? What are you doing here, Flum Apricot? You're supposed to be out on the great quest to take down the Demon Lord! And what happened to your face?!"

Flum moved back a step. "Well, I mean, some things kinda came up..."

Flum and Ottilie had first met when she left her hometown of Patolia to join the quest to slay the Demon Lord. Ottilie had shown up in a horse-drawn carriage to take Flum back to the capital, and they'd gotten to know one another over the course of the three-day journey.

"Hey, what's a member of the royal army doing here anyway?" Ed, Jonny, and Sara looked back and forth at each other during Flum and Ottilie's exchange, barely able to contain their surprise.

"Hey, Sara, does Flum have some sort of connection to the military?"

"It wouldn't be surprising if she did. I mean, Flum here was one of the members of the great party to slay the Demon Lord, y'know."

"Wait a sec... You're not *the* Flum Apricot, are you?" Ed finally put it together.

"What's the great hero Flum Apricot doing here? And with the mark of a slave, no less?" Jonny tilted his head quizzically.

"Something 'came up?' Hardly! What's happened with the journey?! And why are you marked as a slave??" Apparently Ottilie was wondering the same thing.

"I was kicked out of the party, so I'm living in the capital now. I got the mark around the same time."

"Kicked out?? By who?! No, wait, you don't even need to answer that. It was that good-for-nothing scum, wasn't it?" Ottilie immediately knew who was to blame for all this. "Jean Inteige, right?"

Flum laughed darkly. "Good guess."

Apparently, Jean's erratic behavior wasn't restricted to the quest to slay the Demon Lord. He'd behaved much the same way in his time as a royal mage.

"He sold me out to a slave trader. Then there was this perfect storm of useful coincidences, and I busted loose. And here I am."

"A perfect storm..."

"And what about you, Ottilie? What brings you all the way out to the West District? The royal army must keep you busy."

During their long carriage ride to the capital, Ottilie had joked that her sister kept her nose to the grindstone; that the trip to collect Flum was her first real break from being under her watchful gaze. This made sense when you realized that her older sister was Henriette, the highest-ranking general in the royal army. The two were close, and it was treated as a foregone conclusion that Ottilie would follow in her big sister's footsteps.

"Umm, well, you see..." Ottilie seemed unusually hesitant, She looked over toward Sara and her companions. "My sister sent me on patrol."

She was clearly lying, but Flum wasn't about to dig deeper into sensitive military affairs. "A soldier's life is never easy, I guess."

"Nothing compared to you, with that slave marking etched into your face. Aren't you upset about that?"

"I've come to terms with it."

Ottilie let out another heavy sigh at Flum's casual response. "There's still so much I'd like to ask you, but alas, it's about time for me to head back. We'll talk more next time we meet."

"I guess I'll see ya, then."

"...Actually, it's unlikely we'll run into each other again, now that I think about it. Listen, I'm usually in or around the castle, so please stop by when you get the chance, okay?"

"Once I've got some free time, for sure. Is that really okay, though? I can't imagine a lieutenant general like yourself making time for the likes of me..."

"Don't underestimate yourself. A mighty hero that the entire country rallied behind, wandering the roughest part of the capital with a slave brand on her face? Were it anyone else, this would be a scandal."

The conviction behind her words hit Flum deep. She knew very well that she was a plain-looking girl, and that, compared with her lack of talent relative to the other heroes, was probably why no one recognized her until she told them who she was.

"Stop by and see me sometime, seriously. I, and the rest of the royal army, are partially to blame for what's happened to you. We're the ones who brought you here, after all."

With that, Ottilie turned and left. It was rare for a member of the royal army to express any sense of regret, but seeing Flum standing before her marked as a slave must have had quite an impact on her. After all, it was the church that had called together the heroes in the first place.

Once Ottilie was out of sight, the group heaved a collective sigh.

"Huh? What's wrong?" Flum could understand being nervous with the military around, but the reaction seemed a bit much.

Ed was the first to respond. "Don't you know? The royal army and church knights have something of a strained relationship."

"I never knew that. Why?"

"You can't be serious... Look, the military works directly for the royal family, while we serve the church. You still with me? This means there's essentially two armies existing concurrently within the country."

The royal army and the church's knights were evenly matched in terms of numbers, but the knights had light-affinity troops trained in the priesthood of Origin's curative magic. This almost certainly made them the more powerful force.

Jonny and Sara continued on. "Officially speaking, the royal army outranks us. In reality..."

"On the surface, we work hand in hand to ensure the safety of the whole kingdom. But there's a lot of vying for power that happens behind the scenes."

"Huh. So you're officially allies, but there's bad blood between you?"

Flum was starting to realize she truly had no idea of everything that hid beneath the skin of the world she knew. The kingdom encompassed the entire continent, with the exception of the demon lands up north. Alas, it was human nature to battle for supremacy.

Or perhaps there was a greater force at work, playing with the will of man.

A commoner might find serenity in thinking of these things as faraway power struggles, irrelevant to their daily life. Flum no longer had that privilege. After all, someone affiliated with the church was out to get her.

She looked up at the sky as a sinking feeling came over her. It would still be quite some time until peace finally came to the capital.

◇◇◇

After the brief encounter with Ottilie, Flum checked around some stairwells leading into cellars near the church, but her search came up empty. She finally gave up around noon to head back home and have some lunch.

"I'm hoooome!"

Milkit stopped what she was doing and rushed over to meet Flum at the door. She was holding a letter in her hand. "Master, you're safe!"

"Yeah, I didn't really find anything of interest. Hey, what's that letter about?"

Milkit pushed the paper into her hands. "You should read it."

The paper contained only a few scrawled words: *"You killed my father. Now I'm going to take something from you."*

Flum mulled it over. It was probably the work of Dein and his crew, but what were they planning? Milkit looked overcome with concern—not for herself, of course, but for her Master. Flum pulled her into an embrace and ran her fingers through her hair to try and calm her down.

"It's... It's dangerous out there, Master. Perhaps you should just stay in for the rest of the day."

She was right about that; it was dangerous. But that was exactly why Flum needed to go back out and do something about it. From the way the letter was worded, she wasn't the only one in danger here.

"I'm fine, really. And tough, too."

"I... I see." Milkit was clearly unhappy about this decision, so Flum continued on. "But I guess maybe I can stay home for the rest of the day. I've still got a lot to prepare, after all."

Milkit's face instantly lit up. "Master! Yes, I think that's a great idea!"

Her beaming smile showed through all the bandages. Flum couldn't help but smile herself.

◇ ◇ ◇

"It just doesn't make sense..." Eterna frowned, tilting her head to the side as she looked over the chart she'd filled with everything she could measure about Ink. She'd used her water magic to scan every aspect of the girl's body while she slept and found only one anomaly: her heart.

She wasn't sure how the girl was still alive.

"Something's been done to her, but I can't say what that is without a more thorough analysis. The equipment I have here just isn't sensitive enough to do us any good. I guess we could just open her up and then sew her shut, but I dunno about that..."

"What're you mumbling on about, Eterna?"

"I'm thinking here. Now just be quiet, I'm trying to concentrate."

"I know, but...I'm so boooored."

Eterna gave in to Ink's childish demands with a sigh and closed her notebook. She was still a child, after all. She picked up a fish-shaped trinket—a spell focus of hers—and handed it over to Ink.

"Whoa, what is this thing? It's coooold!" Ink held it closely to her chest, where it sat still for a few moments before finally moving, as if it'd gained a life of its own, and squirming out of her grasp. "Aww...it's gone."

Still lying on her back, Ink frantically searched the bed for the mysterious object. Every time she got a hand on it, it would quickly squirm away again.

"Hahaha! I don't know what this is, but I love it! Are you making it move, Eterna?"

"Maybe I am. Or maybe it's moving around all on its own."

Ink giggled. "What kind of answer is that?"

The girl had such a cheerful disposition that it was hard to believe she may have been someone's guinea pig. Maybe it was because she'd grown up with other children in a very similar situation.

"I wonder if they're all like this...assuming they're even alive," Eterna murmured to herself, keeping her voice too low for Ink to overhear. It was practically a given that test subjects would die eventually. It wasn't a matter of lifespan; test subjects were chosen for expendability, not endurance.

She shook her head. It was too soon to assume Ink had been used that way. They still didn't even know where she came from.

"Hey, Ink, I was hoping to ask you a few more questions, if you don't mind."

"Sure, I'll answer as best I can. 'Cause I have amnesia, remember..."

"I know you're lying about that, so you really should just start telling the truth."

"How can you be so sure?"

"If anything, I'm surprised you thought you could stretch the ruse this far. Anyway, I'd like to hear more about the other kids you mentioned this morning."

"Did I say something about that?"

"Yep. Anyway, how many were there?"

"Umm, well..."

"What?"

A look of concern washed over Ink's face. "You won't mention me if you meet any of the kids, will you? Or kick me out and give me back to them?"

It was a difficult question. Ink was still just a child, after all, and if they found her guardian... But Eterna was painfully familiar with the feeling of having lost your home and being all alone. She came to a decision right then and there.

"No, we won't."

It might make things a little more difficult down the road, but Eterna felt an attachment to the young girl.

Maybe it was a fleeting, imagined sensation, but she couldn't turn her back on her.

"I promise you that I won't unquestioningly believe their side of the story, and I won't give you up. So please, trust me and tell me what you can."

Ink looked taken aback by Eterna's words, but her expression quickly relaxed as the meaning behind them finally sunk in. What she lacked in sight, she made up for in insight. The gentle smile gracing the girl's face told Eterna that she'd finally gained Ink's trust.

"There are four other kids, all about two years younger than me."

"Huh, I figured there were more. And the adults?"

"Well, there's Mother, of course, and Papa's off somewhere."

"Off somewhere?"

"I've never actually met him, so I'm not too sure."

"And you're not just pretending you don't know?"

"Nope. I lived there ever since I was born, but I never actually met him. If he's everyone's father, then why am I the only one who hasn't met him?"

If that were true, it would suggest that Ink was being kept away for some reason.

"I couldn't really keep up with everyone, with how they talked. I started to wonder if maybe this Papa person didn't even really exist."

"Why's that?"

"Everyone always made fun of me... Like making up stories and then pretending they all believed them just to trick me. Even Mother said she'd never actually seen his face. How is that even possible?"

Eterna was grateful that Ink was finally opening up to her, though the more she spoke, the deeper the rabbit hole got. She fought to find a pattern in the details. Why was the absentee parent "Papa," and the caregiver "Mother?" Why the two-year gap between her and the other children? What made breakfast so compelling for her?

Eterna was lost in thought as she mulled over all these questions.

"Eterna, Iiiink! Time for lunch!" Milkit's voice calling out from downstairs finally broke her focus.

"Whoa, there's food in the afternoon, too? Hurry up, Eterna! Let's go!!"

"Hold your horses, we'll get down there eventually."

"I'm just so exhausted from hungeeeeeeer...!"

"Heh. You were snoring just a while ago, kid." Eterna reached down and plucked the fish-shaped trinket from the bed, eliciting a frown from the young girl. However, a bright grin immediately overtook her face the moment she took Eterna's outstretched hand.

Hand in hand, the two made their way downstairs for lunch.

◇ ◇ ◇

Flum spent the rest of the day lazing about the house with Milkit. Just holding her hand seemed to do wonders for easing her tension, and Milkit seemed back to her normal self by the time the day came to a close. The letter from earlier was just an empty threat...or so she thought.

When Flum checked the mail early the next morning, she found ten posters plastered to the side of the wall waiting for her.

"Murderer"

"You're to blame"

"You killed Papa"

"I'll have my revenge"

"Enjoy what you have for now—I'll take it all from you"

Flum stared, mouth agape. "Wh-what is all this?"

She immediately went to work tearing the papers down. The specific how and why behind it didn't matter; someone wanted her scared. Dein, obviously.

Reading more closely, it seemed like the writer blamed her for killing the slave trader who'd bought her, rather than anything to do with Dein's crew. But that, Flum reasoned, had been totally justified. She'd clawed her self-worth back from his filthy grasp. She was building a new life with Milkit now. That inhuman sack of flesh, who had killed so many slaves, had deserved to die.

Alas, no matter how strong Flum was, she was still a sixteen-year-old girl. She couldn't easily laugh off such a heinous accusation.

She squeezed the crumpled papers in her fist and bit down hard on her lip.

**ROLL
OVER
AND
DIE**

No Respite for a Slave

EVEN IN THE FACE of such threats, Flum had no intention of backing down. With her chest puffed out and a confident gait, she made her way to Dein's hangout at the West District adventurers' guild to see if there were any job requests issued for finding Ink. Once that was done, she'd immediately make her exit.

Dein smirked as he watched Flum make her entrance. His stare was that of a glutton sizing up their first appetizer, but at least he wasn't hurling insults at her, for once. That was an improvement.

For some reason, possibly precisely because of Dein's behavior, Y'lla would shoot sympathetic glances Flum's way whenever she stopped by. She was, after all, completely outnumbered by Dein's gang.

Y'lla slowly approached Flum as she inspected the job board. She spoke under her breath so Dein and his rowdy group wouldn't hear her. "Why do you insist on coming here with all this going on?"

Flum didn't take her eyes off the papers. "I'm a freed slave. There's nowhere for me to be, other than the West District."

Part of her wondered if she could try to live off her name as the once-famous hero, Flum Apricot, but she suspected this would only put Jean and the church on the offensive. No, her best choice was to live a quiet, peaceful life with Milkit and Eterna here in the West District, while slowly pulling back the curtain on the church's plans.

Not that Y'lla was wrong. Flum couldn't ignore Dein forever. One way or another, she'd have to do something. As it stood, she didn't fancy her current chances against him.

"I don't think there are any good jobs for you here."

"Why?"

"You're a D-Rank adventurer now, aren't you?"

"Well, I've been working hard."

Though she took her fair share of lumps and bruises, Flum had burned through the F-rank assignments. Her recent promotion would mean more jobs and bigger payouts.

"No, that's a bad thing. I used to just tell Dein which jobs you were taking, but he's putting honeypot jobs on the board now, too." Y'lla showed the job list to Flum.

"If you're going to tell me all that, then why don't you just ignore them in the first place?"

"Eww, why would I help you like that? I'm still friends with them, you know."

"You're weird, lady."

"If you're gonna be like that, maybe I'll just make you take the worst job on the list then, huh?"

Y'lla clearly felt no strong attachment to Flum. She was just offering her two cents to a girl who'd impressed her for a moment.

"...Got it. I guess I won't be taking any jobs today, then."

Not that she'd planned to take one, anyway. There was nothing in the list related to Ink, though there was still the possibility that she was mentioned in a job reserved for adventurers above D-Rank or that Dein was purposefully hiding any jobs that might be appealing to her.

"Can I ask you one thing? I was wondering if any jobs came in having to do with a lost child."

"Child? Nope. Pretty sure I hadn't heard about any jobs like that in the Central or East districts either." Y'lla seemed to be telling the truth.

"Got it, thanks." Flum turned away and left the guild, feeling Dein's eyes on her back.

As soon as she was out of sight, Dein shot a glance to some of his men nearby. They stood up in unison, immediately understanding his intent.

◇ ◇ ◇

"Hmm, where to go next? I don't really know the layout of the capital all that well, and it's not like I have any other clues to work from."

With the guild a bust, Flum was fresh out of ideas. If only she were back in her hometown, then she'd have someone she could rely on for...help...

"That's right, Ottilie!"

A high-ranking military officer should have access to information that most normal people wouldn't. In that moment, she felt fate must have conspired to put them back in touch. Besides, Ottilie had insisted that Flum come to see her.

"But I'd draw a lot of attention if I went straight to the castle... Maybe I could sneak into the barracks instead?"

Suddenly, she heard a man shouting up ahead. "Wait for us, kid!"

A young slave boy holding something draped in white cloth was running straight toward her, followed closely by two grown men. In a flash, the trio ran right past Flum. She looked back just in time to catch sight of the boy turning a corner.

Flum had a bad feeling about that. "That's a dead end..."

As she predicted, a scream echoed from around the corner a moment later.

"Why'd a little piece of slave trash like you go and do that, huh?!"

"Die, die! Die, you worthless piece of scum! Just die already and give 'er back!"

"No, please! Stop!! This is... It's important to me! It doesn't belong to you!"

Flum couldn't recall seeing either of the men before, so it was a fairly safe bet that they weren't involved with Dein. In any case, she couldn't just look the other way. "Better get going..."

Just as with Ink, it was clear that Flum wasn't fit to live like the rest of the West District locals. This sort of scene played out daily; it wasn't uncommon to find the bodies of children and vagrants strung up from poles. Those who managed to make it to old age there espoused their own brand of wisdom: don't poke the bear, especially when it's busy mauling someone else. Flum was still too young for that, though she doubted she could ever turn a blind eye to those in need, no matter how old she lived to be.

Flum stood at the entrance to the alley and called out to the two men busily kicking away at the young boy. "Stop it right there!"

"Who the hell're you?"

"You pickin' a fight with us, kid?!"

They were a lot more worked up than Flum originally anticipated. Almost as soon as the words were out of their mouths, they rushed in, fists flailing.

Flum quickly cast Scan and analyzed the situation.

Huh, she thought, *they aren't armed, and it doesn't even look like they have anything hidden on them. They're actually pretty underprepared for the West District. Maybe they just happened to chase the kid out here? Their stats seem too low for adventurers. Best to not arm myself, either.*

She held both fists at the ready, though it was obvious she had no idea what she was doing. The men immediately broke out laughing at the sight.

"Listen, girlie, we don't wanna hurt you. Just get outta here and run along."

"Funny, I was about to say the same thing."

"You wanna play hero, kid? I guess it's 'bout time someone brings you back to reality!"

The gap in stats and actual experience left the man with a snowball's chance in hell of hitting Flum. She ducked clear of his punches, spun, and felt his face deform around her fist.

"Bluaaaugh?!"

The man's nose broke with a crisp snap. Blood flowed down his face as he tumbled backward. His teeth left angry red scrapes on Flum's knuckles, but the wounds closed as quickly as they formed.

"You're done!" The second man lunged in after his friend with a massive kick. Flum caught his leg in both hands and paused. She hadn't quite thought through to the next step. After a moment's consideration, she swung him around and let him fly.

"Waugh!!"

The man tumbled end over end several times before crashing into the wall and collapsing in a motionless heap.

The first man was back on his feet, though there was no fight left in him. "You'll regret this!"

Having gotten the last word in, he limped over to his friend, wrapped an arm around him, and the two men staggered off together. That had been...pretty easy, compared to the usual goons Flum ran across in the West District. She was just glad to have it over with so quickly.

"Pretty spirited for pushovers." Flum clapped her hands together a few times to get the blood and dust off before turning her attention to the boy, who had watched the whole ordeal in stunned silence.

She knelt down and called out to him in the softest voice she could. "Are you okay? Does anything hurt?"

He shook his head.

"Well, that's good. Can you stand up?"

The boy slowly took her proffered hand and rose to his feet.

"You're a real tough one, aren't ya?"

The boy had the same mark as Flum on his own cheek, though it was red and raw, clearly fresh. Flum was more interested in the mysterious cloth-draped object he clung so tightly to.

"That's pretty important to you, huh?"

"...Yeah."

"Did you run away from a slave trader?"

"I hated it there."

Flum laughed gently. "Of course you did. I did, too."

There was almost certainly something nefarious at work for a boy so young to be a slave. Slave merchants usually kept clear of orphanage stock.

"Do you have somewhere to go?"

"No, my family's all dead."

"I'm sorry to hear that. How about I take you to the church, then?" Flum was hardly in any position to take on another kid to look after. She figured Ed and Jonny might be able to help her out. "Whether you decide to stay in the orphanage or not, I'm pretty sure they'll take care of you."

Flum tugged on the boy's hand to lead him back to the main road. To her surprise, he refused to budge. It was then that she noticed a foul odor coming from the cloth-wrapped object the boy carried. In fact, it wasn't even entirely white—a brown liquid was seeping through the white cloth.

That smell... Flum thought, *could it be?*

She could recognize it anywhere. It was the scent that had defined her life since its dark turn.

Aah, she thought, *now things are starting to make sense.*

"Hey, is that..."

"Wanna see it?"

The boy quickly pulled away the cloth, revealing the head of the slave trader who bought Flum. The head, which she had left chopped in half, had been roughly sewn back together. But the state of decomposition was so advanced that a thick, brown pus seeped from the sutures.

"This is my dad. You killed him."

Flum was beginning to understand. Dein had pegged her for the kind of weak child who would break under this type of emotional pressure.

"Ya know, you coulda just run away..." she said. Now that she knew this was all just a farce, Flum felt her composure begin to return.

"Why'd you kill him? That wasn't necessary, you know."

She felt her heart go cold. Even murder didn't faze her. "Wanna call me out? Have at it, kid. But you should know I don't feel even the slightest bit of regret for killing that man."

"It's because of you that I'm a slave!"

"Whatever. Just tell Dein he can stop wasting time on these stupid games." Flum turned her back on the boy and began to walk away. She only made it a few steps before she heard him let out a scream.

"Aaaaaaaaaaaaaaauuugh!!!"

The boy was running full tilt right at her. Undoubtedly, having failed, the least the could do to stay in Dein's good graces was try to kill her. Flum calmly turned and kicked the knife out of the boy's hand.

"Ouch!"

The silver blade arced through the air before landing with a satisfying clink. The young boy huddled down and looked up at Flum, terror in his eyes.

"You guys are *really* overdoing this."

Flum turned around again and walked out of the alley.

Dein's influence reached much further than she ever imagined. When she and Milkit went shopping in the West District, they found plenty of shops that barred them entry for being known enemies of Dein. It had left them with little choice but to take their shopping excursions out to the Central District. It was easy to guess that this was Dein's usual M.O. when he wanted to drive someone out of his territory. Why rely only on violence when emotional and financial incentives worked just as well?

"On the other hand, this is the first time he's gone and done something so bold. I need to be more careful from here on out." Back on the main thoroughfare, Flum gave her cheek a light slap to refocus herself and started for the castle. "I got this!"

A short time later she caught whiff once again of a familiar scent: the smell of fresh blood.

"You've gotta be kidding me."

Flum ever-so-slowly turned her head in the scent's direction, moving stiffly, like a mannequin. Down the alley, she spotted the two men who chased the slave boy earlier, collapsed in a heap on the ground.

They had been cut down from behind.

Huh, she thought. *It seemed strange that Dein would use some random punks like that for his little ploy. I guess he planned on killing them from the jump? Revenge for the boy failing, maybe?*

However, none of this quite fit in with how Dein operated. He might have been underhanded, but he wasn't the type to just casually kill off underlings. In fact, he'd usually play up their failures in order to cement the feeling that they owed him.

While Flum stared on, two soldiers—possibly notified by a passerby who witnessed the crime—came running up. Trying to understand Dein's thought process was a lost cause. She decided to leave the scene to the soldiers and turned to resume her trip to the castle.

Before she could leave, however, one of the soldiers called out to her. "Hold it."

"Why? Listen, I just happened to stumble across the bodies."

The men ignored her plea and drew their swords.

"Whoa, this is a bit much, don't you think?"

"We are holding you on suspicion of murder. Please do not resist."

"Oh, come on. I just showed up a few seconds ago!"

"Shut up! We already know you're the one who did this!"

This was beyond ridiculous.

"...Let me guess, Dein even has some soldiers in his pocket?"

She knew that Dein was growing his power. It was unlikely he'd managed to get anyone in an actual position of command but entirely possible that he'd either bribed or somehow threatened some foot soldiers out in the West District. Regardless of how he did it, it was still enough to frame her. If she let herself get arrested, false evidence and faked confessions would undoubtedly soon follow.

The punishment for killing two innocent men would be execution. Attacking two soldiers would only add to the charges against her. If she couldn't change their minds, then the only option left was to try and escape.

"Hyah!" Without another word, Flum took off running.

"Halt! Murderer!!" The guards cried out just a little louder than they needed to, almost as if to draw attention to the chase.

Flum felt all eyes on her as she barreled past the people milling about in the street.

◇ ◇ ◇

The sight of a young girl chased by soldiers was bound to draw attention. Having the mark of a slave burnt into her cheek only made matters worse. Flum decided to take the narrowest, least populated alleys she could find to minimize attention.

They're doing a good job of making my life hell, huh? she thought.

Flum's only weapon was a broadsword, hardly fit for use in a narrow alley—not that she dared attack the soldiers, anyway. She needed to keep running until she made it back to the house and Eterna, or to one of the churches, where the military would be hesitant to continue their pursuit.

If that wasn't possible, then the only other option would be to find another way to the castle in the North District and Ottilie's assistance.

"You're not gettin' away!" A soldier summoned up a fifty-centimeter-long ice arrow and loosed it at her.

And now they're using magic??

Though the spell was quite weak, it still found its mark, piercing through the back of her leg.

"Nngaaah!" The wound was quick to regenerate, but it still slowed her down. Worse yet, there was an intersection up ahead.

I know the road up ahead is a dead end, she thought, *but where does that side street go?* Flum had a fair grasp of the West District's layout but not a comprehensive one. *Whatever, we're going right!*

She made the correct choice: this was the most direct route to the church.

...Which was probably also why there was another soldier waiting for her, armed with a bow and arrow.

"An ambush?!" Flum's surprise stunned her just long enough for the archer to shoot an arrow straight through her right thigh. "Gaaugh!"

The archer pulled another arrow from his quiver. She could hear the two soldiers closing in behind her. *I can't let something like this hold me back now,* she thought. *Not after what I went through with that ogre!*

She grit her teeth and ripped the arrow out of her leg. "Aaaaaaaaaaaaaaaauugh!!!"

The sound of her scream, and her willingness to cause further injury to herself made her pursuers freeze for a moment. Flum took advantage of the lull to Scan the archer.

Neave Cranfeld
Affinity: Wind
Strength: 450
Magic: 112
Endurance: 381
Agility: 253
Perception: 162

His total stats were 1358—a solid C-Rank. Assuming this was normal for soldiers, then the two men behind her were probably around the same strength.

Including all her gear, that put Flum at...

Flum Apricot
Affinity: Reversal
Strength: 670
Magic: 538
Endurance: 1194
Agility: 920
Perception: 128

A total stat value of 3450, around B-Rank.

One-on-one, she'd have little problem taking these guys down. Three-on-one was something else, and they didn't have her reservations about murder. If she'd left the arrow embedded in her thigh, she risked going into shock from blood loss. If she'd been a normal person, then death would soon follow.

It was looking more and more difficult for her to beat this group without going all out.

There's no way I'm going to come out of this without hurting anyone, so I guess I'll have to take care of the guy up ahead first. Then maybe I can still get away!

Flum took advantage of the lull and rushed ahead, closing in fast on the archer while avoiding more spells from behind. The archer took a few steps back before letting loose another arrow. Flum drew the Souleater and knocked it aside with the flat of the blade.

One of the soldiers behind her knelt down and put his hand to the ground. A moment later, a trail of ice raced across the ground after her.

At the last second, she leapt into the air to avoid the attack and brought her sword down on the archer.

"Hyaaaaaaah!"

He feebly held his bow in front of himself, hoping to soak the blow. The Souleater sent splinters everywhere as it split the bow but stopped short of cleaving through his armor. It was scratched, but his life was spared.

"Listen, I'm sorry, but you attacked me first!" Flum took off again in a mad dash. It didn't seem to stop the former archer from continuing his pursuit.

"Just what does Dein have over these guys?!"

For members of the royal army, they'd put in a pathetic showing, whether or not Dein was holding something over their heads. In terms of sheer speed, the heavily armored men had nothing on Flum. She continued to gain ground on them and was about to finally break away from her pursuers when she turned

the corner to find a two-meter tall barricade blocking the street.

"You can't be serious!!"

Either they somehow figured that she'd take this route, or they barricaded all of the nearby streets. In either case, the lengths they were going to capture one slave beggared belief.

She could still climb it if she tried, though she risked being caught as she climbed up. What's more, there were more soldiers on the other side of the barricade.

That didn't mean she was about to give up just yet. When life gives you lemons...

Flum ran straight at the wall, leapt into the air at the last second, and cleared the wall and the soldiers on the other side.

"How in the... She jumped right over it?!"

"That's no ordinary slave!!"

The soldiers looked on in sheer amazement as Flum made a smooth landing before taking off in another mad sprint. Several of the soldiers took off after her, launching a barrage of fire spells at her back.

I got this... All I need to do is make it to the main road and then I'm practically at the church!

She was in a familiar part of town now. She could even see the exit to the alley up ahead and the wide, open road beyond it. From there she could call on the church knights for help and end this bizarre encounter once and for all.

Most of all, though, she was worried about Milkit and Eterna's safety. She fully expected Dein to try attacking them, too.

With freedom so close at hand, the sight waiting for her out in the road made Flum's spirits crash. There were at least a dozen soldiers waiting for her in a large semi-circle, all of them with arrows nocked and fixed on her. Flum's moment of hesitation was all the time her pursuers needed to close in and finish off the perimeter.

"It was a good chase, Flum, but the game is up." A soldier in decorative armor loped up from behind the wall of men.

"Are you the local commander here in the West District?" she demanded.

He looked a lot like one of Dein's goons. Then again, most people with such rotten personalities tended to look the same.

"Do you really think you can get away with this?!"

"Of course. After all, you're only a slave. It'll be easy to make you disappear."

It was clear none of them recognized her as a former member of the great heroes. They were just following Dein's orders.

"Since when did the royal army serve as thugs for hire for the likes of Dein? Imagine how your generals would react to such a disgraceful sight!"

"Then I guess we'll have to make sure they don't see it."

"So you don't even deny it? I guess he's holding something over you guys, huh? I can't believe it. Do you have no honor?"

"Fire."

Fwip!!

The archers loosed their volley all at once. Flum deflected the first few, but there were too many to block them all. The remainder made a pincushion of her.

She moaned, her face contorting. Even though the wounds were healing, the pain remained. A thin sheen of sweat covered her body. Somehow, possibly through her sheer indignant rage, she kept her wits about her.

"You're a stubborn one, huh. I think it's about time you give up."

"Gaaaaaaaaaaugh!! Haah... Aaaaaugh!!" Flum grunted and howled as she ripped the arrows out of her body, one by one.

With the last of them drawn out and tossed to the ground, she turned her gaze on the soldiers ahead of her. They all took a terrified step back.

"Keep your cool, men! She's just tougher than we

thought!" In spite of his brave words, the commander's voice cracked. He'd only been told they were setting her up, and yet here she was, standing defiantly in the face of a dozen-odd soldiers.

Flum could only imagine what was going through the commander's head at that moment. This wasn't what he signed up for.

"Calm yourselves and fire another volley! Remember your training! Think of her as one of the dummies you use for target practice!!"

"Do you have to act like I'm an inanimate object?! Surely you've had practice murdering real people in cold blood by now!"

"What are you going to do about it? There's nowhere left to run, and killing a soldier is a capital offense. You're only digging yourself deeper."

Her choices weren't looking much better than that day back in the slave trader's underground cell. Give up and die, or put up a fight and die.

Just like last time, the choice was obvious.

"Well, I'm going to die anyway, right?"

"Of course."

"In that case, I might as well die a criminal for living as I choose!!"

Flum rushed the commander.

"Wh-what?! Someone, stop her! Keep her away from me!!"

It was a mystery to her why he was so scared. Wasn't a soldier supposed to embrace death? If he could dish it out, he should be ready to take it, too.

The second volley of arrows wasn't nearly as well aimed. All but one, which struck her calf, went wide.

The archer who'd struck her let out a triumphant cheer. "Yeah!"

Flum stumbled from the pain, just for a moment. She continued her rush straight for the commander and swung the Souleater straight into his head.

It struck his helmet with an awful clang, caving it in instantly. Had she put any more strength behind it, he would have died instantly. The commander's bravado melted away in an instant as he tumbled to the ground and tried to crawl away from her, leaving a puddle between his legs as he went.

The rest of the soldiers were stunned, and the formation began to break up.

Now's my chance!

She'd really wanted to kill him for a moment there, but not enough to put her own life at risk. For now, her only goal was to put as much distance between herself and the soldiers as she could.

Flum took off running, not once looking back.

◇ ◇ ◇

"Here too, huh?"

The closer Flum got to the church, the more barricades and checkpoints she ran across. Her flight was starting to look like a losing endeavor. In fact, it seemed like the royal army had surrounded the entire church. She highly doubted that the knights were okay with this, so they must have come up with some story to explain away their behavior.

Considering how crudely the whole plan was thrown together, it was surprisingly effective. She couldn't run through this many roadblocks, and even though Ed and Jonny would likely be supportive, the royal army and church knights were still allies—publicly, at least. They wouldn't join her in open defiance of the soldiers.

I'd love to meet back up with Eterna and Milkit, but I just don't think that's a good idea right now, she thought. *Maybe I could get Eterna to help me and... No, I can't leave Milkit alone like that.*

Milkit was the most important thing on Flum's mind. Leaving her in Eterna's more than capable hands was the best choice at the moment.

Getting out of the West District is going to be tough, but there's gotta be some way out. I just need to figure out what that is.

Flum crouched in the shadows with her back up against the wall, finally taking a moment to catch her breath. She glanced down to see a paper thrown around by the wind land at her feet.

"What's this?" She picked it up and inspected the discarded paper. Written across the top were the words "Flum–Wanted for Murder," and beneath that was a sinister sketch of her face. Below that was a bounty and the official seal of the royal army.

Flum clicked her tongue in annoyance and crumpled the paper into a ball. "Those scumbags really outdid themselves!"

Dein had really wanted her to kill some soldiers, huh? He wasn't going to stop until she'd been driven from the West District.

"Maybe I should just go kill them all and see how they like it." Flum was taken aback at the murderous tone of her own voice.

A loud voice called out as a man entered the alley. "Well, I'll be! If it isn't the mass-murderer Flum!"

It was just one of Dein's thugs. He was holding one of the wanted posters in his hand. Looking a bit closer, she saw that a nearby wall was practically covered in them. Dein and his crew had taken their time to make sure the whole district knew she was a murderer.

Now she'd have to deal with not only the military but Dein's crew and random street thugs hungry for a payout as well. Even normal people on the street might feed information on Flum's whereabouts back to them for a cut.

"I know I'm no supermodel, but seriously, *someone's* gotta recognize me with all these flyers out there!"

If anyone recognized her as one of the great heroes, it could at least put a damper on Dein's scheme...but she could only leave that up to fate.

More and more low-level street punks began to gather around, drawn in by the man's voice. Flum searched around frantically for an escape route, but the other path away from the men was another dead end. Fortunately for her, the alley was narrow, and the building on her left had a low-hanging roof.

"Up and out!" Flum got a running start and jumped up into the air, bounding off the wall on the right before landing on the roof opposite to it.

"She's on top of the building! Get her!"

She heard an uproar break out below as the men scrambled to climb atop one another in frantic pursuit. Dein must have offered an impressive bonus for killing her.

**ROLL
OVER
AND
DIE**

004

Poetic Justice at Last

THIS LIFE-OR-DEATH game of tag just wouldn't end. Back on ground level, Flum found herself surrounded by soldiers. On the main street, people gawked and pointed at her. In the ghetto, vagrants and street punks tried to chase her down for the bounty. This feeling of having the whole world against her hurt more than the young boy's words or the posters on the side of her house ever could. It'd been a mere two hours since the whole ordeal started, but Flum had been running the entire time; she was down to the last of her reserves.

"They're...not gonna...get me..."

She'd already lost most of the feeling in her feet, and she could feel herself slowing down significantly. Still, she refused to give in to a man as despicable as Dein. She was going to foil every plan he cooked up and get home, one way or another. It was that promise to herself that kept her going.

Flum slowed to a walk, catching her breath on a relatively empty street. Suddenly, she heard a voice call out from above.

"There she is! Fire!"

She frantically turned to look up. Several archers stood atop a roof, already loosing arrows.

"Got her!"

"Ha! Think again!" Flum deftly dodged out of the way and drew her blade with both hands. She gave it a full-body swing, hurling it straight at the roof. The sword spun like a saw blade through the air, scattering the soldiers and catching one hapless man in the back of his head. Chunks of skull and gray matter flew every which way.

The mark on the back of Flum's hand glowed as the Epic weapon disappeared and returned to its parallel dimension, waiting to be summoned again.

The men were shaken. "She killed another one!! You know what we've gotta do, men!"

She'd lost count at this point of how many people she killed. Killing someone for the first time changed you categorically; every death after that was a change in degree. If they were going to try to take her life, they should be prepared to lose their own.

Flum gave up on thinking about right and wrong for now. It wasn't like she was just killing without reason. The more soldiers she killed, the more they began to question whether this was really something they wanted to do. Was following orders worth your life? Was it really worth it to throw everything away for a commander like that? These were the kinds of doubts she hoped to raise in their minds.

In fact, she already felt like the soldiers were being just a little less zealous in their efforts to catch her, though that may have just been wishful thinking. In any case, it made her feel better to think that way.

Flum took off again, leaving the soldiers to grieve for their comrade.

I'm slowly closing in on the Central District, at least...

She kept her wits about her as she continued her mad dash through the city, trying to keep to streets that were less likely to be covered by the soldiers. Block by block, she was edging closer to her goal. Just as she hit the border that separated the West and Central districts, she spotted a group of men standing around. Flum buried herself in the shadows and glanced ahead to get a better look.

The men looked to be part of Dein's crew. They were chatting with a middle-aged merchant who was somehow familiar to Flum. Further back, she saw several kids with slave brands standing there, still and emotionless. Some of the children had no arms, others limped about awkwardly, and others still had burns on their faces. Not a single one of them was without some kind of injury.

The man wrung his hands as he spoke. "I just can't thank Dein enough, ya know? He gets me revenge for my buds *and* buys up my damaged goods in one fell swoop. Be sure to thank him for me, yeah?"

Revenge for your buds... Does that guy have something to do with the slave trader who bought me?

There was really no limit to what Dein would do. Not only was he tight with the local army brass, but now he was trying to build connections in the Central District, too?

"Dying for a cause is about the best this scum could hope for."

"Did you get the little runts ready like we asked?"

"Of course, of course. They're all set up. You can blow them up whenever, wherever you need."

The kids all had belts wrapped around their waists. A bag with a small crystal pin drooped from each belt. Flum hadn't paid it much attention until the merchant mentioned it.

Is that black powder? I get that he doesn't value slaves' lives, but using kids as suicide bombs? Just how far are these guys willing to go?!

She felt her blood begin to boil. She ached to cut the bastards down right now, but she knew that wouldn't save the children. Besides, the street was completely blocked off.

With a heavy sigh, Flum turned away to look for another route.

◇ ◇ ◇

No matter where she went, the roads to the Central District were blocked by soldiers of the royal army, Dein's goons, or kids with bombs. Sometimes a mixture of the three. There just wasn't any way through. Flum wondered if there was any angle Dein *hadn't* leveraged.

"There she is! Kill 'er!!"

She took off running again. Just how many times were they going to repeat this back and forth? The exhaustion was beginning to show on her face.

Glancing around a corner, she saw the words "Give Up" written in large letters on the wall.

She shook her head to banish the thought, but she was reaching the limits of her endurance at this point. She didn't want to hurt anymore. It seemed so tempting to just stop running.

Up ahead, she noticed she was heading straight for a dead end, almost as if her thoughts had surfaced in reality.

Gah, looks like I made a wrong turn...

She was starting to lose her focus. Making matters worse, the walls around her were too high to scale, and she couldn't reach any of the nearby rooftops. Too many people were closing in behind her to make fighting her way out a plausible solution.

"Checkmate."

And there was the mastermind himself, standing among the crowd.

His timing was just too good—almost as if he knew exactly where Flum was going to make a mistake.

"Surprised to see you here, Dein."

"I figured the next time we met, I'd be looking down at your body. But this is quite a happy coincidence."

"Are you sure it's such a good idea to waltz on up here? I could kill you at this distance, you know."

"I'm trembling in my boots, kid. I'm an A-Rank adventurer; you really think you can punch that far above your weight class?"

"Then why are you using such underhanded means to get rid of me?"

"Just wanted to flex my power a bit—see how much I could get out of the army, network with the Central District slavers, y'know? But mostly, I just wanted to watch you suffer."

The men behind him began clapping and cheering at this. She had no idea what they found so amusing.

"You must be tired. To be honest, I'm getting pretty bored chasing you around. Every soldier you kill is another hour I have to spend with their COs bending my ear. Why don't you just give up?"

"Not interested." Flum drew the Souleater and pointed the tip of the blade at Dein. She summoned up the last of her inner strength and fixed him with a defiant gaze. She would go down fighting.

Dein ran a hand through his hair. "Aah, the ignorance of youth. How dreadfully annoying."

He then cast a sidelong glance, hatred clear in his eyes, back at Flum. "It makes me want to beat you down, break you, and teach you how the world really works."

"Must be convenient to decide the world works whichever way is most useful to you."

"What a childish argument, you impudent little runt."

"Funny, that sounds a lot like you. I thought most kids stopped playing gangster well before their teens."

"Shut up, you good-for-nothing wench. Keep mouthing off to me and I won't make your death so easy."

"That's fine. I didn't plan on dying easily anyway!"

Flum lunged toward Dein, though someone stepped in his way before she could reach him. His protector wasn't a brave soldier but a young, one-armed slave who no longer had any value on the open market. A bag filled with black powder hung from the child's waist.

"The mere sight of this kid makes you want to save her, doesn't it, Flum?"

She grit her teeth.

"I get it. Really, I do. I was young once, too, and filled with that righteous zeal. I wasted my days fighting the forces of evil and being an all-around nuisance. And yet you couldn't even protect that little lapdog of yours."

"What did you do to Milkit?!"

"Aaah, yes, that's her name. That little mummy girl with the bandages. Anyway, I'm pretty sure she's already been strung up, violated, and killed by now. It's really a shame you were so nice to her. Gave her something to lose. I bet she wondered why her master didn't come to save her, right at the end."

"Go to hell, Dein!!"

"Oh, I'm *so* scared, just *petrified*. I bet you guys are too, yah?"

The men gathered behind him cackled. They looked more worried about what they would have for dinner once this was all wrapped up.

"All right, I think I'm about done playing around. I'd hate to give you more time to think up another escape

attempt. Could you just hurry up and take care of her for me?"

"What are you going on about?" Flum snarled.

"Suicide, of course. Just think about it—it's almost poetic! Two underdogs of society come together and set themselves free of the pains of this world."

The young girl walked unsteadily toward Flum. Her empty expression reminded Flum of Milkit. Maybe, just maybe, this girl could also find happiness of her own if someone would just reach out to her.

But the only thing anyone ever gave her was a bag of explosives tied to her waist and the instruction to die for these disgusting men's amusement.

"Oh, you're not thinking about trying to save her, are you?"

Flum didn't respond.

"Cat got your tongue? I guess you agree, then. All right, listen, I'm a pretty conscientious guy, so I'll offer you an alternative. I'll take the bag off her, and you can just blow yourself up instead. Then the girl doesn't need to die...though I really can't promise what'll happen to her after that. My boys here are pretty randy and, well, y'know. It takes a certain type of guy to want to make it with a dirty little slave, but I figure there's gotta be about five or so guys here that fit that description. That leaves her about...what, two holes short? Gyahahaha!"

"If you're short on holes, Dein, I'd be happy to make a new one for you."

"With that dinky little knife? Look at little Miss Badass over here!" Dein and his men burst out into a round of raucous laughter. What was it with bastards and their desire to make someone choose their own death? Did it really make you feel superior to lord two awful choices over someone?

Flum didn't hesitate. She walked up to the young girl, took a knee, and removed the bag from her waist. Even relieved from the threat of death, there was no change in the girl's demeanor. She stared back at Flum with empty eyes and cocked her head to the side, probably unsure of what to do now that her one job had been taken from her.

After holding her gaze for a moment, Flum turned around to face Dein.

"Aww, what a sweet little lady you are," he said. "A true shining example. You saved the girl from an explosive death, and now she can learn to enjoy all of the 'love' we can give her. We'll fill her up until she chooses death rather'n endure any more of it. It's gonna be pretty bad, ya know. A whole lot worse than just blowing up. But hey, I'm sure she's thankful."

Flum had a hard time believing she and Dein were even from the same species at this point. Even given years to interpret his words, she doubted she would ever be able to make sense of them beyond their component phonemes.

"That bomb right there, see the crystal on it? All you need to do is give it a little energy and boom! There it goes. It's not all that powerful, really, but strong enough to kill one person. Maybe two."

Dein and the young slave girl took a step back from Flum.

She looked down at the activator. Giving just a bit of magic to the crystal would set off the black powder inside and blow Flum's body to shreds. The pain she felt from the arrows earlier would be nothing compared to being blown apart.

If she did that, then there would be no saving that young girl. The poor girl hadn't done anything wrong other than just happening to be missing an arm, but they saw little value in her life beyond her deficiencies. Returning her to the slave trader wouldn't be much better; all that awaited her was the same death in a miserable cell that Flum and Milkit had so nearly succumbed to.

Such a futile death.

None of the choices available to Flum would open any new doors for the child... If Flum were any normal person, that is.

She let out a breath.

With the bomb in her right hand, she held it out as far away from her heart as she could. Dein watched on with his men, cackling at Flum's impending demise.

She ran her fingers over the crystal. It was cool to the touch. Closing her eyes, she focused on the crystal and felt her fingers tingle slightly as magic flowed freely through them.

KABOOM!

The corners of Dein's lips curled at this, and the young girl's eyes went wide as Flum was consumed by a bright flash of light.

Flum's entire right arm blew clear off her body and landed in a nearby tree. It was easy to follow by the spray of blood that marked its path. Her face and neck were hollowed out, and the heat charred her exposed flesh. The blast sent her flying, jerking around wildly like a rag doll in the wind.

The blowback from the explosion caused Dein's hair to stand on end. A gentle breeze rolled in, filling the alley with the uniquely pungent smell of burnt flesh. A slow, mirthful laugh escaped from the back of his throat.

"Oooooooaaaaaaah!!" The men all let out an excited cheer when Flum's body finally crashed down to the earth.

As far as they were concerned, they'd finally gotten revenge against their comrades' killer. They were beside themselves in their excitement. Some men danced, others undressed, and more than a few began closing in on the young slave girl.

"You're a bunch of idiots, you know that?" Dein said.

"Hey, you're laughin' too, Dein."

"I didn't say I wasn't enjoying myself. It's a party, after all. If we just had some alcohol, we'd be set. Flum here'd make a great appetizer."

"Got a point there! I'll go get the brews!"

He'd said it half in jest, but one of his underlings took off toward the nearest bar.

"There're some real crazy guys out there. But hey, as long as we've got beer, I'm down for a good time."

The crowd of men were already gleefully working over Flum's body, tearing her apart. Once the initial assault died down, the men surrounded her prone form and began discussing what kind of fun they should have with her next as Dein watched.

A man ran up to his side. Dein furrowed his brow in annoyance at the man's presence. "What in the hell are you doing here? I thought I told you to take care of our other problem?"

The man was supposed to be part of the detachment attacking Flum's home.

"What? You finished up your job and figured you'd come join in the festivities? Well, good timing. We just killed Flum a moment ago, and..."

"No, that's not it." The man's face was deathly pale, and he was trembling uncontrollably.

"You look like death warmed over. What happened?"

"We...we failed."

Dein's cheerful demeanor changed completely. "What? How in the hell could you fail in capturing that frail little girl?!"

His outburst immediately caught the attention of the men gathered around Flum. They stopped what they were doing and looked over in his direction.

"Th-there was a burst of water that surrounded us, and the next thing I knew, we were getting thrown all over the place. I...I don't even know where everyone else is."

Dein cut the man short. "Cut the drama and tell me what really happened before—"

They were interrupted by the sound of a man's scream. "Gaaaaaaaaaaaaaaah!!"

All eyes turned in the direction of the sound. The man was stabbed clean through the throat; blood fountained from the wound.

"What the...?"

No one could quite figure out what was going on until, a moment later, a black blade swept through the air and lopped off his head at the neck.

"That really hurt, ya know?"

There was Flum, fully regenerated and holding her sword at the ready.

"Like really, really bad."

She moved lithely across the open square, lopping off one head after the other in short order.

"And here you are, mocking someone else's pain?"

More necks divorced from their heads.

"You're all scumbags. Death will suit you just fine."

With one powerful swing, she severed three more heads. All her pent-up sadness, agony, and resentment were finally being released, exploding forth in this violent outburst.

"You... But you died," Dein babbled. "How are you moving?!"

"It takes more than that to kill me!"

"What the hell are you?!" The mirthful grin on Dein's face was replaced with a look of fear. The corners of Flum's lips twisted up into a forced grin. Her eyes were full of pure, unrestrained bloodlust. "Are you some kind of monster?! Wait...no...is that an enchantment?!"

His men scattered, but Dein stood his ground and drew his weapon before casting Scan. All he could find were debuffs and curses.

"What's going on here? No normal person should even be able to wield that thing!"

Every time Flum had showed her face at the guild, he'd dismissed her as nothing more than a pathetic slave. If he only thought to scan her gear, this never would have happened. Dein cursed himself for his hubris, but now wasn't the time to dwell on it. He changed tactics and focused on the task at hand.

"Get outta here, men! She's some kind of monster!"

The thugs that hung around him ignored his command, still figuring they had the upper hand due to their sheer numbers. "Nah, Dein, she's already killed a bunch of our brothers! Think about what it'd do to our reputation if we let that...gaaaauuuugh!"

Flum waded through the crowd, chopping men down with ease.

"No, please, stop...!"

"Stop? Like hell I will! Now die!!" Flum was beyond caring at this point; she cut down any man within striking distance.

The open square filled with the coppery scent of blood. The Souleater was completely soaked. Dozens of bodies lay on the ground.

Some of the men began to realize the folly of their plan and started to withdraw.

"We're not done yet!!"

But there was no escaping Flum, who struck the men down from behind as they turned to escape.

Where did all that power come from? Dein thought. *She's even outclassed me! And now she's gone and killed pretty much all of my men. It doesn't make any sense; how did she come back to life with nothing but cursed gear? And what's this bizarre story about water attacking my men?? I planned every little thing about this, and now it's going to hell!!*

"Dein, the royal army's here! They're coming to back us up!" One of the men next to him laughed excitedly as he pointed on ahead. Just as he said, there were a dozen or so soldiers closing in. They would be more than enough to take Flum down...

...But there was something strange about them. They looked frightened. In fact, they appeared to be running *away* from something, much like Dein and his cohorts.

"I'm s-sorry! Please forgive us! We were just following orders! Gaaaaaugh!!!"

"Th-this wasn't supposed to happen! N-n-not like this!"

"I don't believe it!"

A serpentine form made of flowing blood flew through the air after the men, tearing straight through one side of their armor and out the other before moving on to its next target. With Flum closing in from behind, Dein and his men had no choice but to stop. A woman in an immaculately white military uniform stood ahead of them.

"Who the hell are you?! You think you can just kill the king's soldiers and get away with it?!" cried one of Dein's goons.

Unfazed, the red-haired woman let out a snort, drew her saber, and pointed it at him. "Who the hell are you to talk to *me* like that, scum?"

"You..." Dein knew who this woman was. Anyone who lived in the capital and didn't have their head buried in the dirt knew her.

"Lieutenant General Ottilie, at your service. I come at my sister's behest to assist Flum in slaying the evildoers out here."

Her name was Ottilie Fohkelpi, the second-highest ranking member of the royal army, and a student of the Genocide Arts fencing style.

◇◇◇

A short time earlier, Ottilie paid a visit to Flum's house. Though Milkit was a gracious host, the young general was still annoyed to find that Flum wasn't there.

"It looks like we must have just missed each other. Do you know when Flum should return?"

"That I don't. She usually comes back in the evenings, once she's finished up whatever job she picked up at the guild. By the way, may I ask how you found Master's home?"

"Do you have any idea who I am? I just had to do a little digging."

Though they parted ways with an agreement that Flum would come see her sometime, Ottilie realized belatedly that she was rarely at the castle. Making matters worse, it was probably no easy feat for Flum to show her face around there, given her unique circumstances. Ottilie decided that it would be easier for her to come visit Flum instead.

"...And two drills..."

Ottilie was taken by complete surprise to hear Eterna's voice coming down the stairs. "Eterna? Eterna Rinebow?!"

"...Yes. What's it to you?"

"What do you mean what's it to me? Why aren't you on the journey?!"

"I got tired of it, so I left the party."

"Just like that?!" Ottilie was beside herself at this point. It was even worse than Flum's departure. "First Flum, now you... The party must be in complete shambles!"

"I think Gadhio will be leaving any day now, too."

"How can you be casual about this?!"

Eterna sat down opposite Ottilie. "I mean, I don't owe anything to the country, really. If it sucks, hit the bricks."

Milkit swooped in and gracefully served the two women tea.

"Thank you, Milkit. By the way, what brings you here, Ottilie?"

"I came to speak with Flum, but I'm comforted by what I've found here."

"And why's that?"

"It's tough for a young girl to live all alone in the West District. I'm glad she has roommates, and especially that you're here. I still have my concerns, but this is better than her living alone."

"That's certainly an interesting assessment." Eterna didn't trust people easily, so it spoke greatly to Ottilie's character that she would take her at face value. Actually, it was surprising how easily Flum and Milkit had agreed to live with her, given her tendency for chaos.

"By the way, does that bandaged girl belong to Flum?"

"I don't fully understand the situation either, but they grew close when they were both slaves, I guess."

"I've since become *her* slave, so Flum is now my master." Milkit's blush showed through the gaps in her bandages. From the way she spoke about Flum, it was clear she was no ordinary slave.

"You're right. I don't get it either," Ottilie said.

"Glad I'm not the only one."

"I guess I'll just have to ask Flum about this myself..." Ottilie's gaze suddenly shifted as she cut herself off. "What do you think about this, Eterna?"

Eterna's expression grew serious. "That's actually why I came downstairs."

"I figured you must have picked up on it."

"It seems like the house is well and truly surrounded now."

"There are quite a few people, too."

"Hmm? I don't understand." Milkit looked quizzically between the two women, completely unable to follow the conversation.

"We should probably split up, and..."

"No can do. Flum left me here to look after this place. Besides, there's not enough guys out there to be a real challenge to me."

"Then what should I do?"

"I'm pretty sure these are some of Dein's goons. He's always out to cause Flum trouble, so I doubt he's only here for Milkit. Flum must be in danger somewhere. I want you to go out and find her."

Ottilie stood up from her chair. "Understood. I'll get right on that, then."

Milkit's face was full of concern. "Has... Has anything bad happened to Master?"

"Don't worry. That girl can't die easily."

"I'll find her as soon as I can, so you just wait here and try not to worry. I'll bring your Master home to you."

Milkit wasn't totally convinced, but she bowed low and thanked Ottilie all the same.

A few minutes later, a crowd of rough looking men had assembled around the front of the house, armed with improvised bottle bombs. After making eye contact with the man at the center of the group, they nodded in unison, then lit their rags and loosed a volley.

The flaming bottles spiraled through the air, rapidly approaching their target. Once they hit the ground, the bottles would break and splash their fuel everywhere, quickly engulfing the house in flames and setting up its occupants for a painful death. If Milkit were to try to escape, Dein had already given his men the orders to do what they liked with her.

The crowd gathered out front eagerly hoped she'd make a break for it.

Unfortunately for them, things weren't going as they planned.

Eterna looked up from her seat and pointed her hand toward the window. "Water Wall!"

A massive plume of water shot up out of the ground, forming a towering protective barrier in front of the house. The bombs bounced right back at the men, smashing down at their own feet.

"No way!!" Some men took off, screaming in terror, while others attempted to knock the bottles back. Unfortunately, this only smashed them, setting fire to the men.

"Water! Into the water!!" Another man immediately dove into the wall.

Eterna watched the goings-on beyond the window, never once setting her tea cup down. Milkit looked absolutely terrified, her hands clasped tightly at her chest.

"A mage?! We didn't hear shit about a mage!!"

The leader of the group looked on in frustration. Eterna wasn't about to let up yet. Considering they'd been ready to torture weak and defenseless Milkit, she decided they deserved no mercy.

She delicately rotated her hand through the air until her palm faced upwards, curling her index finger in like she was offering up a challenge. The wall of water folded into a massive sphere and floated toward the crowd.

"What the hell...?"

Just as it arrived in front of the terrified men, it burst like a balloon, engulfing the attackers and washing them away.

"No way...gyaugh!! Cut it out! Stop!"

Many of Dein's men drowned within moments, their bodies washed out to far-off corners of the West District. After a few brief moments of chaos, the house was once again engulfed in a peaceful silence.

"Where did you send those men?"

"Don't know, don't care. They may've been washed down the sewers. Maybe even out of the capital entirely. If they're particularly unlucky, they're already dead. You worried?"

"No. They were here to hurt Master, after all."

"That's right. Hey, can I get some more tea?"

"Certainly, I'll make you another cup." Milkit grabbed the teapot and made her way back to the kitchen.

◇ ◇ ◇

Dein was completely beside himself at this new development.

"You have got to be kidding me. Lieutenant General Ottilie?? Why are you protecting that slave?! That makes no sense!"

"What doesn't make sense is whatever's going on in that head of yours. Who would send a whole mob after a young girl? In any case, you're done here. I'm going to put an end to your fun once and for all!"

"Ottilie!!" Flum's eyes sparkled at the sight of the young general. Finally, she had someone to fight along her side, and a powerful ally at that. Now that Ottilie had arrived, the West District soldiers had no excuse to follow Dein's orders.

"You sure attract the attention of some strange men."

"I know, right? It's been pretty rough."

"Dammit!" said Dein, "I planned every detail! Victory was so close...but I'm not giving up so easily!!"

"Then I'll just have to make you give up." Ottilie brandished her saber. "Genocide Arts, Blood Anguis!"

A fountain of blood shot from the tip of her sword before forming into a snake and launching toward Dein.

"Dein, no!!!" One of Dein's loyal followers threw himself between the Blood Anguis and his leader, taking the blow head on.

Located in the hilt of Ottilie's sword was a Blood Cartridge, the source of her techniques' power. Genocide

Arts had a lot in common with Gadhio and Flum's Cavalier Arts, though they relied on the energy stored in blood rather than transforming the body's endurance into prana. The Genocide Arts were unique in that they not only directly inflicted wounds on their opponents but also drained their bodies of energy and barred their escape.

The man collapsed, too weak to even let out a cry of pain. His twitching was the only hint that he was still alive.

"Why'd he have go and do something like that?? Now there's no way I can run!" Dein held the buckler affixed to his left arm at the ready. He reached back and wrapped his finger around a thin cord trailing from the small shield.

With a solid yank of the thread, the mechanism connected to the back of the buckler fired, launching a wire with a metal protrusion at the end. The chunk of metal slammed into a nearby roof and opened up like a flower, transforming into a series of prongs. Dein wrapped his thumb around another cord and gave it a twist, causing the wire to reel back in and pull him into the air with it.

"You're a clever little one, aren't you?!"

"I'm not letting you get away that easily!!"

Flum threw her Souleater, and Ottilie shot another Blood Anguis at Dein. Alas, they were only able to score near misses on the wayward adventurer before he pulled himself up onto the roof and disappeared down the other side.

"Damn, he's fast!"

"He's always got something up his sleeve," said Flum.

Even with his comrades falling all around him, Dein somehow managed to keep a cool head and make a daring escape.

"More to the point, how did you find me so easily?"

"Once I found one of my soldiers, he fessed up quick." Ottilie bowed down low. "I'm really sorry for all the hassle my men have caused you today."

Under normal circumstances, Flum would wave the apology off. But... "I wish I could say it was nothing. But the truth is that this was pretty ridiculous."

She quite literally almost died during this ordeal. If Ottilie didn't do something to shut these kinds of problems down in the future, Flum wouldn't be able to trust the army anymore.

"Oh, I absolutely agree. Those guys are going to have to pay. You have my word that the commander of the West District and the rest of his men will be dealt with swiftly and harshly. Is there anything else I can do for you?"

"There's a lot I'd like to discuss, but..." Flum imagined Milkit smiling eagerly as she walked through the door. "Honestly, I'd just like to go home and see Milkit right now."

"I completely understand." Ottilie felt that she had a slightly better understanding of the two girls' relationship. They reminded her a bit of herself and her older sister. "But before you go, I want you to have this."

"Hm?"

Ottilie took off her white coat with its embroidered commissioned-officer's crest and held it out to Flum. "Your clothes look absolutely dreadful right now."

Flum looked down at herself. Her outfit was reduced to clothes in name only, though, all vital parts were covered. Not only had all the arrows left her clothes pockmarked with tears, but the explosion ripped away pretty much everything on the right side of her body from her shoulder to her chest.

"Aah, thanks." Flum couldn't help but laugh at the sight.

She slid her arms through the sleeves and hurriedly buttoned it up tight.

005

Wriggling, Writhing Spirals

SEVERAL HOURS after the battle finally ended, Flum showed back up at the door to find a waiting Milkit.

"Master!!" Milkit dove into Flum's arms and buried her face in her chest. Flum returned the embrace, gently running her fingers through her hair.

"Sorry to worry you."

"That doesn't matter, I'm just so glad you're safe, Master." Milkit rubbed her cheek against Flum's chest, causing a gentle, comfortable warmth to fill her heart.

"You really are close, aren't you?" Ottilie watched the exchange between the two with a feeble spark of envy in her eyes. Eterna, from her place behind Milkit, nodded in agreement.

◇ ◇ ◇

A short time later, Flum sat down at the table with Ottilie, Eterna, and Milkit to regale them with the tale of her day.

Though things calmed down a bit once Ottilie ordered the soldiers stationed at the castle to clean up the area, it was going to be difficult to entirely clear Flum's name among the denizens of the West District. Dein had done irreparable damage to Flum's reputation in the area. No matter how unfair it might have been, that was the reality of it.

"That's dreadful. I wish you'd told me about what you were dealing with, especially with how bad it got."

"I'm sorry. I never figured it'd come to this."

"Who could anticipate something like that? Blamed for a crime you didn't commit and then chased up and down the West District by a whole garrison gone crooked? It nearly defies belief."

Apparently, the local commander and several of his soldiers had enjoyed the companionship of several young girls with connections to Dein.

"I'm just glad you were able to make your way back safe and sound, Master."

"That's because I knew you were here waiting for me, Milkit. I just had to come back."

Milkit's cheeks burned red under the bandages. "Master..."

Flum was telling the truth. If it wasn't for that thought driving her on, she likely would've let her desperation take over.

"Of course, the Souleater's regenerative effects helped a lot, too."

"That's due to the Reversal attribute's effect on negative enchantments, right? Honestly, this is the first time I've ever heard of cursed equipment being used for a purpose other than torture."

"I only learned about it recently myself."

"If only you'd figured it out during your journey. I'm sure you would've never been sold in that case."

"I don't know. In a way, it was a good thing. Or at least, I've started to see it that way."

Eterna looked taken aback to hear this.

"Don't get me wrong," Flum said. "It's not like I *wanted* to get sold! But I'm starting to think this power is why I was tapped to join the other heroes."

"I could see that," said Eterna. "Otherwise, it really doesn't make sense for someone with zeroed out stats across the board to come along."

"You're saying the church might've wanted to get their hands on that kind of power?" Ottilie said. "If that's the case, I can take you there myself."

"I dunno. I feel like there must be some reason I need

to go to the Demon Lord's castle myself." Flum had no clue what that reason might be, but it was pretty obvious that the church was plotting something. Whatever it was, it wasn't good. "Even if I discovered my powers during the journey, it's possible the church might have done even more to limit my movements. Which doesn't mean I'm ready to forgive Jean, of course."

"Of course not."

The passing thought of Jean made her return to imagining the beautiful *click* his jaw would make once it received the haymaker she had in mind for him.

"So, umm..." Ottilie paused for a moment before speaking up, a look of concern on her face. "You don't suspect the church of something, do you?"

"I...uhh, well, I..." Flum faltered.

Even considering the church and military's strained relationship, a lieutenant general like Ottilie doubtless had close connections to the royal family, who were strict adherents of the church of Origin. It seemed best to keep her issues with the church to herself.

"Don't get me wrong," Ottilie said. "I have my own issues with the church. In fact, that's what brought me out to the West District in the first place."

"Oh, really?"

"When the kingdom unified the southern reach, all

of our non-demon rivals were pretty much done for. We lost a lot of influence after that first sortie into demon country thirty years ago. Since then, the royal family's relied more and more on the church. It's gotten to a point where the church now wields power to match, and perhaps even surpass, the throne."

Milkit looked concerned by this revelation. "The church is that powerful?"

Ottilie nodded solemnly before continuing. "Hardly anything comes to us about their activity. Even my sister Henriette, a general of the royal army, can't stand up against them. However, one thing has become clear."

She clenched her fist. Her voice grew strained as she continued. "The church is conducting clandestine experiments in pursuit of some sort of tremendous power. They want a second invasion, and the journey to destroy the Demon King is part of that plan."

Flum averted her gaze. "So the journey was just..."

"It's just a theory for now, but I'm confident there's evidence here in the capital of their experiments. My sister's been working fruitlessly to investigate this for a long time, so I decided I would do whatever I could to help her out."

Thinking back, Flum realized Ottilie had been vague when asked what she was doing in the capital. All she said

was that she was there for her sister. In that sense, she'd been telling the truth.

Flum cast a glance Eterna and Milkit's way to see how they were responding to Ottilie's impassioned speech. More importantly, she wanted to know their thoughts on sharing what they knew. The other two women nodded in agreement. Ottilie could be trusted.

"Actually, we ran across some of the church's monsters out near a small village called Anichidey," Flum said.

"What?!"

Flum went on to explain everything that happened in the research facility. Ottilie listened with great fascination, taking in every word. Once Flum was finished, she sat there in silence for several moments.

"I believe the church has multiple teams of researchers," she said at last. "That place you found was probably just one of their labs."

"So there are more just like it?"

Flum was beginning to realize she was up against something far greater than she originally imagined. Ottilie, meanwhile, seemed surprised to have her fears both confirmed and then expanded on.

Eterna grinned and sipped at her tea, looking like she was giving something great thought. Milkit looked over at Flum, clearly worried for her master.

It was Ink coming down from the second floor that broke the all-consuming silence. The young girl had already become fairly well acquainted with the layout of the house and could navigate it with ease, even without the benefit of sight.

"I can tell Flum's back, but what is that other voice I'm hearing?" she asked.

"That's right. I'm back, Ink. Glad to see you."

"Welcome back, Flum. Soooo...who's the other person?"

Ottilie tensed up. Understandably—Ink was pretty jarring to look at. "Wh-who's that?"

"Dein's men were harassing her; I was in the neighborhood. She ran away from somewhere, but we're not exactly sure where, so she's staying with us for now."

Ink excitedly waved her hand in the air. "Yup, I'm staying here!"

She was always quite energetic right after she woke. It added a certain warmth to the household, livening the mood.

"Hey, Ink, come here for a sec."

"Huh?"

Eterna walked over to Ink, put her arms around the younger girl from behind, and then lifted her and headed to the stairs.

"Whoa, I'm floating! But why are you taking me back upstairs? I just came down to get something to drink, ya know!"

"Listen, I have all the water you could possibly need. That's no problem."

"Huh, you mean your magic, right? I dunno if I wanna drink that!"

"Don't be so picky. Besides, it's far cleaner and safer than what you could get out here."

"Yeah, but it kinda tastes like you, Eterna."

"Does *not*."

The two slowly returned to the second floor, continuing their friendly banter the whole way. Before Eterna left, she gave Flum a glance, silently communicating that she wanted Flum to tell Ottilie all about Ink, and that she would take the girl somewhere she couldn't hear it. She'd grown awfully protective of Ink lately.

"So who was that kid?"

"Her name's Ink Wreathcraft. That's the most concrete thing we know."

"Even if some disease took a toll on her eyes, no normal person would sew them shut like that. Some kind of abuse?"

"It doesn't sound like it," Flum said. At least, Ink never made any mention of abuse. In fact, her whole reason for running away from home was that she felt an odd disconnect with the people she lived with. "I spoke with a friend of mine in the church, and she said she hadn't heard anything about kids in an orphanage going missing. The guild didn't have any jobs mentioning anything like that, either."

"Hmm. So you think she has something to do with the church's research?"

Flum frowned slightly and nodded. Ink still hadn't told them the full story, so she couldn't be completely confident at this point, but every time she looked at Ink's eyes, church involvement was the only logical answer she arrived at.

"According to Ink, she lived together with four other kids, all around eight years old, and a caregiver known as Mother. There was apparently someone she calls Papa around somewhere, too."

"Mother and Papa, huh? Seems pretty obvious they're trying to keep their names under wraps, though I have to admit it doesn't exactly ring any bells."

"Darn..."

"Sorry I couldn't be of any more help. I highly doubt Echidna or Dafydd would go by code names like that."

"Who are Echidna and Dafydd?"

"Researchers who are always coming and going between the cathedral and castle. Considering how hard they work to keep a low profile, I'm almost certain there are other teams, too."

"If you know their names, then maybe we could just follow them back to find this Mother person?"

"No." Ottilie shot down Flum's hopes right at once. "If you're not careful, you'll disappear, too."

"What?" Flum was at a loss for words. This wasn't a threat, nor was Ottilie joking. Someone else probably already met such a fate.

"It's not that simple," Ottilie said. "I'd follow them myself if I could, but if the royal family found out, I'd probably be strung up on some set of false charges."

"So they're beyond the reach of even a lieutenant general?"

"That's the reality. That's what my sister's been fretting over."

The church had clearly made substantial gains in power base if they could cause a general such concern.

"They also spend a lot of time out of the capital," Ottilie continued. "I wonder if they might have some connection to what went on today?"

"Hmm...in that case, why did you decide to come out and look around the West District?"

"It's a place where they could work while easily covering their tracks. If they're conducting research somewhere in a government facility or church, then they'd need to move equipment in and out. I figured the Western District was the most probable location—lots of discreet options, and it's not closely watched by the central government."

The Central and North districts had constant heavy foot traffic to worry about, and as Sara pointed out earlier, any misstep in the East District could bring the wrath of its upper-crust inhabitants down on your head. That pretty much only left the West District.

"Anyway, I'm happy to know there are others out there who share my suspicions about the church," Ottilie said. "I plan to continue my own independent research into the situation, but I hope we can continue to share information."

"Of course! I'm glad to have more allies, too, and especially one as great as yourself, Ottilie."

The two clasped hands and shook on it.

Eterna had been chosen for the heroes more for her raw power than her focus. Paired with Flum they might be unstoppable—so long as Flum could keep her interested. As much as Flum would have liked to count Sara as one of their own, at the end of the day, she was still part of the church and didn't want to lose her position. Ottilie's help was a game changer.

With that out of the way, Ottilie had to return to the castle to report on the day's events. Flum and Milkit walked her to the door, where she took a few steps out before turning around to look back at Flum. "Ah, there's one last important thing I wanted to share with you."

She jogged back to Flum and, making sure no one was nearby, leaned in close. Her voice was barely above a whisper.

"There are others like us out there. People who don't trust the church, who are conducting their own investigations."

"Others? You mean, outside of the army?"

"I don't know them personally, but they exist. There's at least a few. I don't know if we can consider them allies yet, so I recommend you play it safe." With that, Ottilie pulled her white coat back on and left the house behind.

◇ ◇ ◇

Later that evening, as the sun hung low in the sky and cast an orange glow across the West District, Sara showed up at Flum's house again. Within a short time of her arrival, she and Ink were in the bath together.

It started out simply enough, with Sara chattering

casually as she relaxed around the house. "Last time I came over for dinner, I was so late getting back home, I didn't even have time to take a bath before bed."

"Then why don't you take one here?" Ink responded immediately.

She'd started talking and acting like she considered the house her own at this point. It was impressive how quickly she'd adapted. At any rate, things snowballed from there, and before long...

"Cut it out, Ink! That tickles!"

"Soooorry. I can't see, you know."

"Your sight's got nothing to do with it!"

Flum smiled to herself at the voices drifting from the bathroom as she searched the kitchen for a clean knife.

"It seems like those two have grown quite close," Milkit said.

Flum chuckled. "Yeah, the house really brightens up whenever she's here."

Milkit seemed to be enjoying herself as she fussed over a pot on the stove, though it had little to do with the go-ings-on between Ink and Sara. She just enjoyed cooking together with Flum.

"So you just need me to dice up the boar meat, yeah?"

"Right. It's going into a stew, so cut it up however you see fit, Master."

"Gotcha, I'll cut it a bit on the large side then. Don't often get to eat candy boar, so I wanna be able to really sink my teeth in with each bite."

A candy boar was a C-Rank monster that looked akin to a wild boar but much larger. It was just as strong as it looked, yet far faster than its immense size suggested. Killing such a beast was no easy task. Its main flaw was the fact that it was slow to turn, mostly plowing straight ahead, though it more than made up for that with its area-of-effect earth magic.

The "candy" part of its name came from the species' sweet tooth. The boars were often seen eating sugarcane, fruits, honey, and other sugar-rich foods, which lent a sweet taste to their meat, making it a delicacy.

"Isn't C-Rank monster meat really expensive?" Flum asked. "In fact, I remember hearing that candy boars were usually nowhere near the capital."

"It was about to expire soon, so I was able to buy it for half off. Even then, it wasn't cheap. Did I spend too much?"

"Don't worry about it. At half price, that makes it cheaper than goat or buffalo, and besides, candy boar is really tasty. Just looking at it now makes me hungry."

"Oh, please don't eat it before I have a chance to cook it. You'll get sick, Master."

Flum laughed. "Don't worry, I'm not that crazy."

They talked all through dinner prep until Sara and Ink finally got out of the bath. Ink made a mad dash out of the changing room, tracking water into the rest of the house. Eterna dove in and wrapped the girl in a towel. "Hey, you're soaking wet!"

"But I'm hungry!!"

"It's not even ready yet. Just calm down and wait a bit."

Ink and Eterna almost seemed like sisters with their constant back and forth, though their age difference would put them closer to mother and daughter.

"I'm tellin' ya, kids have a lot of energy..." Sara looked exhausted as she slumped down into her chair and rested her head on the table.

"If she's what you'd consider a kid, Sara, I guess that puts the rest of us past our prime."

"Not just youth then, I guess. Ink's just really, really energetic."

Ever since moving into the house, every day had been filled with new experiences for Ink. Each passing second was another fresh, exciting stimulus, so it wasn't hard to imagine she'd be in constant sensory overload.

"Mmm, something smells amazing! I'm huuuungry!"

"Hold it, your hair's still not dry."

"Can't you do it later?"

"Of course not. Listen, it'll just take a moment, so please sit still."

"Okaaaaay!"

Eterna gently toweled Ink's hair dry. It took Flum by surprise to see just how tender Eterna was with her, though now that she thought back, Eterna had always helped Flum out whenever she was in need during their journey. Her offhand speech patterns and laid-back personality—not to mention her fashion sense—caused many to mistake her for cold and aloof. In truth, Eterna was a kind person.

◇ ◇ ◇

Dishes of candy boar stew, salad, and baguettes lined the table. The three women, followed shortly by Ink, put their hands together to bless their meal.

The food was a lot simpler than the last time they came together for dinner, but it was just as delicious. The stew, in particular, was absolutely mind-blowing. With each oversized bite, the juicy boar meat melted beautifully into the stew, filling Flum's mouth with the perfect blend of savory and sweet. Using her tongue to press the meat up against the roof of her mouth, she managed to squeeze out even more of the delightful juices before chewing and swallowing.

Next, she tore a piece off the baguette and dipped it into the stew. She topped it off with a piece of boar meat and shoved it right in her mouth. The stew-soaked bread disintegrated in her mouth, once again bombarding her taste buds with glee. The bread's crisp crust and note of salt added a whole new dimension to the dish.

"Wow..."

"Delishus!!"

"I feel like I've been introduced to a whole new world!"

Eterna, Ink, and Sara were completely bowled over by the stew. Milkit beamed at the praise. She derived far more pleasure from watching people eat something she made than actually eating it herself.

Flum looked over and caught Milkit's gaze.

"Do you like it?"

Flum shot back a thumbs up. "It's amazing. You're the best wife one could ask for, Milkit."

"I'm just happy that you enjoy it, Master."

"All right, that settles it. I guess you're my wife from now on!"

Milkit's face burned red. "What?? I, I...but that's so sudden..."

She'd meant it as a joke, but apparently, Milkit took it quite seriously. Flum laughed and plunged her spoon back into the stew.

◇◇◇

After dinner, while everyone was sitting down to relax for the night, Sara turned her attention to Flum and Eterna. Something was bothering her. "You two traveled with Maria, didn't you?"

She was almost certainly referring to their travel companion and her adoptive elder sister, Maria Affenjenz.

"Yes..."

"How was she doing? Was she happy?"

"We didn't talk a whole lot, so I can't really say."

"It always felt like she was hiding something from me."

"Hiding something...huh." Sara didn't seem all that surprised. "Maria holds an important position in the church. She knows a lot about what's going on."

"I wonder if she knows about the things we witnessed in Anichidey?"

"It's possible. Actually, I'd say it's very likely that the clergy know about it." Sara looked dejected. "But the idea that Maria would be involved in something like that..."

The Maria she knew was kind, warm; the perfect image of a holy woman, and the perfect role model for an aspiring nun like Sara. She didn't want to believe that the woman she admired would have anything to do with sacrificing people in the name of research.

In a way, it was an indictment against the entirety of the church. In public, they were an organization devoted to bringing people to salvation. In private, they worked to consolidate their power base. Even Sara knew that.

"I just wish I knew who was lying and who was telling the truth. The more I think about it, the more my head starts to hurt."

"I don't know either. That's why I need to hunt down the truth."

"The truth..."

Whatever that truth was, it was practically guaranteed to be far worse than Flum could imagine. Not a single good thing had come of what they'd learned so far, but she couldn't help but sense that remaining ignorant would do her no favors in the long run.

"I guess it's the only real choice we got. I'll do whatever I can to help ya," Sara said.

"You don't have to, you know. There are some things you're better off not knowing."

"I can't accept that. I won't be happy until I've got everything completely sorted out."

"I guess you're along for the ride."

"Looks that way. Anyway, first thing tomorrow I'll get right down to seeing what I can find out!"

"Don't overdo it, okay?"

"Same goes for you, Flum. I heard about everything that happened today. Don't forget that Dein's still out on the loose, and wherever he is, you know he's up to no good."

He was injured, sure, but not enough to be fatal. Besides, there were tons of places he could hide out in the West District. The whole place was practically his backyard.

"The problem," Flum said, "is that even if I do figure out what rock he slithered under and report him to the authorities, they wouldn't charge him with anything."

"Why's that?"

"He never actually tried to kill me himself. All he technically did was set the whole sequence of events in motion, which means there's practically no proof that he was even involved. Even Ottilie said they probably couldn't do anything."

"Looks like he found a way out again, huh?"

Flum and Sara sighed in unison.

He'd built his whole little empire on cunning; it wouldn't fall apart all at once. Not that he'd made it out completely unscathed, either. Now that he and his crew were catching heat from the army, they couldn't count on outside support.

But that brought with it new concerns: what would a wild animal do once backed up against a wall?

◇◇◇

Dein's shoulders heaved as he struggled to catch his breath. "I...can't believe...that little punk...managed to do that to me."

He'd found his way back to his hideout, weaving through neighborhoods he knew by heart. The perfect place to lay low and lick his wounds. The injuries Flum and Ottilie managed to inflict upon him during his escape were a lot worse than he thought. Though they were only glancing wounds, the Genocide Arts greatly restricted his movement, and the blow from the massive sword left behind a pretty significant gash—in his thigh, no less.

He'd lost a lot of blood, but he couldn't visit a church for healing. All he could do was bandage up and dip into his herb stash. He narrowly avoided bleeding out, but it left him deathly pale and drenched in sweat. His head ached, and he struggled to stay conscious. It'd be some time until he fully recovered.

"Damn them, damn them all! I'm not going to just take this lying down."

If anything, this only further solidified his desire to crush Flum. Dein's mind raced as he began plotting out his next plan of action. The seed of the idea was something he'd had for a while already. He slowly pulled himself back up to his feet, leaning against the wall for support, and made his way to the door.

This was no time to sleep. He needed to gather his men and put his next plan into motion. He reached out for the door and then froze as the knob turned and someone made their way inside.

It was one of Dein's supporters.

"You made it back. Was worried about you, boss."

"Heh, so you came looking for me. That's great timing. I was about to put my next plan into mo...whoa!" Dein tumbled forward, but the other man caught him and offered his shoulder for Dein to lean on. "Thanks."

"It's nothin'. Anyway, what's our next move?"

"We're going to gather our forces and launch a decisive attack. But before we can do that, we need to bring someone else into the fold."

"You really gonna try that? The first time you brought this up, it was supposed to take a lot more time."

The two slowly made their way out of the hideout as they spoke.

"I've already got a lot of the preparations done.

It should be doable, with some work." Dein's lips curled up into a sinister grin. His breathing was ragged, and his eyes were filled with an impenetrable hatred for Flum. "To the church! With them eating out of my hand, I can crush that Flum Apricot once and for all!"

His compatriot's reaction was more reserved. "That would've been great, yeah."

"Huh?"

They stepped through the threshold. On the other side was a squad of soldiers from the Central District.

"You bastard! You sold me out?!"

The man shot Dein a sly grin. "I'm just a street rat, remember, Dein? I ain't got no loyalty. You really should've known that."

Not all of Dein's men had turned on him, of course. Those who were particularly close to him were probably doing their best to find him right now, but they were in the minority.

"You lying, cheating, son of a..."

"Nah, I'm just a realist, Dein. There's no value following a guy who gets beat by a little kid like that. Now I'm going to walk the path of the righteous with the good ol' royal military."

"Rot in hell!!!"

"Whoa, hey the...gaaaaaaaaugh!"

A person with nothing left to lose is a formidable enemy indeed. Despite his awful state, Dein drew his knife and stabbed out the man's right eye, eliciting a blood-curdling scream from his erstwhile ally.

The soldiers rushed to detain him, but he was able to fire his wire hook into a nearby roof in time to make his escape. The desire to live gave him just enough energy to forget the sheer exhaustion that had taken over his body—but only for a moment.

Dein wheezed. "I'll destroy you, Flum Apricot. Just you wait and see!"

His hatred came from a place deeper, older, and fouler than the rational mind could reach. He clenched his blood-drenched fists as he ran through the darkened streets, his eyes bloodshot.

Alas, he had no way of knowing that decision was the beginning of his end.

◇ ◇ ◇

The next day, Flum woke to the sound of breakfast being made downstairs.

The morning was so tranquil that it was hard to believe the events of the previous day had occurred. She lazily made her way down the stairs, rubbing the backs of her hands against her eyes in an attempt to wake up. She found a smiling Milkit dressed in an apron waiting to greet her.

"Good morning, Master."

A sense of relief washed over Flum when she checked the mail and confirmed that there were no more posters hung up outside their house. A short time later, Eterna and Ink came downstairs to join them at the table.

According to Eterna, Ink put forth a strong argument last night that she wasn't a kid anymore, and way too old to be sharing a bed, so she and Eterna slept in separate rooms. It sounded precisely like something a kid would say, but everyone thought better of saying so in front of their young companion.

After breakfast, everyone split up to carry out their own activities for the day. Flum was flat-out exhausted from the events of the previous day, so she decided to cancel her plans to go to the guild. Instead, she sat down across from Milkit and the two talked the morning away. Eterna spent the morning and afternoon in her room hip-deep in research while Ink alternated between vying for Eterna's room and quietly entertaining herself.

After a quick lunch, Flum and Milkit went to the Central Market. Once their fun (albeit uneventful) shopping trip was over, they made their way home, prepared dinner, and got ready for sleep.

It was, in every possible sense, an unremarkable day. As she lay in bed drifting off to sleep, Flum thought about how great it would be to live out the rest of her days that way.

◇ ◇ ◇

In the middle of the night, long after everyone was already fast asleep, a man's feral screams broke the silence that had settled over the West District.

"Stay back! Stay baaaaaaaaaaaaack!!!"

The man looked to be in his mid-twenties and was dressed in light armor and a cloak, looking in all respects like any other adventurer. Armed with only an axe, he watched uncertainly as a crowd of attackers closed in on him. He didn't know how to fight back.

Were they normal humans, or even monsters for that matter, he'd have some idea. But his pursuers were eyeballs. Human eyeballs, to be more exact, bouncing and rolling after him. They filled the streets, surrounded buildings, and poured over rooftops like a tidal wave in their ceaseless pursuit.

The man took a step back and felt his back touch a cold stone wall. There was nowhere left to run.

"Hyaaaaaaaaaaaaaaaaaaaaaaaaaah!!!!" He dropped to the ground and screamed, resigned to his impending demise.

A dark spot formed at the crotch of his pants as terror took over his body.

Something in the back of his mind fought on, and he swept his axe back and forth in a feeble attempt to save himself. *Squoosh. Squoosh. Squoosh.* The axe smashed open the oncoming eyeballs, drenching the sunbaked stones that paved the streets in aqueous humor. Warm droplets cast off from the axe splattered his body.

The endless procession of eyes reached his knees, then his thighs, then his lower back, climbing higher and higher until they engulfed him.

He felt no pain.

He groaned and choked as the eyeballs filled his every orifice. It was a sensation like nothing else he'd experienced before. Once his body was full, a new arm began to grow out of him. He could feel it, and even move it, just as if it were any other part of him. In fact, it was in every respect like all his other appendages.

"Aaugh... Aaaaaaah!!"

The man was one of Dein's closest allies, whom Dein had immediately sought out after escaping from his hideout, confident that he could trust this man. Dein issued him an order: threaten a member of the church and see how they respond.

The intimidation went off without a hitch, and the

man was on his way back to Dein's new hideout when he suddenly spotted a lone eyeball on the street. That was the beginning of the end for him.

Slowly but surely, the eyes' numbers increased. No matter how fast he ran, they multiplied at such a rate that he couldn't get away. Before he knew it, the street was blocked. His next turn down an alley sealed his fate: it was a dead end.

The alley filled with eyeballs, they surrounded and filled his body, and then he gained a new arm. It had the cadence of a nightmare. What was he fighting against? No matter how many times he asked himself that question, he kept coming up blank.

More eyeballs poured onto him and seeped into his body. It didn't hurt, but it terrified him. If it hurt, he would have been too preoccupied to feel fear.

"Grrrraaaaaaaaoooooowwwl!!"

A second thumb sprouted out of his right hand, followed by a third leg. His stomach began to bulge awkwardly. He felt a dueling rhythm deep in his chest as two hearts beat slightly out of sync.

He'd grown three new arms, and the eyes kept piling on, this time seeping into his neck.

"Waaaaaugh!!"

"Waaoooooooooo!!!"

Two voices screamed in unison as a second, nearly identical head sprouted from his neck, like limbs of a tree growing from the same trunk. A new consciousness filled his body, and it became less clear just who this form belonged to. He no longer had the freedom to try to escape.

If this was revenge for his threats against the church, they were making him pay in spades.

"Cut it out!!"

"Kill me, please!"

"I don't want to die!!"

"Kill me like I was!!!"

None of that was to be.

The eyes continued to surround and force themselves into his body. A third head wormed out, followed quickly by a fourth. He was starting to lose track of who he was. The transformation of his body and mind was complete.

◇ ◇ ◇

On being notified that Phile, the man he sent to the church, hadn't returned, Dein decided to take matters into his own hands. Desperate times called for desperate measures, and besides, just getting up and moving did him some good. Thanks to one of his men's curative magic, his wounds were much better now. He could walk around unaided.

Try as he might, though, he could find no sign of Phile. Could the church possibly have done away with him?

The way Dein saw it, the church was corrupt to its very core. It was why he figured they'd gladly throw their lot in with him...and if they didn't, he had plenty of ways to change their minds. Drug up a nun, get one of the priests addicted to something only he could provide... Maybe even pay a woman to get close to a priest or knight and seduce them into joining the fold. His influence would spread through the cathedral like a plague until he was involved in every aspect of its functioning.

He'd been working on this plan for a while. In fact, he had several church knights and priests firmly in his camp already. Recent events, however, had forced him to skip some of the intermediate steps and cut straight to the chase, which was why he sent Phile out to go threaten the church leadership.

"I guess this was always a risk, though," he muttered to himself.

Were the church as pure and saintly as many were led to believe, there would be no in for him. If they could kill people without a second thought, though, then he should be in good company. It was a shame to lose a good man, but Dein would have Phile to thank for helping to build the foundation of his empire.

"I guess I'll have to avenge Phile's death now, too. I'll keep up the search a bit longer before I call it a day." Dein chuckled to himself. He slid his hands into his pockets and continued his stroll through the dirty streets.

The still, stifling air of the dusty back streets would probably be unbearable to the upper crust of the East District. They likely wouldn't even last half an hour. Dein could never imagine living the life of pompous nobility. He'd much rather live it up just as he was, with his idiot comrades, than live in a way that relied on perpetually reinventing himself for the sake of others.

"Hm?" Walking down a road near the West District church, Dein stopped and took a long sniff of the air. It smelled of a fresh corpse, with one major difference: there wasn't a hint of blood to it. It smelled like sex, waste, and rot.

He let his senses guide him until he turned a corner.

"What in the holy hell..."

The words slipped out of his mouth when he saw the bizarre...*thing* that lay in front of him. The color of the skin and parts of the anatomy were undeniably human—the hands, the feet, the face—but in a volume and arrangement that made no sense, a sick, writhing mass of a dozen people's worth of parts.

Dein put his hand over his mouth, suppressing the urge to vomit. Looking closer, he noticed something familiar about the mass of flesh.

"No...no way. Phile?!"

The face was a dead ringer for the man Dein was looking for. He ran to the creature's side. "Hey, Phile. Phile! It's me, Dein. What happened to you?? Answer me, Phile!!"

There was no response. The face gurgled as a thick liquid squeezed out of its mouth, nose, and eyes. Its other heads seemed equally unaware of Dein's presence.

"Ah, Dein. There you...are...?" One of the men who had accompanied Dein on his search stopped at the entrance to the alley the moment he caught sight of the creature. "Whoa!! What in the hell is that thing?!"

"I just stumbled upon it myself. Anyway, take a look at its face."

"Face? That thing?? I doubt that'd tell me anything but... Hey, wait, is that Phile?!"

"I don't know what happened here, but it looks like those pigs at the church are a lot worse than I figured."

"This is the church's doing??"

"That's my best guess."

This surpassed even his worst estimations. Punishing someone by turning them into a bizarre creature like this was beyond the pale. Dein drew his knife, pushed the thrashing limbs aside, and plunged the blade deep into the creature.

"Dein?!" His compatriot immediately lost his composure, but Dein continued with his task. He pulled his knife out and opened up the wound, laying bare the creature's guts. Dozens of fingers and feet, two hearts, and a pile of parts too numerous and ill-defined to count poured out of the open wound and onto the ground with a wet thump.

Dein scowled and leaned in close.

"Huh, two hearts? Did they just multiply, then?"

He grabbed one of the hearts, cast Scan on it, and quickly confirmed it had Phile's stats. He tossed it aside, grabbed another body part, and did the same.

What really drew his attention were the countless eyeballs. He was hesitant to touch them, so he just cast Scan from afar this time.

> Retribution
> Affinity: origin
> Strength: origin
> Magic: origin
> Endurance: origin
> Agility: origin
> Perception: origin

Dein scowled at the results.

"What the hell is that? Something must be wrong. Hey, get over here and cast Scan on that eyeball for me."

Dein turned back to look at his compatriot. The man was tilting his head at a hard right angle to his neck.

"The hell are you doin'? You trying to show off how flexible you are or something? I don't have time for this crap, just hurry up and cast Scan."

"Umm, I, uh... Dein, what's happening to me? I can't really move my neck or my right arm. Actually, I can't even really move."

Taking a closer look, the man's hand wasn't exactly holding his head. It was embedded in his neck, up to the wrist. When Dein last looked his way, he'd been running his right hand through his hair. The next moment, he lost control of his entire right arm and his head started to tilt, as if beckoned by his hand.

"Why're you lookin' at me like that, Dein? What's happening to me?? Gah, it h-hurts so bad! But I just can't... Help me, help me, Dein!!"

Dein watched on in shock as the situation worsened. The man's arm was now up to the elbow inside his head; his skull began to deform with a sickening squish. His neck was twisted so far to the side that it was going to snap at any moment—and then it did, with a loud snap.

A thick, transparent fluid spilled from the man's mouth, nose, and eyes, drenching the front of his shirt before his body tumbled to the floor.

The transformation wasn't yet complete. His body continued to be shredded before Dein's eyes. It only stopped when there was nothing left but the man's head lying motionless on the ground.

"Just what in the blue blazes is going on here?? What the hell?! Is it some sort of taboo to even get close to the church?? Is that what this is?"

SHLOP.

Dein looked up to see a young boy standing before him. There was a bizarre whirlpool of flesh and muscle tissue where the boy's face should have been. Blood and fluids sputtered out from the spinning helix, staining his white shirt. The boy stood stock-still, his front soaked completely in blood, and stared at Dein.

"Ha...haha...ha..." Dein's hollow laugh echoed off the walls of the alley. He could tell this was a battle he wasn't going to win. "Ha...haha...friends, power, money...none of it matters to you, does it?"

The young boy reached out toward Dein as his screams filled the air.

A Crimson Wind Blows Through the Capital

AFTER MORNING PRAYERS, Sara waved goodbye to her fellow nuns-in-training and left her home in the Central District church off in the direction of the West District. Elune Enjeanar, one of Sara's many caregivers, watched with concern as the girl ran down the road. "She's been heading out a lot lately."

A fellow member of the church nodded next to her. "Maybe she's found a boyfriend?"

"Oh, shush. She's only ten."

"Kids grow up faster nowadays. Who knows, it could be Ed or Jonny..."

Elune clenched a fist and narrowed her gaze in anger. "I'd kill them if they even tried."

"If it were me, I'd be happy to hear that she'd made friends outside the church. I believe it was you who said that keeping yourself secluded would narrow your horizons, wasn't it, Elune?"

"That's right. We need open-minded people now more than ever."

The nuns were all too aware of the corruption running rampant in the church. They had no direct knowledge of its research and experimentation, but the upper echelons—even the pope and his cardinals—had clearly become obsessed with hoarding money and power as of late. They'd outlawed medicinal herbs, raised the costs of healing treatments, and greatly increased the church knights' numbers, all to the detriment of the regular citizens. Though public complaints were now a daily occurrence, the nuns could do little more than look the other way and secretly offer discounts on healing.

"I just hope Sara grows up to be a happy and healthy adult." Elune continued to watch the young nun until she finally faded from view.

◇ ◇ ◇

"Heya!"

Ed and Jonny both waved as Sara approached the church.

"Back so soon? Elune's gonna get pretty mad if you keep leaving like this, ya know."

"It's fine, it's fiiiiine. Unlike you, Ed, I'm actually good at my job."

"Whoa, whatchoo say??" Ed reached out and pulled Sara in close to start mussing up her hair again.

"CUTITOUT!! I'm not here to play today!"

"Fine, fine, I was just sayin' hi."

"Well, you could certainly find less annoying ways to do it! Anyway, why'd you drag me out here?"

The previous evening, Sara had received a letter from the West District church, signed by Ed. The message, written on a single page of paper in his ugly block letters, read: "I heard a rumor about that thing you were talking about. Come over when you can."

"Aaah, about that. So anyway, Jonny and I did a little digging of our own."

"I don't think this is the right place to talk about that, Ed."

"Aah, yeah. Hey, let's go somewhere else, Sara."

"Huh? Is that really necessary?"

Ed and Jonny glanced back at the chapel before prompting Sara out of its line of sight and into the shadows. "Well, I don't exactly want to be seen spreading scandalous rumors about the priests, now do I? They're pretty scary, y'know."

"Scandalous rumors about the priests are already *every-where*, dummy. I'm pretty used to it."

"Yeah, well, this one is a little different. I don't think it has anything to do with that Ink girl you were asking about, though, so just think of it as an urban legend for now."

"An urban legend?"

Tales of inexplicable sightings and occult phenomena spread like wildfire in the city. Taking every story at face value was easier than attempting to discern which monsters and arcane powers were real threats. Regardless, many tall tales held a kernel of truth; Sara refused to write them off right away.

"There are reports of ghost sightings at night in the West District, specifically around the church." Ed waggled his arms around, imitating a ghost.

"Ghosts? What kind?"

"Children, apparently, probably younger than you. Boys and girls, according to the stories."

"So there's more than one?"

"Blonde ones, ones with brown hair, ones with white hair. A few green ones. Accounts vary."

Sara looked suspicious. "Some pretty colorful ghosts, then. But what does that have to do with the church?"

It wasn't exactly unheard of to spot urchins roaming the West District in the middle of the night.

Jonny put his hand to his chin. "That's where the story gets a bit weird. See, urban legend has it that the kids are the church's guinea pigs for all kinds of experiments."

"And where did that story come from?" Sara didn't need any convincing on that particular premise. Could someone have leaked the info on purpose?

"How the hell should I know? Anyway, apparently a side effect of the experiments replaces their faces with this twisting void, like a chunk was carved right out of their heads. Pretty creepy stuff."

"...No way."

The ogre instantly came to Sara's mind. It couldn't be a coincidence. Had their research developed enough in the interim that they could give such immense strength to humans, too?

A look of concern washed over Ed at the sight of Sara's pale complexion. "Hey, you okay, kiddo? Too gross for you?" He patted her gently on the head; Sara made no move to stop him, which only concerned him more.

"So, anyway," Jonny continued. "Apparently, the research facility is somewhere underground in the West District, and the kids they experiment on have these bizarre powers."

"Do you know what kind of powers?"

Jonny shook his head, adding that it seemed anyone who tried investigating the matter just up and disappeared. "Not sure if this helps at all or not, but apparently they're called the 'Spiral Children.'"

"That's definitely interesting. Anyway, uh, thanks for looking into this, guys."

"Huh? I told ya this is all an urban legend, didn't I? Don't go takin' it at face value, kid."

Ed flashed a bright grin at Sara, but the younger girl's usually playful demeanor was nowhere to be seen in response. Putting aside for the time being whether or not these so-called Spiral Children had anything to do with Ink, Sara's fears and Flum's suspicions about the church were all but confirmed now.

"Y-yeah, I got it. Anyway, I think it's best that you guys don't investigate this any further."

"You're talking like you're involved somehow, Sara."

Sara winced at Jonny's pointed observation.

"You're...you're not involved, are you?"

"No, I mean..." Sara had always been an awful liar. Worse still, Ed and Jonny were like family to her. They could read the truth in her face.

"In that case, we definitely can't just leave it be."

"That's right. It's what big brothers gotta do."

"But...if you dig too deep, I'm worried the church might decide they don't need you guys anymore. And then, y'know..."

"That just means that we should... Huh?" Jonny reached back to rub the back of his head. It felt almost like something had touched the back of his neck before melting into his skin. Even now, he could still feel it, like something ticklish moving just underneath the surface.

"What is it, Jonny? Did a bug bite you?"

"Nah, just a funny feeling is all." "It's nothing, no need to worry."

Two different responses came out of his mouth in unison.

"Jonny...?"

"Why're you looking at me like that, Sara?" "What's so scary, Sara?"

Ed and Sara stared at their friend in horror as a second head began growing out of the back of his neck.

"Huh? Something's strange..." "Why are you two looking at me like that?"

"I can't move... What's wrong?" "There's something going on with my body..."

The two stared in horror, unable to speak, as a white ball dropped to the ground behind Jonny. Upon closer inspection, it was a bloodshot eyeball with a deep crimson iris...and it had silently fallen off the church's roof. It rolled toward Jonny, climbing up his body. It embedded itself in his neck, and moments later another head sprouted from the same spot. Now all three mouths spoke at once.

"Wh-wh-what's going on...on...on? I feel st-strange. Sara. Sara strange?" "Don't be so scared not scary. No. I'm fine, it doesn't hurt at all, I'm fine." "Spiral Children. R-ru-run...this is...ga...ngaaaa..."

His words tangled and bent around each other as his mind frayed; long tails of drool dripped from his mouth, and his body began to shudder.

"What the hell... Run, Sara!! Get outta here!!" Ed cried.

"What? But...but we gotta help Jonny! He's gonna die if we don't!"

"He's already a goner!"

"I'm not going to give up just like that! Jonny, Jonnnnny!!!" Sara reached out toward her friend one last time, but Ed grabbed her hand and took off with her in tow.

He wanted to help Jonny, too, but it was clear that there was nothing that could be done at this point. Even if they severed the extra heads and tried to heal him, it was unlikely that would do any good. Jonny was already dead. He just didn't know it.

"R-rrrrrrrr-run!! Sssssssssara...Eddddddddd, runnnnn..."

"Gggaaaaa pluuppppp gaaaaaugh..." "Aaaaaaugh...ssss-sorrrrry...I...w-w-wish we...coulda...spent more...t-t-t-ime t-toge...ther...aaaaaaaaah!"

Tears poured out of Jonny's six eyes. It was unclear if he could still actually process sadness, but liquid streamed from his eyes all the same. He reached out after his escaping friends, though the rest of his body refused to obey his commands. Even with his rational mind turned to mush, something in him he couldn't name stirred at the thought that they would have no future together.

The eyes continued to pour into Jonny, his body the clay that they would mold to their will.

◇◇◇

"Jonny, not Jonny... I can't believe it..." Sara was finally able to run under her own power but still struggled with the immensity of her grief. Tears poured ceaselessly down her cheeks. She doubted she'd forget what she'd just seen as long as she lived.

"Damn damn damn daaaaaamn!! What in the hell was that back there?!"

Sara wasn't alone in her grief. Jonny was also Ed's family, his lifelong partner in crime. He'd always thought they'd rise through the ranks of knighthood together, but that future had been shattered in an instant. All because of one mysterious eyeball.

"Why are they after us?!"

"How should I know? Maybe it was because we said something about the church?!"

If that were true, then the capital should have been littered with corpses. It had to have been something more specific than that. Or maybe there was no reason at all. Maybe it was just pure, cruel coincidence.

Unsatisfied with claiming Jonny for their first victim, the eyeballs poured down the street in pursuit of Ed and Sara as they sprinted for all they were worth, their questions left unanswered. Running at full speed in armor was no easy task; Ed threw off his gauntlets, though it hardly helped. The tide of eyes came in from all directions now, leaving fewer and fewer avenues for escape.

"This is all my fault..."

"Huh? What the hell are you talkin' about??"

"I mean, I asked you to look into this in the first place!" Sara wailed.

"Don't be so stupid! Now's not the time to get down on yourself!" This was the first time Ed had ever actually raised his voice at Sara. "Jonny didn't wake up this morning intending to die, but I'm sure he's glad that it was him and not you!"

Sara began to sob. "B-b-but...!"

"You heard him, right? Even with all that, he still told us to run away. Jonny mustered up all he had to make sure his little sister was safe. I...I just know that he died proud." Ed clenched his jaw, unable to say any more as he fought to keep the fear and anger welling up in him battened down.

Reason and passion did battle in his mind for a moment, before concluding that he needed to protect Sara, no matter the cost. He stopped running.

"Ed?!"

"I also need to protect you, Sara."

His mind was made up. He knew what it meant for him. Ed drew his sword and faced the swarm.

"Stop it! Please!! Don't leave me alone, Ed! I can't lose you, too!!"

The pain in Sara's voice was palpable. Ed hesitated for a moment. His heart ached. He'd love nothing more than to run away with her.

"I really looked forward to seeing you grow up and get married, kiddo. I was hoping to be there as part of your family."

It didn't change his mind. Jonny had wanted nothing more than to protect Sara, and Ed would give his life to make that happen, too. He would make a fine decoy.

189

"Hyaaah! Sa...Hyaaah! Ra...hyah!" He pulped multitudes of eyeballs with each swing of his sword, but it was like trying to bail out a ship with a thimble. It was a matter of moments before they were at Ed's feet, infiltrating his body. A new leg sprouted from where they sank into his flesh. "Nnng...this is...disgusting...!"

"Ed!!!"

He couldn't run anymore. It was all on Sara now.

"I was really hoping to see you in a dress, your makeup done up all nice, and then tell ya that it really didn't suit you and mess up your hair. Then you'd get real mad like you do, and..." Ed's newly-sprouted leg waggled around. "But...aaugh! But...maybe I can still do that from the afterlife. We won't see each other, sure, but I'll watch as you live your life."

"Don't talk like that!"

"Hey, if no one stops 'em, then we're both gonna die, Sara!"

"Please...please don't leave me! I don't care if we both have to die!"

"Don't be so stupid! This isn't the first time I've been selfish, ya know? Now get the hell outta here, Sara, and don't forget that super awesome brother of yours who gave it all to save you!"

Sara bit down hard on her lip till she tasted blood. Tears poured down her cheeks. Every fiber of her being rebelled against this.

"Please? For me?" Ed's soft plea broke down her last wall of resistance.

"Nnnng...fine!"

No matter how much it destroyed her, she couldn't let his loving sacrifice be for nothing. Sara knew that this would be the last time she ever saw him, so she had to make sure her last words counted. She shouted as loud as she could. "I...I love you guys! No matter how many years or decades may pass, I'll always love you, Ed and Jonny. You're my brothers forever!"

Ed let out an embarrassed chuckle. She took one last look at his smiling face, before she finally turned and took off running.

Didja hear me, Jonny? Ed thought. *She said she loves us. That little punk finally said it. And now she's gonna make it and live on for us...*

He and Jonny could share that feeling.

Sure, maybe they weren't connected by blood, but the three of them were family. Though he'd always known that, hearing it straight from Sara's mouth was different. A feeling of ineffable happiness warmed his heart.

I don't know how or why this came to be, but...who the hell cares? At least we got to keep her safe and die without any regrets. Well, some regrets. Dammit, Jonny, I still got a lot of regrets. I'm gonna die a virgin, unlike you and your girlfriend, jerk.

They were far too young to die. They still had so many things left undone, futures and dreams unfulfilled.

Ah well, at least I got to die keeping Sara safe. If not, this would be a really crappy, pointless way to go.

"Love you too, sis!!!"

Ed hacked away with all his might as he felt his body transform into something far beyond human.

◇ ◇ ◇

Sara sniffled and ran as hard and as fast as she could, gritting her teeth and wiping away her tears with the backs of her hands. She ran down unfamiliar streets, never once stopping to take stock of where she was or where she was going.

Her family was dead. Everyone she loved, dead.

Or, rather, they had suffered a fate worse than death.

"Wh-why'd I survive? Ed...Jonny...why?"

She couldn't help but feel at fault for their loss. She groped desperately for ways to absolve herself, but the timing was too damning. When Sara first caught sight of the eye that fell from the roof, she felt the same uncanny pang the ogre gave her back in Anichidey.

If these were part of the church's research, did that mean the Spiral Children were, too? In any case, it seemed someone was out there, working behind the scenes to dispose of anyone who might expose the church's dark secrets.

Sara ran with the sole goal of telling Flum what she'd learned. Ed and Jonny's sacrifices would not be in vain.

"Huff...haaah... Wh-which way...haaah...was it again?"

She was well and truly lost, though she noticed the city wall off in the distance. If she could just make it there, then she'd find herself in a much bigger street—and beyond that, the slums. If the church was trying to keep their creations entirely under wraps, then she could get away as long as she found a crowded place. Under normal circumstances, she'd do her best to steer clear of such a dangerous place, but desperate times called for desperate measures.

She crossed into a large, open square before heading for the west gate. The east and west gates were connected by one long thoroughfare that bisected the capital. There, she could reorient herself and make it back to Flum's house.

Sara mustered the energy to pick up speed and bore for the wall.

The tidal wave of eyes chasing after her grew as she inched ever closer to her objective. They dropped in number briefly thanks to Ed's brave sacrifice, but they were reproducing quickly.

"Thanks, Ed."

No one was there to say "you're welcome," but she didn't have time to dwell on that.

Sara chanced a look back, only to see a ceaseless wave of eyes cascading down the streets, over walls, and off roofs. She doubted she could ever get used to the sight.

"You guys still ain't satisfied?? You already killed two of my friends!"

The hatred in her voice didn't register. Or did it? After all, the eyes must have heard them spreading rumors—that was how it all started. That could only mean their failure to react to her cries of anguish was their own way of agreeing with her. Yes, her two dearest friends hadn't been enough to sate their hunger.

She could feel a white-hot rage building up inside her. She had no idea where to point it.

Sensing that the creatures were looming ever closer, Sara pressed on. Her body was already down to the last of its reserves at this point, and it was hard to keep her balance on the uneven streets. She nearly tripped over herself every few steps, but slowing down was tantamount to death. She had no idea how long she could keep it up, but it was the only choice she had.

"Aaaaaaaaaaaaaaaaaaaaahh!!!" She released her anger and fear in one loud, primal scream.

Undeterred, the eyeballs massed together as they poured off rooftops, out doors and windows, and pushed up and out of the sewers. The way they filled every crevice reminded her of maggots crawling over each other.

She decided to not look back anymore. It only made her situation seem even more dire.

She slapped at her thighs to try and get her mind off the pain in her muscles and the sounds of her own ragged breathing. All she could do was pump her arms as hard as she could to overcome the feeling that her heart was about to explode.

As the slums drew close, the smells around her began to change. Never before had she thought she would welcome the stench of rotting garbage: she was nearing people at last. Sara pulled right onto the thoroughfare at full tilt. Though a small girl dressed in immaculate white garb must have been a rare sight in these parts, no one paid her any mind.

"At...at least th-they won't...haah...chase me out here... haaah..." She finally let herself slow down and cautioned a glance behind her. Her shoulders heaved. "Hah...haah... Wh...what?"

What she saw left her wide-eyed and mouth agape. She was witnessing literal hell on earth.

"There's...there's no way. That's impossible."

Sara had been so focused on running that she must have not heard the voices of everyone around her. She'd gambled on the eyes giving up in the presence of others... and she'd lost. Just as they did before, the grotesque orbs continued their endless procession down the street—and into the innocent people in their way.

"Eww, what are these disgusting things?? Hey, hey... stay back! Staaaay baaaaack! Aaaauuuugh!!" A man standing at a street corner was caught in the leading edge of the swarm. Within moments, his arms multiplied. The shock froze him, and the tide swallowed him up. Within moments, he no longer resembled a human.

"Eyaaaaah!!! God, oh, God Almighty, please spare me from this menace! Please...please, God, I beeeeeeg... Aaaaaugh!!!" A woman kneeled in the street, praying to the mark of Origin; the eyes piled around her waist, causing her body to puff up like a balloon. Her screams of terror were abruptly replaced by drool and froth. The eyes filled her to capacity, and pink organs began to press up and out of her mouth.

"No, please...stay away! Spare my child...at least spare my child!!!"

"Mama! Mamaaaaaa!!"

"Get out of here! Run!!"

"Mama!!! I'll sa..." "Save...mammmma...s-s-save..." "Ssssssaaaaaaa...maaama...saave..."

"What?!"

In spite of her best efforts, the young child in the mother's arms now had three heads. The mother, overcome by horror, dropped her child to the ground momentarily before scooping him back up when she saw the procession looping closer. The young boy continued to contort and transform in her arms.

There would be no attempt to conceal this. If this was a conspiracy's way of hiding the evidence, its methods were inexplicably coarse.

"Sorry!! I'm so sorry!!!!" Even though she'd done nothing wrong, Sara still felt compelled to apologize for the terror unleashed on these people as she took off again. "I'm...I'm so, so sorry...!!"

More and more died in the name of the enemy's pursuit of the last surviving holder of the information they aimed to suppress, as Sara pulled another right onto a small alley. She could still hear the cries for help calling out behind her, but there was nothing she could do about that now. She could stop running and give herself up, but being forced to choose to sacrifice her own life so that others might live was a tough pill for a ten-year-old to swallow.

She balled up her fists, digging her nails deep into her palms to bring herself back to reality. Tears stung her eyes. Run...run...keep on running...

She did her best to stick to largely unused streets in the hopes of avoiding anyone else. At this point she'd completely lost track of how long she'd been running. She'd reached what she thought were the absolute limits of her endurance long ago, and her whole body ached, but she somehow forced herself to keep moving forward.

Her enemy, however, had no such limits. Every time she thought she shook them, more would appear out of nowhere and surround her. Was there really no way to get away? Had her fate been sealed the moment she learned about the research being conducted at the church's underground research lab.

Sara's breath came out in ragged gasps. That was right. It was over. She was destined to die.

Eventually, she ran out of road. She ran her fingers over the rough exterior of the wall before her legs gave out from under her in exhaustion.

That was it. She was done. In a small way, she felt relieved that she no longer needed to run anymore.

"I'm sorry Ed 'n Jonny. It looks like you weren't able to save me after all. I guess I'll see you soon..." Sara sat down and leaned against the wall for support. She would've been concerned about fouling her robes, but it was about to be a moot point.

Her arms dangled limply at her sides as she stared off into the distance at the oncoming parade of eyeballs. They looked to her like a hunter that had finally closed in on its prey. There were already so many of them, and yet, they still insisted on growing in number. They poured through the entrance to the alley. Yet more came tumbling off roofs and crawling up out of the ditches lining the street. There was a kind of vicious cunning to how they got about.

"It's a shame, really. I managed to survive this long, but it looks like my time's up now."

Images of her caregivers back at the Central District, the people who lost their lives during her escape, and Ed, Jonny, Flum, and the rest of her friends ran through Sara's head. She apologized to each one of them for her failure to do more, turned up to face the sky, and closed her eyes.

She felt a crisp breeze caress her cheek. It seemed out of place in the dry, oppressive West District.

007

Lies, Lies, and Yet More Lies

"**G**AAH, I'M SO BORED..." Y'lla, the receptionist for the West District guild, leaned forward with her chin propped up on her hand, twirling a pen to alleviate some of her boredom. Dein always kept the bar lively. Since he'd stopped turning up, the rest of the men drank in silence. It felt like the first time it'd been this quiet since she started working at the guild.

Not that she wanted Dein back, of course. She wasn't particularly loyal to him; she just helped out from time to time. In fact, her job was immensely easier with him and all the fraud and grift he brought with him gone.

"I...umm...have...have some tea."

Y'lla turned to find a mug being offered out to her. "Oh, thanks, Slowe."

"J-just doing my job."

The shy, blond haired man was named Slowe Uradnehs. He was eighteen years old and recently joined the guild as a staff member. He mostly worked in the back office and had little exposure to Dein in the first place. In fact, he'd never even seen Flum before.

"Hey, uh, can I ask you something?"

"What?"

"I'm...I'm not gonna get f-fired, am I?"

Y'lla laughed in spite of herself at the spooked look on her coworker's face. "What, you worried the guild's gonna go out of business without Dein? Don't worry, the government pays our bills. Whether we're super busy or dead quiet doesn't matter."

"Well...that's good to hear." A look of relief washed over Slowe's face before he turned and disappeared into the back office.

Truth be told, Y'lla was so bored that she'd hoped Slowe would stick around for a while longer and chat. He wasn't exactly a people person, so it was probably a lost cause to begin with.

She rested her elbows on the counter again and sipped at her tea as she stared at the wall. "Whoa, that's bitter..." Slowe still had a lot of learning to do.

Y'lla continued to drink the tea, all the same. Suddenly the door opened, and in walked Flum.

"Well, it's pretty quiet 'round these parts." She glanced around, looking pretty pleased with herself at the results.

"And that's all your doing."

"Hey, he brought it on himself. After all, Dein started it, no?" Flum grabbed a stool and set it in front of the counter before sitting to face Y'lla.

"What, you just showed up to hang out?"

"I didn't want to just stand around if this conversation drags on."

"There's no conversation I want to have with you that'd take that long."

"All right, let me ask this then: do you know where Dein is?"

"I don't know...isn't exactly truthful now, is it? I do, in fact."

This took Flum by surprise. Even if Y'lla did know, she'd hardly expected her to come out and admit it. "Wait, can you tell me where he is, then?"

"Sure. He's a scumbag, but offering his soul up to the church is a bit much, even for him."

"The church? Like, is he just playing them? Or is this place so empty because he and his crew are busy offering up prayers?"

"Wow, you're good at this," Y'lla said. Flum had meant it as a joke, but she hit the nail right on the head. "Why, just this morning he came by with one of his long-time companions to say hi and tell me they'd become disciples of Origin."

"He's gotta be planning something."

"How would I know? But hey, it's kept him out of the military's hands, at least. They don't get heavy with members of the church if they can help it."

"Huh. Sounds like he just joined them for the perks." Flum glanced around the bar and scowled. This meant the people still hanging around here were those Dein had left behind.

"He was real excited about eventually taking control of the church," Y'lla said. "But he wasn't going to do it with those backstabbers along for the ride."

The picture was starting to clear up for Flum. "And yet you didn't go with him?"

"Ha! Me? Why would I offer myself up to the church? The only gods I believe in are money and power." It really fit her, though it hardly seemed like something to brag about. "Besides, can you imagine trying to worship with Dein and those lowlifes running around like they own the place?"

"Yeah. I'd probably want to keep my distance, too." For once, they were in agreement.

One thing struck Flum as odd about all this—was it really necessary for Dein to take all of his men with him? She could only hope they weren't going to get Sara involved in whatever they were planning.

"I know I asked you about this before," she said, "but have there been any new jobs about a missing kid?"

"Big nope."

"Could you at least pretend to do your job and look at the books for me?"

"Not up to it, sorry."

"Whoa, hey... I'm pretty sure the guild wouldn't like that."

"The guild master is the one who keeps an eye on stuff, and he's gone, so I can do whatever I want."

"There's no guild master?"

"There's one on paper, sure, but I've never even met the guy. Who would want to be the guild master overseeing the West District? What a drag. They just gave the position to some high-ranking adventurer and let it be."

That explained how Y'lla and Dein got away with so much. Flum figured the main branch in the Central District was probably in charge of assigning guild masters, but even then, the whole process seemed rather haphazard. Was the West District guild not really considered up to snuff with the rest?

"Listen, all I'm saying is that if you don't do your job, it puts us adventurers in a pretty tough spot."

"Hey, you've been earning plenty lately, girl. You can afford to take time off. If you really need some quick cash, make like a slave and sell yourself for a night."

"That joke wasn't even funny the first time."

"Oh? Well I intend to keep making it. Streetwalking fits you much better than the life of an adventurer."

"Strong words from a woman with her tits hanging out like that."

"Whoa, you trying to say I look like a hooker??"

"I mean, it's true, isn't it?" said Flum. "I bet you spread 'em wide open and let Dein and his guys have their fill..."

Y'lla launched to her feet and slapped Flum right across the cheek.

"He said that as long as I was quiet and listened up, I could do whatever I wanted, okay!" she shouted. Y'lla and Dein had overcome a lot of obstacles in their time together. The sheer power in her gaze was impressive, though nothing compared to the hell Flum had endured. Flum just smirked in return.

"Heh, I see you smirking. That's because you know my body's worth some good money."

"Oh? And here I thought you were already in the clearance bin, half off."

"What? I'm top tier, and I always make sure to take care of myself, too!"

Flum chuckled.

"Don't you laugh at me like that! Anyway, it seems like you've misunderstood me, so let me make one thing abundantly clear: I've never slept with a man I wasn't in love with, okay?!"

"Which says a lot about Dein, then, huh? Either you really don't know how to pick 'em, or you like the type of guy that needs a lot of work."

"It wasn't Dein!!!"

"...Really?"

"That's right! He had all the leverage, so I kinda let him do his own thing, but I never actually slept with him!"

Flum calmed down immediately. She'd always figured that the woman behind the counter spent every night with Dein and his men, but now that she really stopped to think about it, she never actually saw any of them come on to Y'lla.

"Why're you looking at me like that?" Y'lla demanded.

"Nothing, really. Something sad just came to mind."

"I don't need that from you!" Y'lla's cheeks flushed red. Maybe Flum was right. "I'm tellin' you, the whole world's gone mad now that those guys are gone. I've got a list of jobs for all the guilds in the city for you if you'll stop."

"You'll let me see it?"

"Even if I don't have a manager here to yell at me, there's a certain adventurer who likes to complain about how slow I am at doing my job."

"You could've just given it to me in the first place, you know."

"Oh, shush. Just look at it and be quiet for once."

Flum had a feeling Y'lla just wanted to keep her around to stave off the crushing boredom. Still, she sighed and looked over the paper, seeking for anything related to Ink. Y'lla just stared on, looking deeply inconvenienced.

While she was scanning the list, Flum heard someone rush into the guild and up to the counter. His breathing was ragged.

"H-hey, Y'lla, where's Dein? Where'd they go??" The man's face was incredibly pale.

"They went to the church and haven't been back. Why?"

"That...that thing is back!"

"And what is this thing, exactly?"

"It looks kinda like Phile! This morning, I saw this bloated creature that looked like Phile moving around."

"Listen, I've never heard anything about that before, okay?"

"Anyway, I also saw more of those creatures off in the slums!"

The word "creature" instantly brought the church to mind. Flum jerked her head up to look at the other man. She didn't know him but figured he was one of Dein's. She didn't exactly want to ask him for a favor, but she needed more information, so she steeled herself and spoke up.

"Hey, do you mind telling me a bit more about that?"

He glared daggers at Flum. Y'lla intervened. "What could it hurt? Weren't you already upset Dein ditched you, anyway?"

The two held each other's eyes for a moment before Y'lla snorted and looked the other way. She wasn't exactly stepping up for Flum's benefit—just striking back at Dein any way she could.

"I guess you have a point." The man looked thoughtfully between the two women's faces. Finally, he clicked his tongue loud enough for Flum to hear, even at her distance, and continued with his story. "Dein ordered Phile to go strong-arm a church official."

"Hmm. So that's how he was planning to get in there."

"Obviously! There's no stronger ally the church could have!"

Flum sighed inwardly. It took a particularly dull-witted person to boast about his group's strength right before the very person they'd tried and failed to kill.

"Anyway, that didn't work out, and now Dein's a member of the church. Pretty lame, if you ask me." Y'lla sounded quite annoyed at the whole ordeal.

"I know how you feel, Y'lla, but no one expected it to turn out like this."

"Hey, could you tell me about that creature you were talking about?" Flum asked.

"Ah, right. Y'know, I never saw it myself exactly, but I hear that it's all arms, legs, and heads mushed together in a pile. Its whole body is distended, 'cause of all the eyes crammed inside."

"A bunch of eyes? Growing new limbs?"

This was a different creature from the one that she dealt with back at the laboratory. It was still entirely plausible that whoever they threatened at the church had something to do with the natural extension of that research.

"When I first heard about it, I kinda just figured Dein had gone mad. But then I saw bodies off in the slums that fit that description and...and...well, I just couldn't doubt it anymore."

"So there is a lab somewhere here in the capital..." Flum muttered.

"Enough with the creepy talking to yourself. Or are you trying to say that you know something about this?" Y'lla demanded.

"Hmm, if you're really interested, then I guess I could tell you."

"No thanks. I don't want to get involved."

That was a wise call. Flum didn't want to have to spend more time with Y'lla, either.

"Back to this Phile guy. You said you saw him this morning. Wouldn't it have caused a ruckus if other people saw him, too?"

"I guess the church got rid of 'im."

"Then there should've been an even bigger stir with all the bodies you saw back in the slums! There had to be tons of witnesses."

The man let out a sigh and shook his head. "Beats me. There were tons of victims everywhere, and a lot of people millin' about, so maybe they just couldn't hide them all?"

"In that case, why attack there in the first place? It just seems odd. Listen, would you be willing to take me there?"

It was a brazen request, given what she knew about the church, but she couldn't really say anything more without seeing it for herself. The man didn't look too keen on this idea, but there was still something left that he wanted to check out himself, so he finally agreed. Y'lla volunteered to join them, too.

"Are you sure you can leave the guild unstaffed?"

"I'm not the only staff you know. Slooooooooowe!" A young man Flum had never met before lumbered out of a back room. "That's Slowe, one of our admin guys."

"N-n-nice to meet you. I'm Slowe Uradnehs." He offered a low, curt bow in their direction.

"Oh, umm, hi. You're certainly not the usual type that lives out here."

"That's probably true. Anyway, I'm gonna head on out for a bit, Slowe. Can I leave you in charge of reception?"

"Huh? Uh, me? I mean, I've never even..."

"You'll figure it out. See ya!"

Y'lla waved her hand excitedly over her shoulder and made for the door. Slowe hesitated for a moment, but it was clear he wasn't the type to argue back. It felt cruel to leave him alone behind the counter like that, but without Dein and his gang around, Flum figured he'd be fine.

With that settled, Flum, Y'lla, and the other man left the guild.

◇ ◇ ◇

Soon after, they found themselves in the middle of the slums, surrounded by a mob vying for good angles on the grisly scene. The stench of death assaulted their noses as the three drew closer.

Y'lla held her hand over her mouth and scowled. "Yuuuuck. I knew the slums smelled bad, but this is *way* out there."

The smell nearly overpowered them by the time they made it to the front of the crowd. The sight waiting for them only made it all the harder to bear.

Y'lla gagged. "Nngaaa...what is that??"

"Y'know, I think it used to be a person."

"That's what you said, but it's hard to believe..."

Flum and the man were also clearly repulsed by the sight.

Arms, legs, and heads stuck out of the mass of flesh at odd angles; it looked like an art piece gone wrong. The road was littered with several of these creatures. Making matters worse, they writhed about like they were still alive.

The guards who had been summoned to the scene stood by, flummoxed. What could they do, anyway? As the three stared on in shock, a soldier finally showed up with a large cloth and draped it gently over the mass of flesh and muscle.

"Hya... hyaaa..." Y'lla threw her hand over her mouth again as she started to gag.

"Don't throw up here."

"How're you so cool, anyway?!"

"I'm an adventurer." Right as those words left Flum's mouth, the man who brought them here—also an adventurer—began to gag, too. "Well, I guess that doesn't entirely explain it."

She was hardly an ordinary adventurer, after all. This was nothing compared to the ogre she'd faced off against before.

It looked like Y'lla was hitting her limit, so the three of them made their way back through the crowd and away from the scene. They all wore dark expressions, though for separate reasons. The overcast sky only strengthened the scene's foul tenor.

"Man, I just dunno. Phile got turned into a freak o' nature like that, and Dein just runs off to the church. Is it really such a good idea to follow him?"

Dein had done everything in his power to increase his reach and power over the entire West District. Adventurers, guilds, merchants, soldiers—he'd managed to gain influence over them all. Though many called him a coward or scoundrel behind his back, there was something about his audacious personality that drew people in. The downside of this was that the moment he was gone, his empire began to crumble like a castle made of sand.

"If you're still not sure which side you fall on, it's best you stay out of the West District for a while," Flum said.

"You never know when or where those eyeballs might show back up."

"Yeah, you're probably right. I should wait until things cool down a bit."

"I'd hate to get caught up in this bullshit and wind up like one of those freaks." Y'lla shuddered.

They were quick to write Dein off after what they'd just seen. No matter how much she still disliked them, Flum wasn't heartless enough to harm anyone willing to break off their ties with Dein.

She watched them make their way back to the guild, and turned towards home.

◇◇◇

"I'm hooooome!"

Flum threw open the door and heard three separate greetings echo back. It sounded like Milkit and Ink were in the living room, while Eterna was still upstairs in her bedroom. She was initially a bit saddened that Milkit didn't come running to the door to greet her as she usually did but got over it once she set foot in the living room and spied Ink sitting in Milkit's lap.

"Welcome home, Master. I'm sorry I couldn't greet you at the door."

"No worries. What're you two doing, anyway?" Flum motioned toward the wooden frame with several inter-locked pieces lying in disarray atop the table.

Ink shouted out excitedly. "We're doin' a puzzle!!"

That made sense. Since each piece was shaped differently, Ink could complete the puzzle by touch. However, something was oddly familiar about the pieces.

"Eterna made it for us using some things around the house, so Ink would have something to play with," Milkit explained.

Flum sat down on a nearby seat to watch. "Wow. She did a great job."

She knew that the previous owner left behind some tools in a closet upstairs, but they were all old and covered in dust, so she didn't look much further. Apparently Eterna had taken the lay of the land when she was squatting.

"And what's that?" Flum motioned toward a metal toy sitting off to the side.

"A ring puzzle. We played with it for a while but grew bored of it eventually."

"Milkit was great at it! I totally couldn't do it at all, but she managed to just take the rings right apart!"

"You've always been pretty good with your hands."

"No, hardly... I've played with one before, and it's... it's just a matter of learning the secret to how it works."

Though she wouldn't admit it, Milkit was quite dexterous. Her knife skills in the kitchen were impressive, and she could cook as well as any professional chef. In the short time Flum had spent with her, she picked up reading and writing quickly.

In Flum's eyes, she was perfect, both inside and out—and talented to boot. It pained Flum to imagine the horrors she must've endured, but it did no one any good to dwell on that anger, especially since there was no one around to be angry at. It would just leave her feeling drained.

After taking a deep breath and clearing her thoughts, Flum slowly glanced around the room. "Now that I think about it, Sara's still not here yet."

"She might be planning on coming just before dinner." They hadn't exactly made any solid plans, but it'd become almost like a tradition for Sara to come over for dinner recently.

"Isn't it tough to keep cooking for so many people, Milkit?"

"I suppose it might be tough on your wallet, Master, spending all of the money that you work so hard for on food, but I... Actually, I quite like it."

"Huh? I guess it's fine, then."

"I love seeing people enjoy the food that I've made. The more people who come to eat my food, the happier I feel."

217

The answer was practically ripped from the pages of a good housekeeping manual. Flum caught the slightest hint of a smile underneath the layers of bandages. It reminded her of just how glad she was to have taken Milkit's hand and brought her along for this journey.

"Hey, Milkit, d'ya like it when I eat, too?" Ink demanded.

Milkit responded cheerfully, "Of course I do."

Ink smiled brightly, relieved to hear it. Judging by the look on her face, it was clear she hoped to stay here and make this her new home.

"Hey, uh, Ink..." There were still things Flum needed to know. It was going to be difficult for them to keep living together as long as Ink kept secrets from them. "Don't you think that Mother, Papa, and the other kids you were living with must miss you?"

"I wonder... I couldn't really talk to Papa, and the other kids always made fun of me, saying I was useless. Mother was nice, of course, but she seemed to think I wasn't of any use, too."

Flum furrowed her brow at this. Useless... Just how were they determining the use of these children? "Ya know, people told me I was useless all the time, too. I understand how you must've felt about wanting to run away."

"You too, Flum?"

Flum laughed bitterly. "But in my case, I was kicked out before I had a chance to run away." She gently traced her finger over the mark of a slave burnt into her cheek.

"Master..."

"Don't look so worried. After all, it's thanks to a certain someone who reminded me we have matching marks that I realized it wasn't as bad as I thought."

It was true—if she'd never received this mark, she and Milkit would never have met. Flum would never have realized her true potential, and Milkit... Well, Milkit would have been eaten alive in a cage by those ghouls. They may have had to travel to the depths of hell to make it happen, but their chance encounter was ultimately what gave them the happiness they had today, even if Flum still wasn't about to forgive Jean for what he did.

"Aww, must be nice to have someone like Milkit..."

"Yup. Honestly, I don't know if I could've gotten myself out of that place if it weren't for her."

Ink looked down, dejected. "I wonder if I could ever live with all of you..."

Flum understood how she felt so well that it hurt. There was a pretty big difference in their situations, though. Flum had been rejected, while Ink chose to run away of her own will.

"If that's what you really want, I'm fine with it," Flum said.

Ink practically pulled herself across the table to face Flum, a broad grin plastered across her face. "Really??"

"But you'll have to start telling us the truth. I know you're still hiding things, aren't you?"

"Well, I, umm..."

"Eterna's worried, too, you know. She'd be pretty broken up if something were to happen to you."

Ink had also grown quite close to Eterna in their time together. Flum didn't enjoy having to use their relationship like that, but it had to be done.

"Well...I used to take some medicine every day, always at the same time."

"Are you sick?"

Ink shook her head. "Mother said I wasn't sick but that I needed to take it."

"Why did you keep that to yourself? It's pretty important."

"I figured Eterna knows a lot about medicine, and she'd make me keep taking it if I told her about it."

"But if something were to happen to you, it'd be too late to help you by the time we figured it out. Anyway, if it wasn't for your health, then why did you take the medicine?"

"Dunno. The second-generation kids didn't have to take it, but I had to because I was from the first generation."

"Generation...?"

"I don't really know, to be honest, other than that I was one of the first generation. Maybe 'cause I'm ten?"

Flum was certain of it now. Ink had to have escaped from a church laboratory.

"I think there's something different about me that kept my friends and family from really accepting me," Ink continued. "That's why I felt like something was off."

"Different?"

"I can talk and play like anyone else, but... I don't know. I just felt like I was different, somehow. Like, not even the same kind of animal as everyone else. That's the best I can explain it."

Ink was probably closer to the truth than she even knew. If the church had performed the same experiments on people that they had on those ogres, these children likely *were* no longer human. And the second generation, likely an improvement over the first, would be far less human than Ink.

If the stories about a wave of eyeballs sweeping over the capital and killing people was the work of this second generation, then whoever was behind it must be looking for Ink. There was something crude, almost childish about the way that the eyeballs murdered without cause or care. Some might argue that Ink may have had something to do with it—she was, after all, missing her own eyes—but she hadn't left the house once since they'd brought her home. What's more, Flum couldn't imagine Ink murdering all those people in the slums.

There was one thing that Flum just couldn't explain: if the people at the laboratory deemed Ink useless, why was she still alive? At least thus far, she hadn't exhibited any of the spiral-based powers that the ogre had. Flum didn't know if Ink had any powers at all.

As far as she could tell, they'd never bothered to keep their failures back in the underground lab. The researchers had discarded every unsuccessful subject like so much trash. Did that mean that Ink *was* a success on some level? And they let her escape from right under their noses?

"Flum?" Ink's voice brought Flum back from her thoughts.

"Huh? Uh, sorry, what was that?"

"Are you suspicious of me?"

Flum couldn't in good faith say no, though she still didn't know *what* she suspected. "I guess...I guess I am. Or at least I don't trust you completely, even though I want to."

"You know, I never left that place, not once in my life. I was stuck in there for ten years. This is the first time in my life I've gotten to enjoy fresh air, taste delicious food, sit on someone's lap, or even talk to new people!"

Ink threw out her arms to express her excitement. Regret stung Flum's heart.

"I'm not blaming you, Flum," Ink said. "I'm saying I get why you'd be suspicious of me."

"What makes you say that?"

"Everything I thought was normal was upside down. Every new thing I experience now, from the moment I wake up to when I go to bed—it makes me realize how strange my life was. Anyway, I'm not hiding anything else, I promise. So...so...please, just trust me, I'll tell you anything you ask, Flum. Just tell me what you want to know."

"I'm sorry, Ink." All Flum could do was apologize.

"Oh, no, no, no. You don't need to apologize, Flum! I mean, you have every right to be mad, even. I mean, from your point of view, I should've told you all this sooner. Maybe it seems ridiculous why I don't know all this obvious stuff."

"Well, Master has a kind heart," Milkit said.

"And that's why I won't hide anything from you. Please, just ask anything you like! I'll answer the best I can!"

◇◇◇

True to her word, Ink told them everything they asked. They started with the details of how she left the facility in the first place.

"Well, I opened the door, walked down some stairs, and stepped outside. Then I ran for a really long time, and I don't remember much after that. I remember thinking that a building near my home seemed really clean; it smelled nice compared to everywhere else."

That sounded a lot like the area around the church.

Next, they asked about life in the facility.

"Like I said, everyone treated me different. I wasn't allowed outside. I was alone a lot, and it was super boring. I used to spend time exploring the place and making up my own rules while I ran around. Hmm, oh, and the food was pretty bland compared to what you eat here. And there was the medicine I mentioned."

Then, Mother.

"All I can say about Mother is that she was...well, Mother. I don't even know her real name. I think she was just a little taller than me, 'cause my face rested against her chest when she hugged me. Judging by her voice, I'd guess she was in her thirties or so. She was kind but always a little cold to me. Now that I think about it, though, I don't think she was actually all that nice."

"Why do you say that?"

"You guys are a lot nicer to me. I dunno, it's embarrassing to put it into words." Ink's cheeks flushed.

Flum blushed at this in kind, and Milkit smiled at the young girl on her lap.

They moved on to the so-called "second-generation" children Ink had been living with.

"Lessee, Nekt was pretty wild and rebellious, Mute never really talked much and was kinda hard for me to read, Luke was a little scary but always loyal, and Fwiss was Mother's favorite. I always felt like I shoulda been like a big sister to the rest, but it never really worked out that way."

"How were you different from the second-generation kids?"

"I mentioned this to Eterna already, but I think the biggest difference was Papa."

"You say you never met him before, right? I guess you don't know his name, either."

"I never really heard his name mentioned specifically, and they didn't really tell any of us kids, but I remember overhearing Nekt once. Everyone was real mad when they found out."

Ink smiled proudly.

"They called Papa 'Origin.'"

Flum and Milkit froze.

This was it—as good proof as any that the church of Origin was behind this. Flum had always considered the Pope to be the leader of the church. She'd never really believed in an actual god. Even if one did exist, it was hard to believe that such a god would be directly involved in the intricate details of their daily lives.

Ink, though... The other children Ink had lived with spoke of Origin like family.

"Uh, hey, Ink, I just want to make sure. Did you say Origin?"

"That's right. Do you know anything about them?"

"Not really, no..." Flum's reply came out much louder than she'd intended it to. It was entirely possible that Ink didn't know what churches were, or anything about the religion that operated them. "All I can say is that Origin is, well, Origin."

I wonder if the people who chose me also heard the voice of Origin...

She'd always figured that the Pope and Cardinals had been the ones choosing the members of the party sent out to slay the Demon Lord. But as she thought back on her encounters—monsters with spiral faces, animated eyeballs, creatures covered in grotesque limbs—Flum couldn't help but feel that they didn't quite seem like the products of a human mind. From the bizarre, spiral-filled notebook she found back in the laboratory to the ogre with her name listed in its stats, she was starting to doubt the church could create all of these things through research alone.

If there *was* some sort of supernatural entity known as Origin out there...well, it would explain a lot. The only question was *why was it looking for her*?

"Flum?"

"You're looking rather pale, Master."

"I'm fine...really. Probably."

And yet, Flum felt an ominous weight in her chest as her pulse quickened.

**ROLL
OVER
AND
DIE**

008

The Pervasive Sense of Helplessness

SARA ULTIMATELY never showed up, but then, they'd never made official dinner plans. Considering recent events, though, Flum couldn't help but worry. The next day, she made her way to Sara's home at the Central District church. She wasn't exactly in a position to walk up to the front door and ask for her, so instead, she hung back in the shadows and watched the building for some time.

"Well, it doesn't seem like anything strange is going on, but..."

There was something about the expression on the face of the knight guarding the entrance. Inside the building, the nuns bustled about anxiously. Was it her imagination, or did it look like they were worried about Sara?

Flum debated for a bit if she should just go up and ask them, but before she had a chance to decide on her plan of action, a nun in her thirties, dressed in the same white robes as Sara, happened to walk right in front of her.

"Um, excuse me, Sister... I was hoping to ask you something."

The nun stopped and turned around, her peach-colored hair swaying gently as she moved. Flum beckoned the nun over, eliciting a suspicious look, but the woman slowly moved in close.

Flum decided to just ask her straight out. "Do you know a kid named Sara?"

The nun instantly lost her composure and clutched onto Flum's shoulders. "You know her?"

Flum felt the vague shape of her anxiety begin to crystallize.

"Ah, I...I'm sorry. I'm just a bit frazzled, is all," the nun apologized.

"Did something happen to Sara?"

"Before I answer that, could you please tell me the nature of your relationship?"

"My name's Flum, and Sara and I..."

"Oh, Flum! Yes, she spoke of you a lot. The nice girl who always let her come over for these great feasts."

Apparently, Sara had told them all about Flum and the others. It seemed very much like her to lead with the food.

"Apologies for not introducing myself further. My name is Elune. I was the one who looked after her, Ed, and Jonny ever since they were little. Ah, excuse me, Ed and Jonny are..."

"I've met them before."

"Oh? Well, then that will speed things up. You see, the Pope himself made a sudden appearance earlier and...well, he informed us that Sara was to be excommunicated."

"Excommunicated?! Why so sudden?"

"Demon worship, apparently. Once they were made aware of it, the church had her taken before the court for judgment."

The ecclesiastical courts operated separately from the royal judiciary. Doctrine called for enforcement; enforcement sometimes called for imprisonment, torture, and execution. Where the law of the nation could not be reconciled with doctrine, the royal family stayed clear of church affairs. Certain regions of the kingdom were managed and overseen wholly by the papacy.

To be found guilty by an ecclesiastical court would leave you branded a criminal throughout the country.

"Obviously there's no way that child was worshipping demons or doing anything of the sort," Elune continued. "I mean, we lived with her; we should know."

Flum bit down hard on her lip to keep her worry in check. Sara had been a valuable asset to the church, of that much she was certain. What could they possibly want to hide so badly that they would sacrifice her like this? Did it have something to do with Ink and the goings-on in the West District?

"Flum, do you happen to know where Sara went or what she's doing? I don't understand how it's come to this!" Elune's voice was unsteady and desperate. She was doing everything in her power to keep the tears from flooding out.

Flum had come here to ask the very same questions. "Actually, I asked Sara to look into the church's orphanages..."

"The orphanages? Why?"

"I found a lost kid out in the West District. I'm taking care of her now, but I was trying to figure out where she'd come from."

"So that's why she left so early in the morning for the West District..."

"She recruited Ed and Jonny to help her out, apparently. However, I was told that the orphanage didn't have any missing kids."

"So Ed and Jonny were involved, too..."

"Did something happen to them?"

"As of this morning, they were suddenly transferred to a neighboring village. It's practically unheard of to transfer knights assigned to the capital unless they committed some kind of offense, but I hadn't heard anything about them being in trouble. When I went to ask them myself, I was told they already departed. It just seems so out of character for them to leave without saying goodbye!" Elune was clearly losing her grip on the fear welling up in her.

Flum ran her thumb and index finger nervously over the front of her blouse. A lot was happening all at once, all for the purposes of keeping something under wraps. She was certain of that much. But why excommunicate Sara and transfer Jonny and Ed? If they just wanted to get rid of them, they could've excommunicated them all.

"Do you know where any of them might be, Elune?"

"All I've been able to learn is that someone saw a blonde girl in a habit out in the slums, near the wall of the West District."

"That's...that's where the bodies were found."

Elune nodded. She must have known she wasn't likely to get a response to her next question, but she had to ask it anyway. "Does that have anything to do with Sara's excommunication?"

Flum had no proof, but the timing, circumstances, and past behavior of the church just fit all too well. "They both seem to be connected with some of the church's less savory dealings, yes."

Elune's eyes went wide in shock and affirmation. You couldn't spend that many years in the church and not be aware of their underhanded dealings, even if you wanted to.

"I...don't want it to be true," Flum said, "but I fear that Ed and Jonny may already be dead."

"What?" Elune cried.

"I have no proof, but I think the story of them being transferred served to cover up their deaths."

"I...I can't believe that. But then, why would they choose to only excommunicate Sara?"

"She might still be alive and on the run. Excommunicating her covers them in case she ever surfaces."

"But what could the Pope possibly be hiding that would necessitate all this?"

"That..." Flum paused. "I'm sorry, but I really don't want to get you involved. You might just meet the same fate as Sara if I do."

"I don't care if I do! I may not be related to them by blood, but Sara, Ed, Jonny... They're my children!"

"Assuming Sara is still on the run, the fact that she hasn't shown herself yet means she doesn't want you involved."

"But...but even then...! Does she even know how much we love and care about her?" The anguish was clear in her voice.

Flum understood. All too well. If this was something Elune could have helped with, Sara would have come to ask for assistance. If she hadn't shown up, it was because she believed there was nothing they could do. She'd chosen to stay out of sight and continue to flee.

The two women stood there, agonized by just how little they could do.

"Then what should I do?" Elune asked. "Would going out to punch the Pope bring my Sara home?"

"I don't think it's that easy, sadly."

"You're right. He's far too strong for me to even..."

"No, not that. I mean that the whole church, well..."

"What about the church? Just go ahead and spit it out, I'm ready to hear it. We already know that the Pope and his inner circle are hiding something."

It was entirely possible that the nuns familiar with the church's inner workings were even more receptive to criticism of the church than those on the outside looking in. Flum decided to tell Elune what she knew.

"I think this incident is the result of someone losing control over...something, whatever that may be."

"So you're saying that the church is disappearing

people to cover up something they were doing in secret? And they've somehow lost control?"

"They created children who possessed the power of Origin through human experimentation. That's all I've been able to figure out, but I suspect the children are acting on their own now."

"Origin's...power? You mean that the Divine Creator gave them his power? But Sara was a rising star in the church; why would Origin target her like that? She, of all people, would have defended Origin's teachings to the last!"

"I suspect power is far more important to these people than scripture."

Elune looked deeply troubled at this revelation. The fact that she would even entertain the idea that Flum—a girl she barely knew, and even then only as an associate of Sara's—was telling the truth spoke to the suspicions she'd already born about the church.

"I...I just can't believe anything the church says anymore. A few hours ago, we were laughing, smiling, and now I might never see them again. This feels like a terrible nightmare."

"We might still be able to save Sara," Flum said.

"We have no idea where she is! Besides, even if we found her, the church would just put on a show trial and sentence her to death."

"And if we don't look for her, she's just as likely to be attacked by those eyes and die anyway."

"Eyes?"

"The victims back in the slums... They were all attacked by a flood of eyeballs that transformed their bodies into abominations. The best explanation I can come up with is that this was Origin's power, and I suspect the same entity is chasing Sara."

"What are you talking about? You mean disembodied *eyeballs* managed to attack people all on their own?"

"Actually...yes."

"That's hard to believe."

"I understand, but this isn't the first time I've fought one of the church's aberrations. Sara was there, too, in fact."

"That...ah, I see now. So then, when Sara..." Something about what Flum had said seemed to resonate with Elune. "That time when Sara went out of town for a few days, right? I knew there was something strange about the way she tried to write it off."

"Sara didn't want to get you involved, I'm sure."

"I see... Even still, I like to think of us as family. But what is happening in the capital, and what does it mean that Origin granted these children his power? Why would God turn his back on his most devout followers?"

The more Elune learned the truth behind Origin, the weaker her faith grew. The church likely anticipated this exact response from their flock and chose to prioritize seizing more power—a decision that culminated in their attempt to eliminate Sara. Once that power was firmly within their grasp, they could dictate what was right and proper. It was inevitable many of the devout would turn on the church when the truth surfaced; better to wipe them out before they could organize or go to ground.

"Do you know why they targeted Sara, Ed, and Jonny?" Elune asked. "None of them were deeply involved in church matters. It's strange you weren't attacked as well, if seeing the creature was enough to do them in."

"I don't have an answer for that, but Sara must have taken the path through the slums because she discovered some of the church's secrets."

"What makes you say that?"

"Sara wouldn't knowingly put innocents in danger. If something attacked her, she wouldn't let it follow her through a busy neighborhood—not unless she thought her attacker wanted to keep something secret and wouldn't follow her where people could see."

"But they continued to pursue her, anyway... Which is why you said earlier that the church lost control of whatever that something is."

"Bingo. These eyeballs they summoned up to keep their secrets under wraps ended up causing a bloodbath of their own. The church must be desperate for a way out. That's where these claims of transfers and excommunications come in."

"And if the church is that flustered, it could mean there's still a chance to save Sara..."

"That's right. Which means we need to start searching for her right away."

"You're right... It's too early to give up now. I'll call on those I can trust and do whatever I can to bring her home."

"Don't draw too much attention to yourself," Flum warned. "We don't know when they might come looking for you, too."

"I don't know. If I was targeted, maybe it would draw Sara out of hiding."

Flum didn't laugh at Elune's attempt at a joke. "Thank you for everything, Elune."

"No, thank you. If I learn anything about Sara's whereabouts, I'll be sure to let you know."

"Please do. I'll let you know if I find her." Flum gave Elune her address, and the two parted ways. Looking up, the sun smiled brightly down on her against a deep blue sky. It felt like it was mocking her.

"I hope you're okay, Sara." She felt ill as she pictured the sweet, innocent girl turned to a bloated tangle of limbs.

She would find Sara and put a stop to the children controlling the tide of eyes. For now, she just had to keep moving.

◇ ◇ ◇

On her way home from the Central District, Flum caught a man's gaze as they walked past, and both parties froze instantly.

Dein's lips turned up into his trademark malevolent grin. "Well, hello there. How've you been?"

There were about twenty other men walking behind him in procession, almost a military formation. All of them looked familiar, though their faces were expressionless as dolls. Flum felt goosebumps rise up all over her body as she walked on past, completely ignoring their presence.

"Aren't you upset to have lost that ankle-biter?"

This stopped Flum in her tracks. She could feel the expressionless men turn and watch her. A chill ran up her spine.

"I figure the little ugly mummy-girl'll be next..."

"Dein, you son of a...!" That was the last push Flum needed. She stepped forward and grabbed Dein's collar, but he only responded with his usual sardonic smile.

"You sure you wanna do that? We're devout servants of the church, ya know. Devoted to our beloved master, Origin. I don't think God Almighty would look too fondly on you hurting me."

"So that's all it took to make you cave? Too scared of working alone now that your underlings abandoned you?"

Dein belted out a boisterous laugh. "You think I'm scared of a runt like you? Ha! The church ain't all that bad. Besides, it's nice knowing I got friends in high places looking out for me."

He brushed her hands away and turned to continue on his way, swaying back and forth and cackling like a drunk.

"Y'know, my client...or should I say 'boss' now...told me to keep my hands off of you, Flum. So I guess I've little else to do with my day but drink the hours away. Not a bad price to pay for keeping my life, really. Low risk, high return, as they say!"

"I have no idea what you're talking about, Dein."

"All in due time, Flum, all in due time. Anyway, we best be off."

With a snap of his fingers, Dein's procession followed after him in two perfect lines.

Suddenly Y'lla's anger at what happened to Dein made sense; Dein's posse was a thing of the past. He'd both figuratively and literally discarded everything and everyone to save his own life.

Flum took some comfort in the removal of a heavy burden from her shoulders. Maybe she could even live a little more freely...to the extent that a captive animal could live free within its cage.

She was happy to see his pride and reckless dreams come crashing down all around him. Dein Phineas, the charismatic thug who ran the West District, was no more. And yet—Dein would continue to make the same choices as before. He would sacrifice his pawns to serve his own ends. All that changed was the means to those ends.

For a second, Flum felt rage burn deep within her. She contemplated cutting him down from behind. Perhaps that would be the best choice, after all.

She averted her gaze. Looking off to the right, she caught sight of an eye staring directly at her.

Just a single eyeball, waiting at the entrance to an alley, staring at her.

Flum swallowed hard. "N-no way."

This was, without a doubt, one of the eyes that created those deformed corpses she saw earlier.

She forgot all about Dein. Drawing her sword, Flum

slowly closed in on the eye, her hand clutched so tightly around the hilt that the entire sword wobbled.

Her mind filled with images of the bodies she saw just the day before: bloated, limbs sticking out everywhere, bodily fluids dripping out of every orifice, eyeballs covering their flesh. The very thought that she could be next left her mouth bone dry.

I have to kill it...

At least there was only one right now. From what she could discern, there needed to be a lot more of them before they could enter her body. As far as she knew, it could be calling out to its friends right now in some language she could neither hear nor understand. Maybe it just had to separate and multiply.

Or maybe splattering it across the walls might in itself start a process that called forth the swarm. There were so many possibilities that Flum found herself unable to commit. Her breathing came out ragged through her nose, and her palms were slick with sweat.

Should she try to catch it? Cut it down? Run away? As Flum worried over her next step, the eyeball rolled off in the other direction, away from her, around a corner, and out of sight.

Flum gave chase, but by the time she rounded the corner, it was already gone.

"So maybe it wasn't after me after all? What was that all about, then?"

It never made any attempt to chase her. The eyeball seemed to simply want her to know it was there. It *did* distract her in time to stop her from cutting down Dein. Could that have been its intent?

No answer was forthcoming, so Flum hurried home.

◇ ◇ ◇

Milkit hurried over as soon as Flum opened the front door. She seemed even more cheerful today as she greeted Flum, like she could pick up on her master's worries.

"What great timing, Master. I just finished making lunch, so why don't you come sit down with us?"

Flum didn't want to spoil the mood, so she kept what she learned to herself as she joined the other three at the table. She didn't need to say it—whatever it was, they knew Flum's news would be bad. Once lunch was finished and the plates were cleared away, Flum brought everyone up to speed.

Ink took the news worse than anyone else, blaming herself for getting Sara involved. The group did what they could to try and make her feel better, but it was to no avail. Ink eventually went back upstairs to her room and shut the door.

Eterna mentioned having work to get back to and left for her own room shortly after, leaving Flum and Milkit alone in the living room. Milkit opened her mouth several times as if to say something to try and cheer Flum up, but she couldn't find the right words.

Flum watched her perplexity play out, offering her up a gentle smile. "Thanks."

"Hm?" Milkit's face more than made up for what she couldn't express in words.

"You really helped a lot, Milkit."

"B-b-but, I didn't do anything, Master."

"Nah, you did more than enough. Just being here next to me, worrying about me, that really helps. So..." Flum stood up, reached over, and took Milkit's hand. "You don't need to say anything special or feel bad about it. As long as you're here, and I can see your beautiful smile, that's enough to cheer me on."

"I...I understand what you're saying, Master...but I just wish that I could give back even a bit of the happiness you bring to me."

"Aww, that's lovely of you to say, Milkit. If that's how you feel, I'm not going to stop you, but never forget that your Master is always looking forward to your delightful smile."

Milkit let out a small, disappointed sigh as Flum drew her hand away. Flum paused and turned back around, stepping in close and wrapping her arms around Milkit's waist, pulling her in close. She gently started to stroke her hair.

"Master..."

After Flum left the room again, Milkit sat back, clutching gently at the bandages that concealed her flushed cheeks as she mumbled all the words she couldn't get out earlier.

◇◇◇

Flum knocked on Eterna's door, pausing for a moment as she waited for permission to enter before slowly turning the doorknob.

"Well, there you are."

"How'd you know?"

"You looked like there was something you wanted to ask me all through lunch. You're really easy to read, Flum."

Flum unconsciously stroked her cheeks, wondering just what kind of face she had made.

"Anyway, go ahead and sit down."

She dragged a chair over from the corner to sit near Eterna. Eterna set down her pen and turned her own chair to face Flum. A floating, fish-shaped object moved in unison with her. Her desk was littered with dried leaves and a menagerie of small carved statues, lending a mysterious air to the room.

"What were you working on?"

"Just some medicine. It doesn't have any effect on illnesses or injuries, but it does boost your spirits."

"Sounds...strange." If it didn't have anything to do with illnesses or injuries, then Flum figured the church would have little interest in it...though there were probably others who would object.

"I'm just making tea, Flum."

"Oh...oooh. I see. I know you drink a lot, but that seems like quite a bit, even for you."

"I'm going to sell it. I can't keep freeloading like this."

Flum smacked her fist into her hand as it all came together. She was about to mention how out of character that was for Eterna to be so considerate but thought better of it. "And what's that carving of?"

"This?" Eterna handed it to Flum. Inspecting it closely for a few seconds, something about its features struck her.

"Hey, this...this kinda looks like me."

"Milkit made it."

"So it is me! I knew she was skilled with her hands, but wow..."

"Apparently she made all kinds of things with stone and wood back when she was a slave. Just one of her many talents."

"And why do you have it?"

"She said she'd be embarrassed if you found it, but she couldn't bear to throw it away. I don't need it, so it's all yours."

Flum didn't know what to do with a carving of herself, either. The strange journey the statue had taken through the house seemed self-defeating. Finally, deciding to pass up on Eterna's offer, she set it back down on the older woman's desk. Eterna pouted at this, apparently also displeased with being stuck with the carving. It was just taking up space.

"Milkit's been trying out a lot of different stuff when you're away, wanting to find a way to be of help," she said.

"Like the carving here?"

"Yup. That girl loves you so much it's kinda maddening."

"I wouldn't exactly call it *love*, actually...but I guess she does like me quite a bit."

"Bragging about your love life, I see."

Flum unconsciously sat up in her chair, voice rising. "Am not!!"

Eterna smiled warmly at this, happy to see Flum shedding some of her glum mood.

"Anyway, back to the subject at hand..." Flum sat back in her chair, let out a deep breath, and clenched her jaw. "I was hoping you could teach me some magic."

The limits of her own power had been bothering her of late. When Dein and his gang cornered her, there was nothing she could do to fight back. If she ever had to face off against a flood of those eyeballs, her only choice would be to run until she dropped from exhaustion. She was beginning to worry that even if she did find Sara, she might not be of any help.

Her Reversal ability meant no amount of ordinary practice or growth would help her stats, but that didn't mean she was without options. Other abilities, like the Cavalier Arts and spellcasting, weren't strictly bound to her stats. She could at least brush up on those. Whenever she had a free moment, she'd been practicing to increase her prana, along with her ability to focus on the latent magical energy within her own body.

However, she still couldn't successfully turn that into "magic."

"Well, I have water affinity, so I don't have a whole lot of spells that I could teach to someone with a rare affinity like yourself. Also, I'm not really a good teacher to begin with...but I feel like I've told you all this before."

"Even just the basics will do."

ROLL OVER AND DIE

"Hmm...but you can use prana, can't you? Honestly, I think that's a whole lot harder to learn. I'm not really sure why you can't use magic, then."

"I can gather up the magical energy inside myself, but I just don't know how to put it into any sort of form outside of my body."

"Hmm...try to direct some of your magic into the palm of your hand for me."

"Sure."

Flum narrowed her gaze and focused on summoning forth all of the magical energy she had. She focused deep inside herself and tried to bring it together in the palm of her hand, as instructed.

Just like Eterna had said, this was the easy part—much simpler than even generating prana.

"Hmm, there's nothing wrong with the amount, quality, or condition... However..." Eterna closely inspected the ball of light in Flum's hand and gently prodded it with her fingers. "I see... So that's what's going on..."

"What is it?"

Eterna quickly stood up from her chair and pointed back at it. "Keep focusing on the magic and touch the chair."

"Huh?" Flum reached out and touched the seat of the chair as instructed.

"I don't know how Reversal works, but you need to have a clear vision in your mind and use it on something."

"So...I should imagine using the magic on your chair?"

"Exactly."

Flum tried to imagine it exactly like she'd been told. Reversal—vertical and horizontal, internal and external. She had a hard time really focusing in on it, since this was her first time, but she figured that the internal and external varieties would have the biggest impact here. It seemed like it would take a lot of energy to destroy a chair, so she decided to start with something simpler.

On her first attempt, all she was able to do was jiggle one of its slats. Finally, the answer—and the name of the spell—popped into her mind.

"Reversion!!"

The chair slowly spun around before stopping with the seat facing down. Flum was at a loss for words at seeing exactly what she imagined take place before her eyes.

"...It worked." It was a lackluster spell, to be fair, but it was still the first time she'd ever cast magic. "So magic's really that easy?"

"How do you feel? Do you feel like you've used up a large amount of your reserves, like there's an empty spot inside you?"

"Not at all!"

"Sounds like you're fine, then. As long as you can summon up the energy, your affinity should work just fine with magic, though I suspect the nature of how you try to reverse something will have a great impact on how much energy you use."

This was in line with what Flum had been thinking. If she tried to reverse the interior and exterior of the chair, she was pretty sure it would've taken a lot more out of her. Besides, Eterna probably wouldn't be too happy to see her chair destroyed.

"But why was I able to use it now?"

"That part's pretty simple." Eterna took Flum's hand and began to massage her palm. "What you can use your magic on is incredibly limited in range, to the extent that you need to be in contact with it if you want to use any magic at all. That means that you won't be able to use it for ranged attacks, like with other affinities."

Come to think of it, Flum had always tried using magic against distant targets when practicing. Since she was already able to use a sword in combat, she'd wanted to supplement that with ranged magical attacks.

"I was hoping to find some way of fighting that didn't involve getting hurt so much..." She was, at her core, still a child. Though the healing factor Souleater let her endure more pain than anyone, she preferred to avoid it.

"Well, that can't be helped. The rest all comes down to how you use the magic. For example, if there was something connected to the object you intended to use your magic on, you should be able to do it just fine, at the expense of using more magical energy."

"Like using magic on the floorboards, for example?"

"Flipping the whole floorboard? Sure."

That would open options up to her for attacking enemies at range. If she used her magic on a long board, she could easily flip it around as soon as her opponent set foot on it. Whether that would actually be useful in battle was another story entirely.

"What about solid earth?"

"Depends on your abilities and imagination. Even assuming limitless magic reserves, you're still not at a point where you could do it unless you limit the scope by focusing on a specific area and depth."

Flum decided to give it a shot. She gazed hard at the floor beneath her but absolutely nothing happened. Obviously, she'd need to keep practicing. Even if she were still just restricted to that which she could touch for the moment, that kind of magic still greatly increased her options.

"Listen Flum, just because you can use magic doesn't mean you should try doing everything on your own, okay?

I've said it countless times, but I'm more than willing to help out."

"I know. I just need to be able to protect Milkit on my own." The opponents she would be up against now defied logic.

"You're always going just a step too far, you know. You were like that back on the journey, too."

"I have to make up for what I can't do with effort and perseverance."

"Sacrificing yourself on the field of battle as a fighting style is fine on your own, but try to keep it to a minimum when you have allies around, okay? Milkit would be pretty broken up if you get yourself hurt."

"I know that...or...I try to keep it in mind, at least."

All Flum wanted, from the very bottom of her heart, was for Milkit to always have a reason to smile. Getting herself hurt to protect that smile brought Milkit sadness. And yet, if she ever needed to sacrifice herself to protect Milkit...

Her mind went around and around over this conundrum, though it didn't change the reality that she had to fight. As long as she stayed alive, she'd have a chance to help ease that sadness once more.

009

The Missing Piece

AFTER THE INITIAL LESSON, Eterna lectured Flum on magic use for a few hours more. By the time she left, the sun was hanging low in the sky, illuminating the hallway with a deep orange glow. Flum took another brief trip out of the house to look for Sara but once again came back empty-handed. It was getting dark by the time she came home for dinner.

She left again once dinner was finished, in spite of Eterna's warnings. She couldn't keep sitting around the house doing nothing.

This trip, too, proved fruitless, and Flum returned home to find everyone asleep except Milkit. As had become tradition, Milkit met her master with a bright smile right at the entryway. Flum felt bad for not being able to give her the attention she deserved, but her heart was in turmoil at this point over her lack of leads on Sara.

She took a quick bath and headed upstairs, only to notice Ink sticking her head out of the door to her room. She must have heard Flum's footsteps. She was wearing a pair of Flum's old pink pajamas. They suited Ink quite well, even if they hung loosely off her tiny frame.

It always pained Flum to look at her sewn-shut eyes, though through her easy smile and cheerful demeanor, her dismay had worn off greatly since the first time they met.

"'Night, Flum!" Apparently, that was the whole reason she'd popped out.

"Good night, Ink."

Flum reached out and rubbed the young girl's head. She'd been doing that with Ink a lot lately; it had kind of become a force of habit. Ink didn't seem to mind. She smiled brightly at the gesture.

With that done, Ink and Flum both returned to their respective rooms.

Milkit was sitting at the desk in their shared room with a pen in her hand, a serious expression on her face. It looked like she was practicing her reading and writing. She had already changed from her usual maid attire into light green pajamas that matched with a pair Flum owned.

Flum inched closer and closer from behind, though the other girl was too focused on her task to take notice.

She leaned in close over Milkit's shoulder until their faces were right next to each other—still no reaction. Usually Milkit was all smiles around Flum. It was rare to see her looking so serious. Yet her eyes were still as beautiful as ever, and the soft cheeks that peeked out through the bandages...

Flum could no longer resist the urge. She slid her fingers under the bandages to rest against Milkit's soft cheek.

"Eep!" Milkit let out an adorable cry and hopped up in her chair at the sudden contact, causing Flum to break out into a laugh.

"How ya doing?"

"M-master, please tell me when you come in."

"I mean, you didn't even notice me when I got so close. Who could resist the chance to tease you a little bit?"

"Even so..."

Milkit pouted at Flum. Her repertoire of expressions had grown exponentially in the time they'd spent together. Not only that, but thanks to actually being able to eat food meant for people now, her scrawny, unhealthy frame had filled out a lot. Knowing she'd helped grow the girl's spirit and body through her hard work brought Flum great joy.

She looked over the results of Milkit's practice session. Bit by bit, Milkit had gained more and more skills, and with them, more possibilities for the future. Flum was immensely proud of her companion and felt each achievement as if it were her own. This was the kind of happiness she'd never experienced back home, even before she was sent off on the great journey. She wanted to share it, to protect it.

She wanted it so badly.

"...Master?" Milkit's voice drew her back to reality.

"Ah, sorry, sorry. I was just kinda lost in thought for a second there. Anyway, shall we get to it?"

Flum dropped heavily on the bed and waved Milkit over to sit next to her. A moment later they sat shoulder to shoulder.

Flum reached behind Milkit's head and started to undo the knot holding her bandages together. They came loose with a faint rustle, revealing Milkit's soft, pale cheeks. This was something of a ritual for them now. Milkit was shy about it at first, but as time went by, they got it down to a well-rehearsed procedure.

Her skin, under the bandages, was nearly unblemished by the sun. It stood in contrast with Flum's, which was weathered from her years of adventure. While she was jealous on one level, she was secretly excited that she had such a beautiful face all to herself. This was what Milkit wanted, too: for her beauty and innocence to be seen by Flum and Flum alone.

On some level, Flum knew it was unfair. She wanted to open up as many doors to Milkit as possible. On the other hand, Milkit was important enough to her that she could easily brush off such concerns. Night after night, Flum found herself gasping at the sheer beauty exposed to her.

"Is the sight of my face that exciting for you, Master?" Milkit looked down, fidgeting under Flum's gaze. Flum didn't hesitate before replying.

"Yep. I look forward to it all day."

This only embarrassed Milkit all the more. This wasn't the first time they'd had this exchange, either—though with time, Milkit slowly came to doubt her Master less and less, even if she sometimes still rationalized it away as her Master having a strange fetish with which her face just happened to align. It was difficult for her to admit she was pretty.

"You're absolutely stunning today, Milkit...as always." Flum reached out and traced her thumb gently over the slave mark on Milkit's cheek, as if to put an end to the conversation.

She wanted to take her to a place that even words could never reach. She wanted to build up a sense of love and affection so deeply ingrained in Milkit that it could never be taken away.

Even Milkit's fear of loss slowly lessened, day by day. The deep-seated belief that she would one day be discarded was being replaced with a sense that things would probably be okay. In time, this feeling would be replaced with a steely conviction.

She will never leave my side or abandon me.

As they went through their nightly ritual, their bond grew stronger and stronger, and Milkit became ever more confident in their relationship. Once the bandages were off, the two would chitchat, break out into smiles when their eyes happened to meet, tease each other, and otherwise waste the evening away enjoying each other's company.

Flum propped herself up on the bed and glanced out the window. Milkit followed her gaze, seeing nothing but boundless darkness beyond the glass. But Flum had caught sight of something lurking out there. In an instant, she stood up and crept to the window before opening it for a better look.

"Ow!" She placed her hand on the sill to lean outside before jerking it back.

"Did something poke you?"

"It looks like a knife... There's a letter wrapped around it."

As best she could tell, someone who'd been watching them through the window had thrown the knife. Flum unraveled the letter to find a simple message in sloppy handwriting. All it said was: "stay inside."

"What is this, some kind of threat? Bit late for that."

"But why would they attach it to a knife, I wonder? And that handwriting is pretty awful, too..."

"Guess they couldn't use the mail slot. As for the writing, it looks like they were in a hurry." Flum racked her brain for who could have written such a message, but no one came to mind. "Maybe it's just a stupid prank by one of Dein's goons."

No matter what she did to them, those guys never seemed to learn.

"Ah well, I guess it's about time to go to bed."

"You're right. Another day awaits tomorrow."

After extinguishing the light, the two returned to their respective beds.

Even as Milkit's breathing slowed and she began to snore lightly, sleep still wouldn't come to Flum. Her anxiety was just too great to let herself relax.

Krakka...krakka...

Every little rattle of the window seemed to keep her right at the cusp of sleep and consciousness until finally, mercifully, whatever was making the noise outside moved far enough away that she could no longer hear it, and she fell into a proper slumber.

By the time she woke up, she forgot all about it.

◇ ◇ ◇

The next morning, Milkit saw Flum off at the door as she headed to the West District church to see if she could trace Sara's steps. She didn't come across anything strange along the way—in fact, it was almost too serene and quiet, in her opinion. It may have just been because people thought it wiser to stay indoors after the discovery of the bodies out in the slums.

Once she arrived near the church grounds, Flum decided to hang back a bit and keep watch for a while. Compared to the compound out in the Central District, the church here was quite a bit older, smaller, and more austere. She noted that there were two church knights she'd never seen before standing guard where Ed and Jonny used to be.

Their expressions looked dark. They had, after all, just lost two of their coworkers and friends. Perhaps even heard rumor of the real reason behind their sudden transfer.

"Hi there." Flum finally approached the men and

offered up a cheerful greeting. The men froze for a moment at the sight of a slave mark on her cheek—the church forbid the practice of slavery—before smiling and offering up a greeting in return.

They didn't seem to recognize her, so she offered up a quick introduction before getting down to business. "So I understand there used to be two knights here named Ed and Jonny."

The knights visibly tensed up at this.

"They really did a ton to help me out, y'know. I guess they're not on duty today, but do you know if I could talk to them tomorrow?"

"They're, uh, they're not here anymore. They've been reassigned to another village."

"Oh yeah? That was pretty sudden."

"Yeah, you could say that."

Flum took a step closer. "So what really happened?"

The church knights hesitated.

"So they were taken care of, huh?"

One of the men scowled in annoyance. "What're you going on about? I don't know who the hell you are, little girl, but watch your mouth."

"No worries, I didn't hear anything. Anyway, I'll be back another time, so I guess I'll see ya, then." Flum bowed politely to the men before making her exit.

So, even the knights were talking about it, though it didn't look like any of them knew exactly what was going on for sure. It lined up with what she learned from talking to Elune.

Flum turned onto a parallel street and walked until she spotted a gap in the surrounding fence where she could peek through the church's windows. What she saw was a priest, looking preoccupied as he delivered a sermon before a crowd of men who looked like they had absolutely no business in a place of worship.

Dein was sitting right in the front row.

One of the men with him glanced around, eyes stopping to look in Flum's direction.

"Oh, shoot!" Flum dropped out of sight and slunk off to make her way to the orphanage right next door.

There she found a group of children running around in the church yard, playing games. Far more than four children, to be exact. Once she was done constructing a mental map of the church grounds, she started off in the direction she figured Sara was most likely to have taken to the slums.

The streets grew filthier as she got farther from the church. The crowds grew rougher: tough-looking men with tattoos and piercings covering their faces and bodies, eyes sunken deep into their skulls from prolonged drug use, some clearly on the look for their next mark. Even Dein's men were a step up from what she encountered out here.

It seemed unlikely she would encounter any of the eyes that chased Sara with so many people around, so she decided to take a different route.

"I can only imagine how scared Sara must've been running down these narrow, dark alleyways..." It pained Flum just to think about it.

After coming up empty-handed once again, she took to the slums to check out the place where the bodies were found. Though she should have fit right in as a slave, Flum's nice, clean clothes instantly made her draw more than her fair share of attention. Some looked at her in jealousy, while others eyed her as a potential mark. The children running past were just interested in the coins they could hear jangling in her pockets.

Despite being cleaned up, nobody wanted to linger near the site of so many grisly deaths. Even the lean-tos built up against the wall seemed deserted.

"Hey, you." A middle-aged man dressed in ragged clothes called out to Flum. "You lookin' fer that girl that came through here when this all went down?"

"You know something about that?" Flum's expression was neutral, her posture conveying confidence. She knew

he was going to ask for something, probably money, in exchange for information. If he had something note-worthy to offer, she'd be happy to pay.

"That I do, that I do."

"Mind telling me what you know, then? If it's money you're after, I have some I could spare."

The man let out a raspy laugh.

"You're a smart 'un. I guess I'll tell you what I know, then. So that blonde kid, yeah? She was being chased by a whole swarm of these beady fucking eyeballs. As soon as she got what the things were doin' to us, she took off down those side streets."

Flum pointed to make sure. "That way?"

The man nodded.

"Got it, thanks." She dropped a few coins in the man's hand. It wasn't much, but it was more than she had to work with before.

"Thank you kindly."

He smiled a broad, toothless smile and went back into his shanty. Flum, a little surprised at how cheaply he'd been bought off, turned in the direction he'd pointed and made her way down the side streets. She could probably have stumbled across this route herself, but this saved her some time.

...Or so she thought, until she realized just how convoluted the maze of side streets was. "This is going to take a while."

She'd have to scour every corner of this area to make sure she didn't miss anything.

As she made her way back and forth through the twisting alleys, Flum finally arrived at a dead end. The walls were marked with countless gashes made by some kind of sharpened blade.

"Looks like a battle took place here." In fact, even the ground itself was marred with deep cuts. Flum ran her finger along one of the grooves in an attempt to figure out what could have left them behind. "Huh, the depth and length vary a lot, so it clearly wasn't all done with the same weapon. Magic?"

She couldn't tell which affinity had been used, but it was apparent that whoever cast the spell was powerful.

"Sara couldn't do this with her mace. But then, who did?"

After exploring a few more routes and expanding her search, Flum was no closer to learning anything about Sara's whereabouts. Feeling dejected, she made her way toward the North District next. She just wanted to head back home at this point, but there was one last thing she wanted to follow up on, and it was at the castle.

Ottilie was conducting her own investigation into the church. Flum had to see if she'd learned anything about Sara.

◇◇◇

With a little bit of work, she was able to make it to the North District without getting recognized. She crossed paths with clergy on a few occasions, but other than a scowl or offhanded remark about a slave being in these parts, no one took much notice of her.

That was the easy part.

Getting up to the barracks next to the castle wasn't in and of itself an impressive feat—until you considered the fact that armed guards stood watch over the entrance. Flum spent a moment gauging the odds they'd just let her in if she said she was here to speak with Ottilie. If she could convince them that she was the hero Flum Apricot, she might stand a chance, but so far no one had even given her a second glance.

"Well, I'll never know if I don't try." Deciding to stay positive and give it a go, she stepped in front of the guards.

The mark on her cheek instantly drew derisive looks from the soldiers standing watch. "State your purpose, slave."

"My name is Flum Apricot. I'm here to see Lieutenant General Ottilie."

"Ha! Don't make me laugh, kid. You think a slave can just drop the name of a hero and gain access so easily? Next time, come up with a more believable lie!"

That had gone about as well as she predicted, though she didn't plan on giving up just yet. Just as Flum was about to bring up some fact about the journey that only she would know, a man stepped out of the barracks. He was so burly that the guards had to move aside for him to pass, and she had to crane her neck just to look up at his face. He was even buffer than Gadhio.

"Herrmann Zavenyu...?"

Together with Ottilie, he was one of the royal military's three lieutenant generals. Unlike Ottilie, Flum had never actually met him in person, though she doubted she'd forget his massive figure anytime soon.

Zavenyu was currently in his civvies. His signature warhammer was nowhere to be seen, but even without it, he struck an imposing figure. He walked up in silence until he stood immediately in front of the guard. "Let her in."

His voice was so low and deep that you could feel it thrum deep in your rib cage. The soldier swallowed hard. "B-but, she's a sl-slave, and..."

"She speaks the truth."

"That miserable little slave is the Flum Apricot?! But how?"

"Miserable?" The look on Herrmann's face said more than words could. "Watch your mouth."

"I-I'm sorry!"

"She's the real deal. Now let her pass."

"Yessir. P-please come in, Miss Flum."

Flum wasn't sure how to feel about this, but she happily followed Herrmann's massive form back into the barracks all the same. "Thanks."

"It's nothing."

Herrmann continued through the halls in silence, Flum following behind him. They walked for a few minutes before he stopped suddenly.

"Waugh!" Flum only barely managed to stop herself before crashing into his back.

"Who are you here for?"

"Oh? Um, I wanted to see Ottilie..."

"Ottilie, hm." A deep crease formed in Herrmann's brow, causing Flum's face to cloud over in uncertainty. Everything about Herrmann, from his voice to his face, seemed designed to inspire nightmares in children. She knew he couldn't be all bad, based on their earlier situation with the guards, but still... "That's a problem."

It seemed no matter what he was talking about, he always spoke in a monotone. Though that was probably fine—suitable even—for a lieutenant general.

Herrmann put his hand to his chin and thought for a moment before he began walking again. Flum hurried after him without saying another word. The two eventually found themselves in front of an ornately decorated door on the third floor of the barracks.

Herrmann raised a massive fist and rapped on the door. "I have a guest."

He didn't bother to introduce himself, though the person on the other side of the door didn't seem to take notice.

"Aah, Herrmann. Come in, come in."

The door opened, revealing not Ottilie, but the head of the entire royal army, General Henriette Bachsenheim.

"H-Henriette??!"

Flum couldn't contain her surprise.

"Well, if it isn't Flum Apricot, in the flesh. Judging by the look on your face, I'd venture a guess that you're not here to see me. Why did you bring her here, Herrmann?"

"She came for Ottilie."

"Ottilie? Ahh, I suppose that makes sense. Thank you, Lieutenant General Herrmann. Now, why don't you have a seat, Flum Apricot?" Henriette stood from her exquisite chair and motioned Flum toward a sofa. Flum hesitated for a moment before she sat down where indicated.

Herrmann bowed his head and left the room, leaving Flum alone with the General—a woman she'd never even met before. She was a bundle of nerves at this point.

"Thank you for having me, General Henriette!"

"No need to be so polite. You can call me by my first name, as you do with my sister. Besides, I, too, am in the presence of a hero."

Henriette's frankness helped smooth over at least some of Flum's nervousness. "I'm just a normal person."

"And I'm the head of a fallen military. They may call me General, but I have no real power." A tinge of sadness entered Henriette's voice. Her face softened as she changed the subject. "So what brings you here to see Ottilie?"

"Right. I was hoping to talk to her about an incident in the West District I was involved in a few days ago. Perhaps you'd be willing to listen?"

"Of course. The incident in question was quite a black mark against us. The royal family and the cardinals gave us a piece of their mind; it hasn't done much to improve our status. I suppose we brought it upon ourselves."

"That sounds pretty tough."

"I'm sure things were far more difficult for you. On that note, I must thank you for exposing the corruption in the West District. Is that when you met Ottilie?"

"That's correct. If it weren't for her, I wouldn't be standing before you right now."

"I'd love to be proud of that, but considering that my forces were the cause of the problem to begin with, that's not exactly appropriate. Anyway, I've already heard from Ottilie about how you were dismissed from the party and became a slave." Come to think of it, neither Henriette nor Herrmann seemed surprised by the mark on her face. "I see Jean hasn't changed at all."

Flum laughed darkly. "I guess you could say that."

"If you run into any difficulties at all here in the capital, please don't hesitate to reach out to the military. I know Ottilie has offered her help, but Herrmann and I will also do whatever we can to support you."

"That's not actually why I'm here today."

"Oh? Then what brings you here?"

"The last time I met with Ottilie, she mentioned she was investigating the church."

"Ottilie? Now why would she go and do something like that..."

"She said it was for her sister. Are you two not in agreement on this?"

"Ah, yes. Ottilie and I have been close all our lives. She's also quite stubborn." An understatement as far as Flum was concerned. "She was never a gifted fencer, but she worked herself to the bone to follow my example. She certainly serves under me in the chain of command, but she also works for me on a personal level. So you came to speak with her about the church?"

"That's correct. One of my friends, Sara Anvilen, was recently excommunicated."

"Ah, yes, her. I recall hearing that she was following in the footsteps of Maria Affenjenz herself. I also hear that two church knights were reassigned at the same time."

"Then you must know about what happened in the slums?"

"Of course. I suspected the church might be involved, so I had the corpses collected."

Huh. Henriette was on the ball. Flum was impressed, though she was speaking to a general, after all. Maybe this was par for the course.

"I think my friend is wrapped up in all of this," she said. "so now I'm looking for her. I was hoping to see if Ottilie knew anything about it."

"I'm sure you've already guessed this by now, but Ottilie isn't here."

"She's missing?"

Henriette nodded gravely.

Ottilie and Sara had been chasing the same prey. Flum

took a deep breath and brought her hands to her face. She felt light-headed.

Why would the church go this far? Doing away with one of your own was one thing, but a powerful member of the royal military—a lieutenant general, even? She felt like she was up against a wall so high that she could no longer see the top. Her opponent was just too powerful for her to face alone like this.

"But why isn't there more commotion over the disappearance of a lieutenant general?" Flum barely managed to force the words out.

Henriette bit her lip momentarily before she let her annoyance show on her face. "Because some idiot told me to keep it under wraps."

"Who is this idiot?"

"Why, King Dian Carole, of course."

Flum swallowed hard, left at a complete loss for words by the fact that a member of the royal army—the kingdom's shield—would call her liege an "idiot."

"The army lost the King's trust ages ago," Henriette said. "The church has its hooks in him, and he affords them every convenience. Apparently, that includes disappearing a lieutenant general!"

"I can't believe this..."

"Ottilie is honorable. Always has been. I imagine she went off on her own to do what she thought was in my best interest. Had I known, I would have put a stop to her activities—and she must have known that I would have stopped her. It's really quite frustrating. I suspect she felt compelled to do everything she could to help me."

A slight smile graced Henriette's face. Though they spoke of their relationship in a different manner, it was clear the bond between the sisters was mutual.

"Forgive my sentimentality. As I'm sure you've guessed by now, we don't have the information you seek. In fact, I, too would like to know where Ottilie is."

"I understand."

She was at a dead end. Her investigation proving fruitless, Flum decided to leave the barracks and continue on.

More

010

THE SUN WAS JUST STARTING to set by the time Flum made it home for the day. She could barely muster a greeting as she stumbled in through the door.

Milkit jogged over to greet her master with a cheerful smile. "Welcome back, Master."

This raised Flum's spirits. A grin came to her face.

"I was just about to go out shopping for tonight's dinner. Would you like to come along?" Milkit, who was holding a shopping bag, must've been waiting for Flum to get home. She peered closer into Flum's face, seeing her exhaustion. "Or would you rather stay here and rest?"

Today, Milkit wore a mostly white maid uniform with a bright red ribbon tied at her chest. It was different from her usual style, lending an adorable air to her serious demeanor. She looked more like a waitress than the maid to some rich noble.

Milkit tended to rotate through her collection of uniforms, making each day unique. Flum loved seeing the variations. More than anything, though, it helped alleviate the heavy emotional blows she'd been dealt throughout the day.

"I think I'll stay and rest up. Sorry, Milkit." She suspected Milkit had been looking forward to going out shopping together, and a part of Flum wanted to as well, but she just couldn't work up the energy to go.

"Of course, Master. Please get some rest. Eterna and I will go out."

Eterna popped her head out of the living room. "See ya!"

After seeing them off, Flum made her way to the dining table and dropped heavily into one of the chairs before resting her head on the tabletop.

"Hiya, Flum!" Ink was busily working her way through a puzzle across from Flum.

"Hey, Ink."

"How did it go? Find out anything about Sara?"

"Nada. Zilch. Worse yet, apparently Ottilie is missing, too. It's all just...a lot to take in."

"Oh, that's too bad. But I'm sure you'll find them. Both of 'em."

"Me too, kid." If she didn't believe that, then she wouldn't be able to continue looking.

Flum finally gave in to her exhaustion and closed her eyes. Ink paused for a moment out of concern for her weary friend and decided to let her relax. It was the least she could do. She rolled up her sleeves and continued playing with the puzzle, this time slower and more methodically, to avoid making any sound.

◇ ◇ ◇

"You're done already?" Eterna was surprised at just how quickly Milkit finished up the night's shopping.

"Yes, I'd like to get back to Master's side as soon as I can."

"She did look pretty down and out." Whatever it was, she figured Flum's news was going to be bad.

"Umm, Eterna...?"

"Yeah?"

"Are you sure I can't carry that?" Milkit seemed to be feeling guilty about Eterna carrying the food-laden shopping bag.

"It's no big deal." Milkit had a Strength of 11. Eterna's was an impressive 668. Her arms may have looked thin, but she was a great deal stronger than your average passerby. "I'm stronger than you, Milkit."

Eterna flexed her left bicep to punctuate her point, though there wasn't actually much to show. This only made Milkit look even more worried.

"It looks like you grabbed all of Flum's favorite foods," Eterna said.

"I was thinking it would lift Master's spirits to have these tonight."

"Like two little lovebirds, I'm telling you…"

"It's not like that at all, Miss Eterna. It's just… It's just that I want to give back to Master at least some of the happiness she's given to me. That's it."

"Well, isn't that sweet."

"I am Master's slave, after all." Milkit brought her hand to her chest, a smile gracing her lips.

"Sounds like a really fortunate meeting for the both of you, then."

"Absolutely."

They'd met in a place that could charitably be described as hell on earth. It was only by pure happenstance that she'd happened to survive and that Flum had chosen to take her along. Milkit had just gone with the flow, as she always did, never knowing when or how her life would change. It had never occurred to her to try otherwise. Looking back on her time with Flum, now it all seemed like a miracle.

Before she could dwell on this much further, however, she noticed a man standing right in front of them.

The man was tall and slender, with a crop of light brown hair atop his head. He threw out his arms in a dramatic fashion, like an actor in a stage play. "Well, I'll be. What an unexpected sight to behold. I figured she'd be easy pickings if she were alone, but this really messes things up. Is that really the legendary hero, Eterna Rinebow, accompanying the brat?"

Dressed in leather armor with a buckler fastened tightly to his arm, the man was armed with a twenty-centimeter dagger and a heavy crossbow strapped to his back. This was no casual encounter. He was here to carry out a job assigned to him as an adventurer.

Milkit recognized him immediately. "Dein Phineas!" She glared at him, a rare look of angry defiance plastered across her face.

"Bring it on." Eterna's voice was cold and even. She started to gather magic energy in the palm of her hand.

"Whoa, whoa, hold up there for a second. I'm not here to fight. I'm at least smart enough to know when I'm completely outclassed."

"Then what are you doing here?"

"I just want to talk. I have some information that could prove useful...to both of us."

"No, thank you. Let's go, Eterna."

Eterna readily agreed. The two didn't even give him a second glance as they began to walk past.

Dein's lips curled up into his signature grin. He leapt back into his monologue. "Well, that's really a shame. And here I had all this information about our dear Sara Anvilen. Flum spent all day running around the West District looking for her, didn't she? I'm sure your Master would be overjoyed to learn whatever became of that brat, why she disappeared, and where she is now..."

"Sara?" Milkit stopped dead in her tracks.

"Milkit, just keep going."

"But...!"

Milkit loved Sara. She longed for the day when they could chat, play, and eat together again. What's more, the image of Flum's exhausted face came to mind. Her master had put so much into finding her. If she could just be useful to Flum...

"Gotta say, I love a slave with a good head on her shoulders. She's plumped up a bit, too. Did her face get better? Sure looks that way. Y'know, you could sell her for quite a bit now, I'm sure."

"Shut up, you pathetic lowlife." Eterna glared daggers at Dein.

Where was he getting his information on Milkit and Sara? Even if his network of contacts had taken a hit, it seemed to be working well enough.

"Wow, real scary. Gotta say, it'd be nice to just live the life of luxury, always under someone's watchful gaze, and not need to worry about anything. Alas, I'm more the type to want to protect others, myself."

"Cut the crap and get to the point. What do you know about Sara?"

Dein chuckled.

"Testy, testy. I'm going to tell you, all in due time." The sly grin never left his face, though something about his expression changed.

Milkit narrowed her eyes, face scrunching in displeasure.

"She stopped by the West District church to dig up information on some Ink kid the day she went missing. Some of the knights told her these rumors they'd heard about secret church research."

Dein paused to take in their expressions, almost like he was trying to gauge their reactions at dropping Ink's name. Eterna and Milkit stayed stone-faced. No matter what happened, they weren't going to let on that Ink was living with them. Eterna knew this on a logical level, while it was a more intuitive, emotional response from

Milkit. He and his goons may well have been looking for Ink, which was all the more reason for them to play it cool.

Dein clicked his tongue in annoyance before continuing with his story.

"Alas, this story was more than a mere rumor. It actually happened to be way closer to the truth than anyone figured, which triggered what happened next."

"Triggered? What do you mean?"

"You might call it an overreaction, I guess. A knee-jerk attempt to protect their allies. I guess it depends on which side of the line you stand on, huh?"

Neither Eterna nor Milkit could follow what Dein was talking about anymore. He shot them another one of his charming smiles and opened his mouth to explain.

Before he could start, Eterna's finger twitched. Milkit cocked her head quizzically to the side as she heard an unfamiliar sound.

Dein continued. "It's not the church or someone related to them, no. It's the children. If anyone learns they exist, they chase them down, multiply, and kill them. That's why I've decided to ally myself with them. It was really my only choice if I wanted their protection."

"Children? Are you talking about the place that's experimenting on people?"

"Right, exactly! But wait, you knew about it, too? Hmm, that means you meet all the criteria as well. In that case, maybe it's not the children... Maybe it's another team."

"Another research team?"

"Bingo. You see, the Spiral Children are given cores instead of hearts at birth, turning them into heartless creatures with a black crystal buried deep within their bodies. There's a lab right beneath this very city where the church creates them in droves."

It was unclear to Eterna why Dein was sharing this clearly vital information with them so freely, but she was convinced now that she knew what the bizarre presence she sensed earlier was.

"Hm?" Milkit looked around quizzically. She hadn't heard a word Dein said. After all, Eterna had used her water magic to block off the younger girl's ears and shut out all noise.

It didn't take long for Dein to reveal his true intentions. "I bet you're wondering why I'd be telling you all this, aren't you? Well, I'm actually quite smart, if I say so myself. Even if you don't stumble on rumors like that little nun girl, or start sticking your nose where it doesn't belong like those other guys, all I had to do was tell you. And then you'd meet all the criteria."

He tapped his finger against his forehead several times before, a moment later, something began to pour off the side of a nearby roof. They slapped to the ground with a sickening *fwump*.

Eterna's cheek twitched when she caught sight of the eyeballs. They seemed to come out of nowhere, rolling along the ground toward Eterna. Making matters even worse, they started to pour out of windows and spring out of holes in the ground, further closing the distance.

Dein began to cackle in delight. "Looks like they're already here! Guess you better start running before you become one of those stinkin' corpses, huh?"

Eterna already heard of the dead mounds of flesh that Flum encountered in the West District slums. Assuming Dein was speaking the truth, that meant the same awful fate awaited them if they let the eyes touch them.

"E-E-E-Eteeeeerna!! Look!!"

"Milkit, get back! Aqua Garum!" A sphere of water manifested in front of Eterna. It twisted and contorted in the air until, a moment later, it took the form of a dog that towered over its conjurer.

"Wh-wha?! Eeeeeek!!"

The giant dog ducked its head down, clamping its

jaws lightly around Milkit's frame before throwing her up onto its back.

"Go!!!" Eterna waved her hand in the direction of Flum's house, and the dog took off in a straight line, leaping over and onto any building in its way.

Dein continued to laugh hysterically at this turn of events. "That's a complete waste, ya know!"

Eterna looked back at him coolly. "Hardly."

"And what makes you say that?"

"Milkit didn't hear a thing. I used my magic to block her ears."

"Why you...! So you noticed what I was doing?!"

"Looks like I'm even smarter than you, huh?"

"Shut it, you old hag!" Dein whipped out his crossbow and leveled it toward Eterna.

"Looks like someone's got a pretty low boiling point."

"Well, look who's in hot water now, Eterna Rinebow!"

Eterna was now fully surrounded by the eyeballs. Now that she had nowhere left to run to, Dein pulled the trigger on his crossbow.

In the exact same moment, Eterna cast a spell of her own. "Aqua Spear!"

Spears of water lanced out of the ground, piercing through the incoming eyeballs and spearing the crossbow bolt midair.

"Aqua Tentacles!" Wasting no time, Eterna called up tendrils of water near her feet. A moment later, they shot straight toward Dein.

"Hnng!!" Dein dove backward and shot a wire from his buckler toward a nearby building. Once the grappling hook found purchase, he yanked another wire to start it reeling in. "It's a shame I missed out on the little slave girl, but at least you're done for! At least give us all a good show before you kick it, eh hero? Gyahahaha!"

His voice echoed through the streets as the wire grew taut and he flew through the air toward the rooftop. Before Eterna had a chance to shoot off an attack after him, she noticed the eyes regathering, rapidly increasing in number.

"Hmph. I don't have the time to fight on two fronts right now."

Though the eyes were slow, their sheer numbers made them formidable opponents. Focusing all of her energy in her feet, Eterna stomped several times as she cast her next spell. "Aqua Shelter!"

Water began to bubble up out of the ground before forming a liquid barrier around her. In an instant, it turned hard as ice, though still flexible enough to rebound with each incoming attack.

Eterna was renowned for her magical abilities. But the eyes continued to multiply, and her energy wasn't infinite. Turning Aqua Shelter back on her enemy and doing enough damage to wipe them all out was beyond her means, if not her skill.

The eyeballs slammed again and again into the wall of water, trying to climb it as they did with human bodies.

"It doesn't look like they're going to give up any time soon. Guess running's my only option." Eterna once again focused magic in her feet and tapped the ground.

"Splash!" A fountain of water shot out of the ground, rocketing her through the hole in the ceiling of her Aqua Shelter.

"Aqua Tentacles!" Tentacles of water wrapped around her, pulling her to a nearby roof.

As soon as she landed, she cast Aqua Tentacles again and again, carrying her from rooftop to rooftop.

The eyes continued to chase after her. Every time she thought she'd shaken them, even more came flooding in from some new angle, and Eterna would once again find herself nearly surrounded. As she pressed on through the darkening streets, her thoughts went out to Flum, Milkit, and Ink. She knew Dein wouldn't give up so easily. Worse still, she knew that he wasn't the one behind the eyes, which meant they had yet another enemy to contend with.

All she could do was hope and pray for her friends as she ran for her life.

◇ ◇ ◇

"Master!!!"

Flum's heart skipped a beat as soon as she saw Milkit come running through the door. She was completely soaked from head to toe and didn't have her shopping bag with her.

"What happened?! And where's Eterna??"

"Eterna...she's...she's being chased by those same eye-ball things...that got Sara!"

"Eterna, too?? But why?!" Ink seemed to take this news especially badly.

"Why'd they let you get away, Milkit? And what even caused all this? You guys were just out shopping...!"

"Dein showed up out of nowhere and rambled at us for a while. The next thing I knew, eyeballs started to show up everywhere."

"That son of a...! Do you remember what he said?"

"No, I don't. Halfway through the conversation, I think Eterna used her magic to plug my ears. I couldn't hear anything at all for a bit, and then she made me ride a magic dog, and now I'm here."

"Plugged your ears... So just hearing what he said was enough to make Eterna a target?" If that was true, simply looking into the church's dealings wasn't enough to set them off. You drew the eyes' ire only after learning something specific.

And yet Dein knew about it but wasn't a victim himself.

"Maybe it's because Dein is a member of the church?" Flum fretted. "But no, that doesn't make sense. Sara was, too."

The other day, Dein had mentioned that his "boss" told him to keep his hands off Flum. Was this boss a member of the team experimenting on humans? If so, it could only mean that their reason for keeping their hands off Flum was not just to keep her alive but because they wanted to capture her.

"So it's all my fault..."

"Master, don't talk like that!"

"Milkit..." While Flum appreciated the sentiment, she couldn't overlook her own involvement so easily. "Listen, you should get yourself out of those clothes before you catch a cold. We'll figure out the rest later."

If even a powerful mage like Eterna was on the run from these enemies, Flum didn't think she'd stand much of a chance on her own either. She felt absolutely crushed. Looking over, she saw Ink curled up, her face buried in her hands. The air in the entire house had grown dark and foreboding in a matter of seconds.

But no matter what, she still had Milkit. That was enough to keep Flum pushing forward.

◇◇◇

Flum grabbed a fresh set of clothes from their shared bedroom and passed them to Milkit in the changing room. She originally planned to wait outside while Milkit changed, but they were both insecure about being alone, so Flum decided to wait in there with her. She felt awkward gawking at the other woman as she changed, so she turned her back to give her some privacy.

"It's not your fault, Master. They're the ones who are wrong here."

She heard the sounds of Milkit undressing and drying off with a towel.

"I think those bastards are in the wrong, too, but I'm the one who's at the center of it all," Flum said.

"You shouldn't feel bad just because they decided to make your life so hard, Master."

"Yeah, but...well...I guess."

The church was after her, after all. And now Sara, Ottilie, and even Eterna had been dragged into it. The logical conclusion was to offer herself up to the church...

The room was silent except for the sounds of Milkit finishing with the towel and the rustle of fabric as she pulled her underwear on.

"At the very least, I should take care of this Dein issue once and for all," Flum said.

"He seems different now."

"I thought so, too. I guess that's what happens when you lose everything. That's what makes him all the scarier."

Milkit grabbed her maid outfit and slowly began to dress herself with well-practiced motions. The elaborate clothing, with its multiple layers, took time to get in place, but she'd become used to it by now. What's more, these were clothes that Flum gifted to her, so Milkit was more than happy to spend every second in them that she could.

"Finished."

Flum turned around, but Milkit was nowhere to be seen.

"Huh?"

There was just...nothing. A blank space where she should have been. Milkit's wet clothes sat in the hamper ready for the wash. They were still slightly warm to the touch. That proved Milkit was there at least a few moments prior.

"Um...hello?"

No one was there.

"M-Milkit? Hey, Milkit! Where are you?? Are you hiding? You're just hiding...right??"

Flum could feel goosebumps prickling across her skin as a cold sweat beaded at the back of her neck. Her breathing grew ragged, and she felt lightheaded. "Say something! Milkit!!"

No response. Flum searched the bath before tearing off to check the hall, kitchen, and even second floor. She found nothing, no matter where she looked.

"What's wrong, Flum?" Ink, looking concerned, had to tug at her sleeve just to get her attention.

"Milkit... I can't find her anywhere! She was just changing right behind me a second ago, and now she's gone!!"

"Calm down, Flum. What are you talking about? Why would she just disappear?"

"If I knew that, I wouldn't be looking!!" Flum was half-crazed with worry at this point. Everyone she knew was going missing, one after another. Without Milkit, she was a building without its support pillars. She felt like she could crumble at any moment.

Without Milkit, she was little more than an average sixteen-year-old girl.

She could hang on a little longer. Her heart might be breaking, but she hadn't completely lost control yet.

That was why she needed to find Milkit before the last of her companion's emotional support wore off.

"Milkit!! Milkit!! Milkiiiiiiiiiit!! Milkit!! Miiiiiiiiiil-kit!! Milkit!! Milkit!!!!!!" Flum screamed her name over and over, even going so far as to crawl under the house in her maddening search. But she wasn't there. She wasn't anywhere.

How was it that someone who was there just moments ago could disappear without a trace?

One hour stretched into two, and then three. No matter where she looked, she couldn't find a shred of evidence of Milkit's whereabouts. Cold and forlorn, Flum made her way back home on uneasy legs, buffeted by the chilly night wind.

"Are...are you okay?" Ink fumbled for a moment before finally taking Flum's hand into her own and giving it a reassuring squeeze.

The young girl's warmth managed to reach Flum's slowly chilling heart. She heard the sound of Ink's stomach growling. That was right. Dinnertime had passed a long time ago...

On any normal night, they would be sitting around the dinner table, enjoying a delicious meal Milkit prepared.

But not tonight. Milkit, Eterna, even Sara...none of them were here tonight.

Flum dropped to her knees and broke down. She began to bawl uncontrollably.

What did she do to deserve all this? All she did was brush away the embers of the world as it burnt around her. Was she supposed to take the abuse in silence? If this was God's way of getting revenge, it was beyond unfair. Flum had no idea where she went wrong, what she could have done differently. What could have justified robbing her of everything she held dear?

All she and Milkit did was support each other. Thrown into the depths of hell, she'd tried to crawl out to the only light she could see. Was that so wrong? Was it worthy of punishment?

"Waaaaah! Milkit...I shouldn't have taken my eyes off of you. But...but...why?!"

They'd been so close that she could still feel the warmth radiating from Milkit's body. It seemed impossible that Milkit could disappear when she'd been right there. How could Flum stand a chance against someone who was capable of this?

She felt completely and utterly powerless. No matter how far she'd come, she was still a good-for-nothing, useless piece of garbage. Just like she'd been on the journey.

"And here I am, back in hell..." She scratched at the slave mark burnt into her cheek, driving her nails into it until she drew blood. This was all the proof that she needed that nothing had changed. The shallow cuts healed nearly as soon as she'd inflicted them. "Even with all these powers, I still couldn't protect her...!"

"Flum..." Flum seemed so far gone that Ink didn't know what to say. She wanted to comfort her, but no words came to mind. All she could do was clench her fists in frustration.

Flum abruptly stopped her crying and looked straight ahead at nothing. "I'm going out to look for her again."

"It's already night, Flum. It's too dangerous."

"I'm going out. Stay indoors, Ink, and don't leave for anything."

"...Okay. I'll wait here."

It was already dark out, and it seemed unlikely to Flum that she would find anything running around alone through the empty city, but she couldn't sit still knowing that she hadn't done everything in her power for Milkit. She'd go insane if she didn't.

◇◇◇

It was past midnight when Flum finally returned home empty-handed.

"...I'm back." Her voice was barely a hollow whisper.

There was no reply from Ink, so she figured the girl must already be asleep. She must've left the light on downstairs for Flum's benefit.

Her body was well past the point of exhaustion. All she wanted to do was stumble to bed and fall into fitful sleep. Flum's legs felt leaden as she thumped her way up the stairs, one step at a time. If she was lucky, maybe she'd never wake up.

The second floor was pitch-black. On closer inspection, she noticed the door to Ink's room was only half-closed. She figured Ink had hoped to hear Flum's return so she could greet her when she came home.

Just as she walked past Ink's room, she heard a thumping from inside.

"Ah, so you're awake?"

The thumping sounded like the window was being shaken, though that was entirely unnecessary; Flum was already inside.

"Hey, Ink, I'm home." Flum gave a light knock on the door before peering into the room.

No response. The incessant rattling continued.

"Hey, Ink, can I come in?"

Once again, there was no reply.

"All right then, I'm coming in." After a moment's hesitation, Flum stepped through.

The first thing she noticed in the darkness was that Ink had climbed up onto the windowsill and was staring out at the backyard down below.

"What're you doing, Ink? Are you...are you looking for Milkit?"

She took a few steps closer before stopping short.

Baloosh. Sploosh.

There was something about the noise that sounded very familiar.

She froze. All the muscles in her face tensed up. Flum felt instantly cold, like all the blood drained from her body.

"...Ink?"

It couldn't be. It had to be her imagination.

After building up the courage to move, Flum forced herself to take a step forward.

The sound only grew louder. It sounded like the slapping of wet meat combined with some sort of liquid spewing out.

Spwoosh... Jabloosh... Drip... Drip...

What was happening? Just what was Ink doing?

She didn't want to know, didn't even want to look. But she couldn't turn away, either.

She took another step forward, and the noise grew louder still. Flum heard the floorboards creak. The motion resonated through her feet and up her legs. She swallowed hard. The saliva that built up in her mouth traveled down her throat in rhythm with her own pounding heartbeat. Sweat beaded and poured down the sides of her forehead, down her cheeks, accumulating at her jaw before dropping to the floor. Her lungs felt nearly paralyzed, leaving her only able to breathe in ragged gasps.

All of her senses were on high alert, giving the world around her an uncomfortable novelty. Her heart was pounding so hard in her chest that she began to feel lightheaded. Finally, she reached out toward Ink, gingerly resting a finger on the pajama top she lent her.

The fabric collapsed around her finger, and she could feel Ink's skin through the thin cloth. Ink seemed to take notice of her presence and slowly turned around to look at Flum.

Ploosh... Ploosh... Bwoosh...

Looking back at her was a spiral of flesh—the same disgusting sight she'd seen back during her encounter with the ogre. It spat blood indiscriminately as it pulsated.

The seams between each whorl of corded muscle wept eyeballs.

"Aaa...aaaaaah..."

Where did she go wrong? Had she taken a wrong turn somewhere? Flum knew the answer to these questions

before even asking. The old shirt she'd lent Ink was drenched with blood. Eyes tumbled down its front and onto the floor.

The sight in front of her overrode every memory, every thought that Flum had ever had of Ink up until now.

"Uwaaaugh...aaaaah...aaaaah!" A choked scream fought its way from her throat, joining the slow fountain of eyes and gore. Sweat and tears flowed freely down Flum's cheeks. And yet, despite her terror, she still knew the figure sitting in front of her was Ink.

They stared at each other for some time before the figure lost interest in Flum and turned back toward the window.

"Aaaaugh... Ha... Hiiihaa... Aaaaauuuuuaaaaaaaaaaagh!" Flum screamed in frustration, unable to stand it any longer. She dashed out of the room and slammed the door behind her in the hope of forgetting the scene she just witnessed. The sound of the slamming door echoed through the narrow hallway.

She sat in the hall with her back pressed firmly against the door as she struggled to catch her breath. Holding her head firmly in her hands and staring down at the ground, she focused in on the sounds of her own shallow breathing.

However, that did little to change the reality of the situation. She could still hear the sloshing, dripping, slapping sounds from the other side of the door. Flum clamped her slick hands tightly against her ears, though the wet, sticky feeling fixed her mind on the image she was avoiding. It was still an improvement over having to hear the noises.

"Why, why, whyyyyyy?!"

She didn't even care who answered the question at this point. She just wanted an answer. Even a bad answer was better than nothing at all.

She was all alone now. No Sara, Ottilie, Milkit, and now even Ink. Her home was completely empty except for herself and that...creature she was certain had been Ink, once.

"Uuaaagh...aaaaah...haaaauuugh...gwaaaaup...pluuup... haaaaaah..."

Even her hands were no longer enough to drown out the moans now. Curled up in the hallway, the volcanic churn of her pulse filling her ears, she let it all spill from her: sweat, tears, spittle, vomit.

**ROLL
OVER
AND
DIE**

011

Breaking Through the Darkness

FLUM LOST TRACK of the passage of time as she sat there, cradling her head and staring at the floor. She could have sworn it was an eternity, though a few hours seemed more likely. The sun still hadn't risen and the hallway was dark, which told her something.

Her throat was bone dry. She stopped sweating a long time ago. Though her body fiercely demanded water, she couldn't work up the will to stand and go to the kitchen.

Clack.

Flum felt the door shake behind her. The doorknob rattled, and the door smacked against her back several times.

"Huh? That's strange, the door won't open. I know I didn't lock it..."

Flum's whole body tensed up immediately. That was Ink's voice echoing out from the room.

Should she move? Should she step back and face the girl?

She had to. It wasn't even a question. Ink was one and the same as the creature she encountered back at the research lab.

Which could only mean...

"Hey, it's open. Uh, hey, is someone there?"

Flum took to a knee off to the side of the door, her Souleater ready at hand. She heard a faint, steely ringing as she tightened her grip. The black blade glowed with captured moonlight.

Her breath came out in ragged gasps as the door opened and Ink stepped out.

"I hear breathing. Is that you, Flum? Hey, don't be so quiet. Are you there?"

Her face...was back to normal. She looked just like the Ink she'd seen so many times before. Was there some sort of condition that had to be met for her to transform? Or did she do it at will? Flum had no way of knowing, nor did she know what to believe anymore. She knew Ink's transformation was no dream. Of that much she could be certain.

Sara was gone. Ed and Jonny were dead. Ottilie was

missing. Eterna still wasn't home. Milkit disappeared. There were countless other victims, too.

If Ink was somehow at the center of this…

Flum stood up, clasped the hilt with both hands, and raised her sword high into the air.

All it would take was one swing. But would it kill her? It seemed doubtful. These things didn't die until their core was destroyed. Was it in her heart or somewhere else?

Cut her in two and find out…

Flum's arms shook. Logic obliged her to attack; compassion implored her to stop.

"You're out there, aren't you, Flum? Anyway, welcome home. I'm sorry I didn't stay up for you. It looks like I fell asleep and just suddenly woke up here on the second floor. I must've been really tired. Y'know, that used to happen to me a lot. They always yelled at me for sleepwalking like that."

"Hn…"

"C'mon Flum, stop playing around. I have sharp ears, y'know. It's so quiet that I can hear your heart beating."

Should she kill her? *Could* she kill her? Maybe, just maybe, that thing she saw earlier wasn't even Ink. Maybe the creature just waited until Ink was asleep and then traded places with her in order to scare Flum.

It made sense, in a way. That didn't mean that it was true.

"Ink..." Flum called out to her. A look of relief spread across Ink's face before her cheeks puffed out an instant later in annoyance.

"Took you long enough! I was starting to wonder what I'd do if it wasn't actually you here!" She sounded just like a normal, ten-year-old human girl.

A human...

If she wasn't a human, then what was she?

What was the point of looking human again after revealing that *thing*? Was it to keep pushing Flum's buttons? Or perhaps to make her let down her guard? If that was the case, then why didn't it kill her earlier? They were living together, after all. There must've been a reason. Why, why, why?

She just didn't understand any of what was going on, and no matter how hard she thought about it, no answers were forthcoming. It didn't make sense.

"It seems like you didn't find Milkit, I guess. I'm really sorry 'bout that, but who knows, maybe she'll come back in the morning..."

"You don't remember anything?" Flum figured she may as well open Pandora's Box herself.

Ink cocked her head to the side. "Remember what?"

Flum swallowed. Her throat was dry, and her voice raspy. "There were... You turned into a creature, and eyeballs were coming out of your face."

"What?! What're you talking about, Flum?! That's a really mean joke to try and play on someone!"

"No, I'm not joking at all! And I know what I saw. Just a little while ago, I saw you with my own two eyes, and you were some sort of bizarre creature! I saw it, I know!" Flum's cries reverberated through the empty house and escaped out to the streets.

"There's just no way, Flum..."

"You were, I'm not mistaken. I heard it; I could *smell* it. I can even remember the warmth coming off of you! Ink, you definitely weren't human! You were some kind of creature that was spitting out eyeballs!!"

Ink could tell by Flum's tone that she was serious. She began to shake her head aggressively, murmuring to herself. "No...no no no... I'm a human."

"No, you're not."

They were at an impasse.

"I am, I really am a human..."

"You stopped being a human when they experimented on you like they did with the second-generation children."

"They didn't do anything to me. I would've remembered that!"

"I've finally figured out what that medicine was. It was to suppress your powers."

"You've got it all wrong!"

"Now that your powers aren't suppressed anymore, you chased Sara down with those eyeball things."

"No! I'd never do anything to hurt Sara. You, Sara... you're all very important to me!"

Flum's anger got the best of her. "How many people died at your hands?!"

Ink could only stand there dumbfounded in the face of her sudden outburst. Perhaps deep down, she knew that Flum wasn't wrong.

"Maybe you're right."

That feeling quickly turned to self-doubt. Her eyes were sewn shut. There was nothing normal about her body. The eyes chasing everyone had to come from *someone*.

The evidence, though circumstantial, pointed to Ink.

"I don't know... I really don't know!!" Ink wailed.

"Milkit disappeared, Eterna's still not home! And Sara, Ed, Jonny, Ottilie... They're all gone!!"

"No, no, no! Why won't you believe me?!"

"Just look at yourself! How could I possibly believe you after I saw you as that...that creature?!"

Flum had never wanted to say these things to her. She always figured that, if it was what Ink wanted, she could live with them just like how she and Milkit made their home together. But now that future was crumbling around her.

"I'm not... I'm not a monster!"

With that, Ink took off toward the stairs. However, she missed a step on the way down and tumbled all the way to the first floor.

She hurt all over. Ink began to sob bitterly, grabbing the edge of the shirt Flum lent her to dry her eyes. She caught a whiff of Flum's scent in the process. This brought back another wave of sadness as the memories of the time they spent together flooded her mind.

The force of that sadness somehow pushed her back up to her feet and sent her running down the hallway, slamming into the walls as she went, before she finally found the entrance to the house and stepped out into the street, not even bothering with her shoes. The cool night air was a bitter reminder that she was all alone.

Flum made no attempt to stop her. The Souleater dropped from her hand with a dull thud, and Flum collapsed next to it. She closed her eyes and angled her face toward the ceiling.

She was crying, too, though she couldn't say for sure why. Her cries, screams, and sobs came together into a cacophony of her pain, fighting for some way out into the

world. Flum buried her head in her hands and bent over until her forehead hit the floor. Then again, but harder. Again, again, and over again until she could feel blood staining the floor with each blow. The pain was its own punishment.

Through it all, she screamed herself hoarse.

Outside, Ink stopped running as Flum's screams caught up with her.

She wasn't the only one crying. She wasn't the only one in pain right now. This wasn't some attempt to play on Ink's emotions. Flum was crying with her whole heart and soul, which could only mean one thing: she was telling the truth. Ink knew then that Flum really had seen her as a monster.

Ink bit down hard on her lip. Her whole body shook, wracked by sobs. She didn't want to believe it, but she knew the place she was raised was anything but normal. She had no idea what they did to her while she was there or why she was raised like that.

This was all her fault. It was all because she'd been useless, not allowed to be like the rest. If she'd known it would come to this, she would never have run away. She could've lived the rest of her life in her walled garden, like a domesticated animal. She probably would've never found happiness, but she would've been spared this misery.

Ink turned around to make her way back to the house. "Flu...*nng*?!"

A figure came up behind her, pulled her arms tight behind her back, and placed a hand over her mouth. She tried to resist, but there was little she could do.

For the split second that she managed to get her mouth free, she screamed with all her might.

◇ ◇ ◇

"Noooooooooooo!!"

Ink's cry for help found its way to Flum's ears from her place on the floor, her head still pressed against the floorboards. The cry stopped nearly as quickly as it started, but Flum knew what she heard. She reflexively leapt to her feet to help the young girl but didn't move any further.

She'd already called Ink a monster, kicked her out of the house. It seemed pointless to chase after her now. And yet...

With Milkit gone, what reason did she have to play hero? Flum Apricot was just like any other girl her age. There was no need for her to put herself on the line.

And yet, she couldn't suppress the feeling welling up within her.

"If I don't help her, I know I'll regret it!"

Maybe it didn't make sense. She knew that already. Flum resolved not to try make sense of it for now. She would save Ink. Whether it was to let her live or kill her herself...was yet to be seen.

She dashed into Ink's room and dove out the open window. Her Epic-class leather boots began to glow as she leapt through the air. She skidded along the ground, braking with her free hand. Now it was time to look for Ink.

"Over there!" She instantly recognized the man pinning Ink's arms back. "Ink!"

"Mmmph! Mmpphh!!"

"Hey, you did show up."

"What the hell are you doing here, Dein?!"

"What am I doing here? Why, looking for our escaped guinea pig, of course. I thought she might be here and, wouldn't ya know it, I was right. I've got a pretty keen eye for these things." Dein put further pressure on Ink's body, pressing her arms even further back. Her face contorted in pain.

"Let Ink go!!"

"Not gonna happen. Besides, didn't you two get in a fight or something? I'm pretty sure I heard you calling her a *creature*. The sad thing is that it's all true, though. Gyahahaha!"

"Damn you, Dein!!"

"Whoa, you're looking pretty scary there, Flum. Did I hit a bit too close to home?" He didn't look scared at all. In fact, he looked relaxed. "Hey, Flum, did you know she's a failed experiment?"

"I don't know, nor do I care to!"

"Well, I'm going to tell you anyway. As you realized, she's got no idea she's a living weapon! That's absolutely deplorable, for one of the children!"

"Mmmmppphh!!"

A creature. A murderer.

Ink shook her head vigorously at this. She didn't want to believe it.

Dein didn't care. In fact, he took great joy in continuing, "There are conditions you gotta meet to release Origin's power. In her case, that's when her medicine wears off and she's fallen into a deep sleep. I guess 'release' ain't the right word. It's more like her body succumbs to Origin's power, yeah? Just imagine: while you were all sleeping soundly in your beds, she'd turn into that disgusting *thing* and spew eyeballs. It's funny as hell when you think about it, considering she was the one that chased down your friends, your guardian, and even your little slave! Gyahahaha!!"

He really seemed to be enjoying himself, though there was something in his laugh that rang hollow.

"Do you know where Milkit went?!"

Dein belted out a cruel laugh. "Oh, but I do! I know all too well, in fact. Right now, she's in a place where her beloved master will find her, being transformed into one of those fleshy abominations!"

"I'm going to kill you, you miserable son of a...!" Flum drew her sword and launched toward Dein.

"Listen kid, I'm just here to bring back a creature that escaped. You really should be more worried about those guys."

Right on cue, the men Flum saw following Dein around on his duties with the church stepped out of the shadows. Their eyes were glassy and distant—dead men's eyes. The church must have done something to them.

"How pathetic...! Even when you're at your lowest, you still manage to muster up some people to do your bidding!"

"Hey, they're just happy to be of some use to me."

"Are you sure you didn't brainwash them and turn them into your pawns?!"

"I dunno why you're so angry, kid. These guys were out to kill you before. What, you some kind of champion of justice now?" Dein's anger reeked of projection. Overcome with emotion for a moment, he finally regained his composure and let out an awkward laugh.

"Well, as long as I'm okay, that's all that matters. At least that much is true."

"You've discarded away everything but your own cowardice. Just what value do you bring to the world?"

"Nng...shut up!!!" Dein leveled his crossbow toward Flum. "What the hell do you know?! What does anyone know about all I've lost?!"

"Are you going to shoot or not?"

"Grr..."

Dein clenched his hands in white-hot rage. If he didn't shoot, he was letting her tread all over his pride yet again. After several deep breaths, his anger seemed to melt away.

"Well, my client told me not to kill you, Flum. So I guess that's that." He gave a weak, unconvincing laugh and forced a grin to his face. "I'd love to see you dead, but they'll kill me too if I disobey orders. And let me tell you, I'm really not keen on being murdered. Hahaha! Anyway, let me leave you with a warning, then."

"A warning?"

"What can I say, I'm a nice guy. See those guys over there? Don't harm them and don't even think about chasing after me. Just run. You see, they're a lot more like this girl here than you know."

"Is this how you plead for your life?"

"Gahaha! Hardly! I'm just thinking about you, Flum.

Not like I think you could hold yourself back anyway. But hey, just try to stay alive, huh?"

"Mmmmmpph!!"

With that, Dein hefted Ink up and took off running. Ink reached out for Flum, begging to be saved.

"Ink!!"

Flum tried to take up chase but quickly found her path blocked by Dein's men. There were at least ten of them closing in around her, armed to the teeth. Further off, there were yet more men with bows, crossbows, and slingshots standing atop nearby roofs. It seemed like a bit much for just one girl.

Flum cast Scan on the nearest man. He was a top-tier C-Rank, with a total stat value of 2,482. His strength and endurance were around 600 each, while his magic, agility, and perception were all over 400. Considering that Dein's stats made him a solid B-Rank adventurer on his own, she figured this made this C-rank dude the leader of the throng currently surrounding her. Just to be sure, she decided to cast Scan on another person.

What she saw left her without words. "They're exactly the same??"

He, too, had a total stat value of 2,482. Flum felt a sense of dread creep up on her as she cast Scan on each one. One thing quickly became evident:

"These guys all have the same name, affinities, and stats!"

Dein's men were all copies of each other in every sense except their physical appearances. Past the initial confusion, nothing really surprised Flum anymore. She'd been through too much.

"This has to be the church's doing."

Dein must have betrayed the men who followed him even after he lost his influence in his bid to join the church. Flum clenched her jaw so hard she could hear her teeth grind. Dein was right; these men were hardly innocents. At the same time, that was partially out of their loyalty to Dein—loyalty he betrayed so he could save his own hide.

"I can't let this keep happening!"

Flum refocused her growing rage into strength and lunged straight into the fray.

This was the first time she'd ever fought so many opponents at once. Even though she was stronger than each of them individually, as a group, the gap in power was immense. She didn't know if she stood a chance. She'd need to make the most of her ability to regenerate and her Reversal magic if she planned on seeing this through.

The first matter of business was to thin them out.

Fwooosh! Flum drew her Souleater and swept it in a wide arc. As the men on the ground fell back in unison, an archer on the neighboring rooftop fired. Flum caught the movement out of the corner of her eye and focused her magic energy down into her feet, casting her spell fractions of a second before the arrow found its mark.

"Reversion!"

The arrow swiveled in place and reversed course, spearing the archer in the neck. He grabbed at the bolt, stumbling back and pitching over the eaves.

"Well, that's one!"

The small victory emboldened her, but she knew her Reversal magic would only be useful against attacks she could anticipate. A surprise attack would neutralize her advantage.

The next attack came from one of the men with her in the street. He rushed her with his spear set, trying to run her through.

Shwick! The spear caught her square in the shoulder. He had her beat for reach; she couldn't hide inside Souleater's circle of blood.

The battle seemed unlikely to end any time soon as long as they kept up this hit-and-run style. She was left with only one choice: take the blows as they came and focus on getting in hits of her own. Blood sprayed from the wound as intense pain radiated through her body. Flum's grip on the Souleater loosened for a moment, but then she quickly found her footing again and grabbed the spear's shaft, wrenching it from the man's hand. As soon as it was free, she yanked it out of her shoulder and threw it to the ground.

The now-unarmed man fled while two more, each armed with swords, rushed in to fill his place and another spearman advanced from the rear.

She decided to press the attack. Ducking between the swords, Flum launched toward the ex-spearman who landed a blow on her earlier. Just as she got in close, he spun around and held his fists at the ready.

"C'mere, you li'l punk!" Flum brought the Souleater down on him in an overhead slash; he caught the blow with his bracer, then closed in on Flum and punched her in the gut. "Gyauuh?!"

He went through the motions so easily, like a born grappler. But the way he'd handled the spear earlier was also the work of no novice. It was bizarre that such a talented adventurer, skilled in so many forms of combat, would so willingly accept such a low position in Dein's camp. Not impossible, of course, but highly unlikely.

A startling realization slowly came to her. *Could they share their fighting abilities, too?*

That would mean they were all experts at pretty much any style of combat.

While her attention was diverted, another spear skewered her from behind.

"Aaauugh!!" She yanked it out and focused on the next attack, this time from a man angling to sever her head. Flum caught the blow with her right gauntlet, though the force behind it still shattered her wrist. Another archer up ahead scored a direct blow on her shoulder.

Another man on a rooftop to her left shot a fireball at her left foot, blasting right through her flesh and sending Flum tumbling to the ground.

"Nnngaaaaauuuugh!"

As pain ripped through her body, she lost more and more fine control of her movements. There was no surviving a fight with these parameters. Flum frantically scanned her surroundings for an alleyway leading away from the clearing, but every option was just too far to be of any use.

In the interest of lightening her load, she decided to send the Souleater back to its parallel dimension. She rolled clear of an arrow and used her momentum to get back up onto her feet, popping up behind one of the incoming men. His guard was down, probably figuring she would make a run for the alley—

"Have at it!!" The Souleater flashed back into her hands as she swung at his neck. *FWOOSH!*

The man dropped into a crouch, effortlessly dodging her blow.

You can't be serious?

Flum was completely taken aback. The man's movements were so smooth she could've sworn he had eyes in the back of his head. Maybe he did, in a way. Maybe in addition to their stats and skills, the men were sharing their senses as well. That was the only explanation that made any sense to her.

Yet more arrows and magic attacks rained down on her while Flum stood dumbfounded. She had to stay out of the ranged fighters' line of sight, but if she stayed in cover for too long, the men in the square would surround her.

Dein's words came back to her: "Don't harm them or even think about chasing after me. Just try and escape."

It annoyed her to no end to have to follow Dein's advice, but that was beginning to seem like the only appropriate choice left.

Flum stumbled forward on unsteady feet as she made her way to the nearest alley. Though many of her wounds had already begun to heal, the pain was still so extreme that it hampered her ability to move.

She heard the men giving chase intermingling with the sounds of magic, arrows, and stones flying all around her. As long as she could break out of their trap, she knew that she was fast enough to get clear. Even if they did catch up, the alleys were narrow enough that she could limit it to one-on-one combat.

Just a little farther...

Flum felt spells blast past either side of her and watched as fireballs slammed through the exterior wall of a nearby house and exploded. The wall crumbled in front of her, blocking her path. She could probably still climb it, but that would give her pursuers even more time to catch up. Flum glanced over her shoulder in desperation, only to catch two more arrows: one in her stomach and another in her thigh.

"Hnnnnghph!"

She yanked them both out, creating openings for more arrows, spells, and a man with a bludgeon closing in fast. Feeling desperation set in, Flum struck wildly.

The man easily dodged her attack and lunged in with his metal club. Flum considered launching a counter-strike of her own, but he would weave past it thanks to the men's shared vision. What choice did she have but to take the blow?

Her lips curled into a grin. Maybe this was her chance.

She concentrated all of her energy down into her legs and touched the tips of her boots against a stone around ten centimeters square.

"Reversion!"

CRACK!

The stone flipped around, catching the man's leg in the empty space as it turned, and snapped the bone in an instant. He lost his balance and crumpled to the floor. No matter how good their vision may have been, they couldn't avoid an attack like that.

"Hyaaaaaaaaaaaaaaaaa!!" Flum brought her blade down with all her might and chopped the man in two along a neat diagonal from shoulder to gut. "That's two down!"

They still had a massive numbers advantage, but even two fewer opponents to worry about lessened the pressure. The men showed no reaction to the loss of their comrade. As one cohesive being, it was hard to call them human anymore. They functioned like puppets, living only to serve Dein's commands.

She couldn't let her guard down just yet. Flum danced around one magic attack after another as she drew closer toward her next opponent. Now that she'd tipped her hand, she probably couldn't use the same trick again.

She heard something drop down next to her as she mulled over how she could stop her next opponent.

"Huh?"

There was an eye in the street. It didn't stop there. One after another, they flooded in from every direction: from the sky, out of gutters, from behind her, from the same direction as the oncoming men.

Dein's words resonated in her mind again: "Don't harm them."

"Is this what he meant?"

Ink had no recollection of killing anyone; no idea what she became at night. Her power activated without her input. The eyes were probably a self-defense mechanism to protect the church's secrets that took advantage of Ink's lack of control.

Why didn't the first man she'd killed count, then? Flum figured it could've been because he died from his own arrow.

"I was having a tough enough time fighting them on their own!"

She dove out of the way, hoping to get clear, but it was too late. An eye latched onto her boot and began to seep through the leather. It didn't exactly hurt, but it made her skin crawl.

"Eyaugh!" Flum's body stiffened as she felt the eyeball make its way deep into her leg. A moment later, she heard an awful sound as her leather boot expanded. Something was growing out of her ankle.

Making matters worse, a man armed with a dagger chose that moment to lunge in, aiming straight for her heart.

PWUUSH! The blade bit way clean through her hand as she threw it up in front of her. "Aauughh…"

Her opponent yanked the blade out to prepare for a second strike, but Flum grabbed it by the hilt. She kicked the man's legs out from under him, sending him tumbling into the sea of eyeballs. They did their best to avoid their fallen ally, scattering like roaches in a newly lit room, but weren't completely successful. His torso began to bulge where it touched the ground, almost as if new organs were rapidly forming inside him. He tried to get back to his feet but just flailed on the ground like a wounded bug.

"Aw'right, that's three!" There were still quite a few more for her to deal with, though.

The next round of arrows and spells grazed past her. Every dodge was a small miracle for Flum with the new leg weighing her down. The eyes put an end to her plan to escape to the alleys. Her options were looking thin on the ground.

If I were up against normal human opponents, I might stand a chance here. Since this new limb isn't technically an

injury, the Souleater isn't helping me recover from it. That
only leaves one real option...

Flum stabbed the Souleater into the ground and
launched a powerful kick toward the blade.

"Nngaaaaaaaaaaaaaaugh!!!"

SHWAAACK!

Her leg went flying off, along with its newly-grown
appendage.

She had to prop herself up with her sword as she made
her escape. If she stopped, the eyes would be on her in a
matter of moments. It would be a little while longer before her leg fully regenerated, but it was still an improvement over having to stick it out with that double limb.

As she'd hoped, Flum's leg regenerated before the men
were able to catch up to her, and she was finally able to
get a sizable lead on them. But just as things were starting
to look up, she caught sight of six figures—all dressed in
the white plate armor of church knights—approaching
from up ahead. She figured they were probably drawn by
the sudden racket.

"Listen, it's dangerous back there, so..." She tried her
best to warn them but was only met with weapons held
at the ready.

As her options dwindled, Flum clicked her tongue
in annoyance and cast Scan. Though they differed from

Dein's men, all of the church knights had exactly the same stats.

"A pincer attack?!"

They were really going all out. Whether they intended to murder her or just capture her, Flum couldn't say. But regardless of their intentions, it was clear they didn't want her to escape.

She clenched her Souleater tightly and looked between the groups of enemies closing in from both sides.

Adventurers, knights, eyes... There were just too many for her to deal with on her own. Her hands shook and the blade's tip wavered. All of her allies were missing. Her loneliness only made her imminent demise that much more terrifying. There was no one standing by her side, waiting for her to come home, or even for her to protect, anymore.

"I don't want to die... I... I don't want to die!!"

Flum gathered every ounce of will she had left, preparing for one final show of her unbreakable spirit. She raised her sword in the knights' direction and focused on centering all the energy in her body and transforming it into prana. It flowed up through her arms like a bubbling spring before transferring from her fingers into her sword.

Prana Shaker? She considered it for a moment but began to doubt it would be enough to stop them in a single blow. Launching multiple attacks in rapid succession was another option, but she never trained to do that.

Her palms started to sweat, and the prana faded as she lost control of her breathing. No. No, she couldn't let despair take over again. She wouldn't give up. Not until she'd given it her all.

The adventurers were almost on her, and the eyes would be right behind them. Once the knights joined the battle, her chances of winning were all but nil.

"Flum, send all your prana into the ground!"

Right at her darkest hour, she heard the voice of a brave hero echo inside her head.

"Hyaaaaaaaaaaaaaaaaaaaaaaaah!!" Flum slammed her Souleater straight into the earth. Her prana erupted and began to stir into a massive cyclone.

The wind whipped straight toward the knights. No mortal shield could block the wind; they'd have as much luck wrestling an inferno. Explosive prana found its way through every gap in their armor and tore them asunder.

Prana Storm was an area-of-effect Cavalier Art that bent the wielder's prana to send waves of cutting force at the enemies in front of you. It required a great deal more prana than Prana Shaker, but Flum was more than capable of that—especially with her back against the wall like this.

A man encased in heavy armor the color of a moonless night landed on the road with a heavy thud, throwing up a cloud of broken flagstones. He drew his massive broadsword and stepped around Flum to face off against the adventurers and eyeballs closing in.

"Hmph."

A second later, Flum heard the roaring winds of another, far more powerful Prana Storm. It spared nothing in its wake. Not the ground, not the buildings, and certainly not her pursuers. The eyes began to fill the streets once again, though the remaining adventurers were less eager to take up the chase.

"Gadhio!!" Flum's voice shook.

"Don't let your guard down yet, Flum. There're more coming!" His voice was powerful, though it still held a gentle undertone. It brightened Flum's spirits.

He was right: the battle wasn't over yet. She was happy to see him, but the reunion would have to wait.

"R-right!" Flum wiped away the tears forming at the corners of her eyes and turned her attention to the knights that just rounded the corner.

Both fighters raised their blades and prepared to strike.

"Haaaaaaaaaaaaaaaah!!"

"Gyaaaaaaaaaaaaaaaa!"

Their swords hit the ground in perfect unison.

012

Counterattack

THE SIX CHURCH KNIGHTS left standing on Flum's side had Dein's men beat for stats—and she wasn't the least bit worried. She had no intention of losing.

CLAAAANG!

Her blade thrummed with prana as it caved in a knight's armor. She could hear the shock wave liquefy his insides. He spewed blood, keeling over onto his back. Another knight lunged, his spear leveled at Flum's head. She leaned back as far as she could, and it left a deep gash in her nose as it passed.

Yet another pressed in with his own spear while she was still off-balance. It was hard to keep track of the remaining knights all at the same time, but Flum channeled prana into her legs and somersaulted through the air to evade the strike. Riding the inertia of her jump, she drove her black blade into the spear-wielding knight, crushing his helmet and scattering its contents.

The moment she landed, Flum heard the familiar *fwip* of an arrow barely missing her, but she stopped to steady her breathing and regenerate her prana anyway.

Gadhio, on the other hand, was relentless in his attack on the remaining adventurers and eyes. He unleashed his massive reserves of prana energy in another powerful storm that cleared away everything ahead of him.

"Remember, visualize the strike! Focus all of your energy on one point and push it through!" His instructions were blunt but clear.

Following his lead, Flum turned back to the knights and focused on Gadhio's instructions.

This technique was called Prana Sting. It was meant to pierce through to the soft, mortal part of an armored foe. The knight took a few halting steps, trying to cover the hole in his armor with his free hand before he fell with a heavy *thud*.

Only three more to go.

The knights hesitated for a moment, giving Flum a chance to catch her breath again. "Hey, Gadhio, what're you doing here?"

"It should be obvious." Gadhio motioned with his

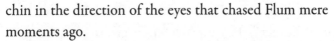

chin in the direction of the eyes that chased Flum mere moments ago.

"You mean they were chasing after you, too?"

He laughed sheepishly. "Yep."

Flum thought back to her last conversation with Ottilie. Could Gadhio have been the other person looking into the church?

He looked absolutely exhausted, like he'd been on the run for several days now, and yet, he could still unleash such powerful attacks. She was beyond impressed. She decided to put the specifics aside for now and focus on the remaining knights. This was a chance for her to finally use all the techniques Gadhio taught her.

Gadhio slammed his blade into the ground, and a wave of prana battered the oncoming enemies; Flum followed suit. Next, with two strokes, they each left a protective cross of prana hanging in the air in front of them. Try as they might, none of the knights' spells could get through.

Flum generated yet more prana, letting it flow straight into her blade; her next cut split a knight from stem to stern.

"Last one!"

Against a single opponent, Flum was assured of her victory. She cleaved the man in two. His left and right sides fell to the ground with a wet thud. Thanks to her enchantment, the man's remains began to freeze over.

Her battle resolved, Flum turned her attention back to Gadhio.

"Hyaaaaaah!!" He tore through the wave of eyes and made the incoming adventurers falter. "Anngh!"

Gadhio cut the men down with a single slash. It wasn't even a battle at this point. Flum knew he was powerful, but she was still impressed. He'd always been kind to her throughout their entire journey, showing little care for whether she was actually "useful" to the party or not. He always held a special place in her heart.

"Looks like you've finished up too, yeah?"

"Yeah, pretty much. Thanks a lot for saving me, Gadhio. I don't know what I would've done if you hadn't shown up."

Gadhio smiled warmly. "Heh, I certainly didn't do it alone. You've gotten a lot stronger, Flum."

Hearing that made her so happy she could dance, but Flum decided to show a little restraint for now. She was still weak. She couldn't save anyone, after all.

"I'd love to talk over everything that's happened, but I don't think we have time for that quite yet..." she said. The eyes continued their ceaseless procession toward the two heroes.

"We'd better go," Gadhio agreed.

Together, they took off in search of Dein.

◇ ◇ ◇

The peculiar pair ran all over the darkened town but found no trace of Dein. As they searched, the two exchanged the scraps of information they gathered.

"So that Ink girl is the one who's making all these eyeballs?"

"That's right. She's one of the church's creations."

"A Spiral Child..."

"These Spiral...things, do they have something to do with the church's research?"

"So you're investigating the church as well, Flum? To answer your question, they replace the children's hearts with Origin cores."

"An Origin core...in place of their heart?"

If Flum were to destroy the core inside Ink, the young girl would die. But as long as the core survived inside her, she would continue to create eyes.

"How do you know this Ink girl?"

"I just happened across her in the street and helped her out a few days ago. She's been living together with us ever since."

"So you want to help her, then."

Flum looked down and nodded weakly. "...Yes."

If there was a chance Ink could survive without her core, Flum had to save her, regardless of how hard it would be.

"I don't know how to do that. But I do know we can't leave her in Dein's hands. He sold his soul and his friends to the church."

"That won't do him any good. That man is drawn to whatever benefits him most. He'll never be able to turn his back on wealth and power." Gadhio practically spat out the words. It seemed he had at least a passing familiarity with Dein.

Once again, eyes began to shower from nearby rooftops on either side of them.

"Hyaa!"

"Haaah!"

In a flurry of blades, the two reduced the incoming wave to burst membranes and spattered humors before they touched the ground.

"By the way, were you the one who threw the knife at my windowsill?"

"That's right. I'd figured out you were living there, but I didn't think it wise to talk to you directly. Was it that confusing?"

"Well, the handwriting was pretty awful, and you didn't exactly leave your name."

"Sorry, I was in a bit of a hurry."

"I thought it was one of Dein's pranks."

"Looks like it didn't have much effect, then."

"I mean, it's a little late to tell me not to go outside. I'm pretty well involved in this whole situation."

"You're involved?"

"As far as I can tell, Origin is after me. Honestly, it seemed strange that a weakling like me would even be put on the party to slay the Demon Lord in the first place. It's the only thing that makes sense."

Flum hopped over another group of eyes that appeared at her feet. The two ran full tilt and took the next available left.

"I don't know why that'd be, but I assume it's something to do with my affinity."

"Reversal?"

"Right. You know those Origin cores you mentioned? I'm pretty sure they can't be destroyed through any normal means." Flum remembered Neigass's reaction when they met at the research facility.

"That's correct." Gadhio had learned as much through his previous research into the church.

"But I was able to destroy one."

"You've already fought one?"

"I was getting pretty desperate, and I dumped everything I had into the core."

"So, you think your magic may be the key?"

"If Origin is involved with these spiral beings, then I've been thinking—something might happen if my Reversal power was used to change the spirals' direction."

"I can't say I fully understand it, but if you were able to destroy one, that definitely says something. If it were prana alone, then someone else should have been able to do it already."

"Only I can do it. Which means that Ink..." Flum glanced down at her palm. Even if she wasn't able to save Ink, she could at least put an end to her suffering. Was that really the right choice?

Gadhio's booming voice interrupted her thoughts. "What's that?! Flum, jump to the side!!"

Flum didn't know what was going on but did as she was told. Looking ahead, she spotted two young boys in their path, holding their hands out and chanting.

"Rotation!!"

"Distortion!!"

The air around them began to twist and deform.

One of the boys unleashed a blast of energy that swirled like a tornado, blasting past Flum and boring a hole straight through a nearby wall. When the other's energy blast hit the wall, it twisted into a large spiral pattern.

Flum had seen both of these abilities before. "Spiral Children!"

"Eh, you know 'bout us? Are the church's secrets already out?"

"We best tell Mother to give them a good scolding. Ha!"

Though they sounded like any other kids, they had the same gory, pulsing spiral where their faces belonged.

"I'm Luke, the scary one. This here's Fwiss, the oblivious klutz."

"Man, I can't believe how much that dummy Ink told you about us."

"At least she's only a first ge-ne-ra-tion. She doesn't know anything important."

"Listen, you're not allowed to go any farther, 'kay?"

"So we're gonna stop ya! Rotation!"

The boy punched his fist into the air, sending another cyclone after Flum. She dodged, mowing down more eyeballs that were getting too close for comfort.

"Well, guess you've left me no other choice!" Flum cast Scan on the children.

Fwiss Tours
Affinity: Wind
Strength: 2341
Magic: 3923
Endurance: 2371
Agility: 5712
Perception: 4117

Luke Fuloop
Affinity: Earth
Strength: 3298
Magic: 3792
Endurance: 3512
Agility: 3148
Perception: 4215

She was completely stunned by these. Ink had completely normal stats. These second-generation kids were something else entirely.

"I've got this, Flum."

"There's no way you can take them on your own, Gadhio!"

His voice was unwavering and confident. "They're just kids. I can make up for the stat difference with skill and experience."

Gadhio held his sword at the ready. He looked completely confident in his victory. Luke and Fwiss looked unbothered.

"Whaaat? You think you know it all just 'cause you looked at our stats? Papa's power can't be measured, y'know."

"Papa's amazing! Even just a small connection to him can make you more powerful than any human ever known. A hero doesn't stand a chance against us."

Could Flum really leave Gadhio behind and continue her search for Dein alone? Should she stay here and fight them together, even if that meant Dein's trail might go cold? She stood there, paralyzed with indecision, when she heard several voices call out from above.

"Who do you think you are?"

"Try getting a bit older before you talk big, huh?"

Flum looked to the rooftop, where two women were silhouetted against the night sky. "Eterna... Ottilie?!"

The newest arrivals wasted no time going on the offensive. Their ice arrows and blood slashes only missed by the slightest of margins as the Spiral Children jumped away.

"I thought I heard a ruckus, but I never expected to find you here, Gadhio," Eterna said.

"Flum and I reunited under similar circumstances."

"We'll take care of these brats. You two go on ahead!"

"Whooooa, you're still alive?" one of the children marveled.

"Who do you think I am?" Ottilie demanded. "I refuse to die at the hands of even God himself until I win my sister's approval!"

"I guess Ink really isn't strong enough. We should report back to Mother."

"No way. I'm beat from running around all night, and those eyeballs are super gross. I wanna have some fun with these ladies!"

So the boys were *also* being pursued by the eyes? They didn't have time to figure it out, or to have a longer reunion, as the terrifying orbs in question were still closing in. "Let's go, Flum!" Gadhio said.

"Right! Good luck, Eterna and Ottilie!"

They took off, resuming the hunt for Dein.

◇◇◇

The pair still continued to come up empty-handed as they continued their search, though it was becoming evident where Dein was headed.

Milkit's still okay...right? All Flum could do was hope and pray for now.

"Flum, there's one thing I need to ask you."

"What is it?"

"I'm guessing you already heard those Children's names from Ink, right? Has she ever told you any of the others?"

"Hmm... I'm pretty sure she said something about some other kids named Nekt and Mute. Why do you ask?"

"Nothing, really. I was just wondering if maybe that was them."

A boy's laughter echoed from the dark behind them. He clenched his small hand into a fist as he cast a spell. "Connection!"

Gadhio stopped and turned.

"Gadhio...?"

"Keep going, Flum!"

Flum wasn't sure what just happened, but she did as she was told.

BWAFWOOOOOOOOOOOM! A massive explosion shattered the silence that hung over the city as the walls on either side of them blew in.

"Aauuunnnnngggg..." Gadhio's arms shook and veins bulged furiously in his forehead as he struggled to hold the collapsing slabs of brick and stone at bay. Making matters worse, eyes crept ever closer to his feet. He desperately wanted to join in the battle against Dein and help Flum...but if he let up his grip now, the walls would crush him. At least Flum had made it to the far side by now—though this also meant they were completely cut off from each other.

"What happened to the walls??"

The young boy in the dark replied, "They're trying to connect, you see. Physical object or empty air, it makes no difference to me. That's my special ability."

Gadhio finally got a good look at the kid. He looked young, not even ten years old, and was wearing a white hospital gown.

"So...you were the one who teleported...those other Children out to us...earlier...weren't you?" Gadhio got out through gritted teeth. Something had seemed off to him about their earlier encounter, as if Luke and Fwiss had appeared out of nowhere. "Teleport...wait. You did it to Milkit, too?!"

"My, my...how observant you are, hero. Yes, that was me."

"So Milkit's still alive??"

"Hm, who can say? Perhaps you should ask Dein. I just did as I was asked. I have no interest in what he did with her."

Knowing Dein, he would have held off on killing her, just to do it in front of Flum. At the very least, if the boy hadn't killed her, it was likely Milkit was still alive.

"You've probably already heard about me from Ink," the boy said. "I'm Nekt Lyncage, the leader of the Children."

"How polite of you to actually bother with introductions."

"I figure my victims should know who killed them, no?"

Gadhio snorted, earning a scowl from Nekt. "Precocious little punk."

There was one last thing he needed to tell Flum. He shouted as loud as he could, hoping Flum could hear him through the wall.

"Flum! Sara Anvilen is still alive!"

"Sara's alive...?"

Flum's shock gave way to tears that stung the corners of her eyes and blurred her vision. She desperately wanted to ask how he knew, but with the eyes closing in, they didn't have the luxury of continuing the conversation. Some of the crushing weight on her heart was finally lifted.

"She's...she's alive! Sara's alive! Thanks, Gadhio!!"

She shouted loud enough to be sure he heard her before taking off again, weaving her way through the pooling eyeballs and pushing herself even further than she'd gone before. Somehow, all her exhaustion had drained away.

◇◇◇

"Heh." Gadhio smirked at the sound of Flum's voice as he readjusted to press his back up against the wall.

"Still able to work up a smile, old man?"

"Eh, I'm hanging in there."

Gadhio's swift answer only seemed to annoy Nekt even more. He reached up to run a hand through his chin-length hair and shot Gadhio a menacing look as he sized up his opponent. "I think you're underestimating me, no? I could kill you anytime I want, Gramps."

"Confidence is a good thing, kid, but too much will get you hurt."

"Gah. I hate when adults treat me like a little kid." A cold, cunning grin came to Nekt's face as he slowly stuck his arm out, palm to the sky. His face began to twist into a blood-red spiral.

Gadhio drew his sword and stood at the ready. He let out a deep breath and summoned up his prana, letting it loose as a blast of force that held the eyes at bay. "Well, let's get going."

Nekt lifted up his hand and balled it up into a fist. "Connection!" His voice rumbled from deep in his throat. It faded almost as quickly as it came.

The young boy moved so fast that even Gadhio couldn't keep track of him. More accurately, he never moved—he simply *was elsewhere*. Gadhio sensed a presence behind him and brought his sword down in its direction.

"Wow, pretty good for an old man." The blade only barely missed Nekt. "But... Connection!"

He disappeared again, reappearing where he was just a moment ago. Nekt formed another fist. He put some more force into his voice this time.

"Here you go... Connection!!"

The gyrating muscles in his face twitched, and the very air around them trembled under the immense power. Both walls of the alley crumbled and bowed once more, straining to come together and crush Gadhio in the process.

"I've seen this trick before, kid."

"Oh, but I added a little something extra to make it more interesting. Now, prepare to be crushed! Connection!!"

An entire house materialized above Gadhio's head. With massive forces bearing down on him from all sides, Gadhio had few options left to him. It seemed impossible for a mere mortal to survive.

Nekt laughed, confident in his victory. "Looks like you're done for, hero!"

However...

"Resolute Cavalier Arts Expansion!"

Even under such tremendous pressure, Gadhio kept his cool and steadied his breathing enough to launch an attack of his own. His technique wedded his prana to his earth affinity; magic coursed up his arms and into his blade, enveloping it in stone until it was three times its original size. Without the prana running through him, he could never lift such a weapon.

Once the first step was complete, he let his prana flow into the sword itself. This was an expansion of his very will, his personal capstone to the Cavalier Arts.

"Titan Blade!"

Time seemed to stand still and the world was silent as he shifted the immense blade. That silence was destroyed a moment later by an ear-shattering explosion as the walls and house were blown to rubble. With a single swing, he'd undone Nekt's best attack.

Yet the boy only laughed as bricks rained down around them. "Huh, I guess I should take back what I said. That's pretty impressive for an old guy."

"Now that I don't need to worry about Flum getting hurt, I can show you what I'm really made of."

"Well, well, I'd love to see it. Though I should tell you now that I'm far superior to any normal human."

◇ ◇ ◇

Flum could hear an epic battle unfolding off in the distance. She worried whether Gadhio could really hold his own but suppressed the urge to turn back. Somehow, she knew that Dein was waiting for her at the West District church. The nave was almost certainly empty at this hour. What better place was there to meet in secret?

The more she thought about it, the more exhausted she felt. Without the possibility of her friends' survival dangling in front of her, she doubted she ever could have pushed herself this far.

Flum shoved through the church's massive wooden door and into the darkened nave. On the other side, a statue of Origin's human aspect stood watch. She felt its eyes on her.

A man lounged with his legs crossed at the head of the pews.

Flum closed the door behind her and readjusted her equipment to buy herself just a bit more time before approaching. About halfway down the carpeted aisle, the man finally spoke up.

"I figured you'd be here any minute now. You're just that annoyingly persistent. Besides, as you know, I've had quite an illustrious adventuring career. I've got a good sense for this kind of stuff."

Flum had no interest in hearing his speech. She was here for his head, not answers. There weren't any eyes in the church yet, but she knew that was just a matter of time. She needed to take care of this before her fortunes reversed.

"I didn't figure you'd show up before I had a chance to meet with my boss, though," Dein continued. "That was a miscalculation on my part. Man, I'd just crawl in a hole out of embarrassment if I could. I'm sure you're probably thinking the same thing, huh? Who can tell with you. I don't get you."

Flum didn't stop.

"Oh, right. That little brat and the bandaged girl are in the room in the back. I made a promise to that little punk Nekt not to hurt either of them, so rest assured they're all fine and dandy. Though who can say when she'll lose consciousness and that creature will reawaken, eh Flum?"

Flum raised the Souleater and brought it down on his neck.

"Whoa!" Somehow, Dein anticipated the attack and dove out of the way.

The two finally faced each other—Flum with a murderous look in her eye and Dein with his usual sly grin. They couldn't continue like this. One of them was going to kill the other soon.

"You look different. Something good happen?"

"You could say that. Knowing that Milkit and Ink are all right has finally put my heart at rest."

"Huh, well, good for you. Not that it matters much." Dein leveled his crossbow at Flum. "You're going to die here."

Even staring down the tip of the bolt didn't shake Flum's resolve. "Not today, Dein!"

She ran full tilt toward her opponent. Dein smiled and squeezed the trigger. The bolt shot straight for her heart. She made no attempt to block, taking the broad tip straight to her chest.

Until...

"Reversion!!"

The bolt flew back at Dein. He jerked out of the way fast enough to avoid being skewered through the head, but it left a gash along his cheek. His expression contorted with rage.

Flum was closing in by the second. The moment she was within striking distance, she swung for him. Dein stepped around her blow, composed and smiling again. "You need to try harder than that, Flum!"

She glared back at him. All the hate in her heart crystallized around his widening grin.

The battle had only just begun.

**ROLL
OVER
AND
DIE**

013

A Little Bit of Love

FLUM BROUGHT THE SOULEATER down with all her might time and again, Dein only barely evading her head-lopping blows.

Fwooo-SMASH!

The sword whiffed past his head and crashed right into the wooden floor. She may have missed, but Dein's back was against the wall now. What's more, she was far too close for him to use his crossbow. If he didn't discard it and draw the short sword hanging from his waist now, he'd be all out of options.

Flum decided to press the attack, not once considering that he might be luring her into a trap. As she came in with another powerful swing, Dein pointed his buckler up and jerked his finger.

Fwish! A wire shot out, dragging him up into the air.

From his spot up on the wall, Dein shot another bolt at Flum.

"You expect to take me out with one shot, Dein?!" Flum held her sword at the ready, prepared to knock the bolt right out of the air.

"You don't give me enough credit, Flum. Spread!"

Dein cast a spell that burnt the bolt up in midair, causing it to split and barrage Flum with fireballs. Realizing there was no way she could take them all out with her sword, Flum dove to the side.

Dein loosed arrow after arrow.

"Spread, spread, spread!!! Gyahahaha!! I didn't intend to finish this battle with magic, but you should've known better than to think a slave could stand up against the likes of me!"

Flum continued her desperate run, only a step ahead of the wave of fireballs that rained down on her. She felt one skim past her shoulder, her burnt clothes sticking to her body as blood soaked the cloth. The wound would heal shortly, but she still winced at the pain.

But Dein was slowing down, too. She wasn't about to let the opportunity go to waste.

"Hyaaaaaaaaaah!!" She steadied herself and let loose a Prana Shaker. A crescent-shaped blast shot straight toward Dein as he pulled yet another wire to release his hook, dropping him back down. "I can get off more than one attack too, Dein!"

As soon as Dein's feet touched the ground, she unleashed another Prana Shaker in his direction.

"Gyahaha! Thinking you can beat me in a battle of force is where you're wrong, girl!" Dein shot another bolt straight into the Prana Shaker's crescent beam. "Burst!!"

The magic-infused explosion left nothing but a white cloud in its place. Flum lunged through the smoke to press the attack once again.

"Whoa, hey! I'm not really interested in a melee battle." Rappelling into the air once more, Dein rained fireballs down on Flum as he rose. "Gahahahaha!!! Take that, and that! Die, you disgusting little maggot! Try some of this!"

Each fireball he sent her way exploded in a cloud of thick smoke once it hit the ground. A Burst-infused bolt sailed straight at her.

"...Perfect."

This was just what Flum was waiting for. She took the bolt head on with her Souleater, much to Dein's cackling delight.

"That won't save you from being blown away, Flum!"

He was right—under normal circumstances, she would have been blown apart.

"Reversion!"

She sent it flying right back at him.

"How'd...?!"

Dein hurriedly released his tether and let himself plummet before firing the grappling hook once more in midair. BWAFOOOM! The bolt detonated, blowing a hole through the wall where he'd been only a fraction of a second before.

"Whoa, pretty impressive, kid. I guess that's what Reversal does."

Flum ignored Dein's nattering and cast Scan on him.

Dein Phineas
Affinity: Fire
Strength: 802
Magic: 1265
Endurance: 710
Agility: 1454
Perception: 741

His total stat value of 2,669 made him a low-level B-Rank. However, Dein's gear boosted him to a top-tier B-Rank, with a final stat value of 4,972. Under normal circumstances, his Magic should have been well below the 1,000 mark. This explained how he was keeping her on her toes.

Adding to her problems, all of his equipment except for his autoloading crossbow was Legendary class—a tier even rarer than the Epic class items that Flum was equipped with. She only managed to get her equipment thanks to the fact that it was all cursed and of no use to most people. Insolent Leather Armor, Sage Iron Buckler, Wild Iron Dagger... All with powerful enchantments on them, too. It would have been rare to find even an A-Rank adventurer with gear so impressive.

"What're you using Scan on me for, kid? I mean, I guess it doesn't matter. It doesn't change the difference in our abilities one bit."

"Is all that gear actually yours?"

"Of course. I've got some real nice friends who gave it to me fair and square. I guess you could say it's a sign of our friendship, yeah?"

"Pretty ironic, coming from a man who sold out his friends and his soul."

Dein snorted at Flum's pointed remark. "Heh, I know you want to make me out to be some kind of villain, but really, look at it from my point of view. You make a man choose his life or his friends, you're not really giving him a choice. Or do you mean to tell me that a little goody two-shoes like yourself would choose friendship?"

Milkit's smile came to mind. Flum knew her answer in an instant. "If it was a choice between that and sacrificing dozens of others, I'd choose friendship."

She'd sooner stab herself right through the heart than hurt Milkit to save her own life.

"Wow, you're really somethin' else. A real piece of work!" Perhaps it was her confidence that bothered Dein so much. Maybe, deep down, he knew she was telling the truth. "You really don't know anything about the world, d'ya, kid? I don't even know why I waste my time with you...!"

Flum could sense desperation in his voice. It wasn't like he chose to join the church of his own will. He was driven to it out of a realization of his own flaws and a desire to save his life. The choice still ate at him.

"Everything I've built up over all these years, bam! Just laid to waste at the hands of an eight-year-old punk. Pretty hilarious, huh? Right??" Dein just couldn't stop talking. "But ya know what? I found something even better than money and influence. A power so great that I could bend the very world to my whim!"

He was still reliving the days before he had to obey the whims of an eight-year-old child and serve the church. Now he was a puppet. A dog serving its master. His pride was ripped to shreds.

"So, Dein..."

"What?" The man shot her a cold glare. His mind was clearly stuck on the tragedy of his fall from grace.

"Are you looking for sympathy?"

"Huh?" His face went blank.

After a brief pause, he laughed so hard his whole body shook.

Just as it looked like he was about to rein in his emotions, his face flushed, and a vein bulged in his forehead.

"Ha...haha...ha! Like I'd ever want that from the likes of you!" He was howling with anger now, his screams echoing through the darkened city.

But Flum could see through him. Dein had succumbed to his desire to have his anxieties heard. It didn't matter if the person on the other end was a friend or foe; he wanted someone to hear his woes. He wanted someone to tell him they understood, that he was justified in feeling so wronged, that he'd endured a lot.

Absurd. Why would she ever entertain the idea of providing him that relief?

"To hell with the Spiral Children, with Origin, and with this damnable church! Screw you all!!" Dein ranted and raved like a crazed man. He had nothing left. There would be no going back. "I'm the king of the West District! From the day I got dumped in this god-awful slum, I knew I would have my revenge on this world!

And I did it! I crawled my way to the top! With these hands, with my own wit and intellect, with my charisma— I brought myself all the way here! Don't you see? If I didn't give myself up to them, I never would've been able to kill you!!"

An eye peered through the hole that his last Burst made in the wall. Within moments, eyes squeezed into the hole until they fused into a vile wad. The sight made Flum tense up.

Flum glanced over at the wall. "What're you trying to say, then?"

The eyes streamed down the sides of the wall, finding new paths wherever they could. Their irises were locked on Flum. At their current pace, they would burst through the wall and fill the church in a matter of moments.

She wondered if Dein was just trying to buy himself time but then rejected that possibility. *The look of anguish on his face is just too real.*

"What? You having a hard time following along?" Dein's hollow laugh echoed throughout the empty building. "Gyahaha...ha...haaa..."

His voice trailed off, and his arms hung limp at his sides.

"I...I don't even know, either. Aaah...aaaaaaaah... I don't... I don't know anything anymore. What do I even want to do with myself? Some brat shows me up, and I lose everything. I sell out everyone who didn't turn on me, just so I can spend my days singing for my supper. This is the last place I ever wanted to be. Gah—hey, Flum. Those guys messin' around with ya, are they all dead now?"

She figured he was referring to the adventurers that attacked her earlier. Her response was cold and even. "I wouldn't call attempted murder 'messing around,' but yes, they're dead. I think they were already dead when I faced them."

"I see, I see..." Dein mumbled to himself, his eyes glassy. "Hey, wait a minute. What do you mean already dead? Are you trying to say I killed them? What the hell do you know?! You wanna die right here??"

His face stayed empty of feeling, even as he forced a smirk and leveled his crossbow at Flum. What an awful way to go: neither alive nor dead, just cornered with his back to the wall. Without Gadhio, Flum would've been in exactly the same spot.

Maybe she actually could empathize with him in that regard, though he would never quite see it that way. There was, after all, a barrier between them that he believed they could never cross.

"Hey, Dein. About what I said earlier."

"Huh?" He kept his finger on the trigger.

Flum smiled. "Don't come crying to me for sympathy, okay? It's gross."

Dein froze. His pride was in ruins, and now she stomped on whatever was left.

"Come crying? To you? No... I... I wouldn't. Gaaaah!!!"

He screamed at the top of his lungs and shook his head frantically, trying to deny the reality dawning on him. He pulled the trigger. There was no magic behind the attack this time. Flum didn't even need to dodge—the shot went wide.

"I'll kill you!!" His second shot veered the other way. Flum hadn't moved. "DIE!"

He missed again.

"Die, die, DIE!" Dein's hands were shaking so badly that he couldn't find his target. He steadied his aim with his free hand and drew a bead on her forehead. "Die, runt! It's your fault I ended up like this!!"

Flum batted the arrow aside with her blade and started to advance. Dein finally regained some fraction of his senses and loosed a Spread-imbued bolt. Flum dashed, her sword hanging low at her side, building prana as she went.

She released all of her stored prana into a furious Prana Storm as she struck. The powerful winds tore up floorboards and ripped apart eyes as they buffeted Dein.

The burning Spread shots went out and fell limply to the ground.

"Nngaah!" Dein threw his arms in front of his face to block out the wind. Flum took the opportunity to close the distance.

She brought the sword down in a powerful slash. THWANK!

Dein managed to block the blow with his crossbow, though it sent his weapon flying across the room. Realizing he wouldn't have a chance to retrieve it, Dein decided to fall back on his wire trick.

Flum summoned up her prana again. Her repeated use of the Cavalier Arts had already taken a lot out of her, but she still had just enough left in her to give it one last go.

"You're not getting away that easily!" The sword felt even heavier than usual in her hands as she rushed after Dein.

SWHICK! Her Prana Sting sliced right through Dein's wire.

"Whooooa!!" He briefly considered casting Float to slow his fall, but that would just make him an easier target. Instead he chose to let gravity have its way while he extended his hand out toward his enemy. "Fireball!!"

It was a minor spell, meant to make Flum pause for the moment he needed. Flum had been dodging arrows all night; she easily ducked out of the way.

Safely on solid ground, Dein turned tail and dashed for the entrance. He had no plan to escape. He was trying to put as many of the eyes blanketing the floor between them as possible.

After all, they only seemed to be interested in Flum.

She gripped the hilt of the Souleater in both hands and pushed at full speed toward Dein, only skirting around the eyes at the very last second.

Her sword skimmed just shy of the floor; with all the grit and prana she could muster in one blow, she heaved it high, whipping up a mighty gale. The eyes surrounding her burst, and the wind cut Dein's arms and body to ribbons in spite of his best attempts to shield himself.

"Nnngaaaaah!!" Dein gritted his teeth in pain.

His buckler protected his vitals from any significant damage. Everything else was left wide open.

Flum still didn't slow down.

"Hyaaaaaaaaaaaaah!!"

"Damn you, brat! I'm not gonna die just yet!"

He tried to catch her follow-through with his buckler, but the blow forced him to one side. Ice spread from the point of impact, locking his shield down for good.

"Dammit!" A variety of unique curses flew from Dein's mouth.

Dein had been playing coy about his buckler's poison darts, just in case, but that mechanism froze over with the grapnel.

Even with Dein backed up against a wall, Flum still didn't let up.

"Now that we've come this far...!"

Flum brought down her sword, smashing Dein's buckler to frost and flinders. All Dein could do was scramble backward on the floor.

"You're not getting away! This! Ends! Here!!" Flum punctuated her sentence by slashing his shoulder, his leg, and his other cheek.

"FIIIIIIREBAAAAAALL!!!" Dein loosed one last spell in desperation. His odds of hitting Flum at this point were practically non-existent.

True to form, she tilted her head to the side, and the fireball swept past before exploding on contact with the ceiling.

BWOOOOOMF!!!

The thunderous explosion echoed through the church.

"Wha?!"

Flum looked up just in time to see the falling debris. She barely managed to dodge out of the way in time, suffering only a gash in her nose from a tumbling beam.

Dein cackled. "I lured you out here, and you thought

I wouldn't use the environment to be best of my ability??
Fool!"

"You don't know when to quit!"

"That's how I've stayed alive this long, in spite of
everything I've been through!" He shot another fireball
at Flum's feet.

Flum tried to dash out of the way, but the fireball exploded the instant it made contact with the floorboards,
blasting her leg away in the process and sending her
body flying.

The moment she landed, she looked down to find her
hand touching an eye.

"Oh no..."

She felt it crawl into her left arm.

She tried to get to her feet, but it was already too late.
A new arm was already growing; the old one refused to
do as she willed.

Dein loosed another fireball. Flum knew there was no
way she could get out of the way in time...unless...

She took the blast head-on, leading with her deformed arm.

Blood and flesh scattered with the blast. She grit her
teeth through the agony.

"You impertinent little brat!!"

"That's rich, coming from you!"

Flum's new left arm throbbed, whole and unmutated. *Back in the lead,* she thought.

Dein was covered in wounds; he struggled to put distance between himself and Flum, inching closer to his discarded crossbow.

Flum changed direction, diving in to intercept him.. She won out by a fraction of a second and threw the crossbow as hard as she could.

Out of options, Dein dove straight into Flum.

"Waaaugh?!"

"Heh, you scream like a little girl, even out here on the battlefield!" Dein was on top of Flum; he wrapped his fingers around her neck.

"You sure have a big mouth on you, kid. Cryin' to you? Pshaw. Don't make me laugh."

"I was just making an observation."

"Just think about it. This is all your fault. Everything only started going wrong after you showed up. You're to blame for everything that's happened. Deny it, just try!"

His actions with regard to the church had nothing to do with her. Honestly, she barely cared what Dein thought anyway. All he was trying to do was get back at Flum and ruin her name for mocking him.

"Haha! Look, look! Those darling li'l eyeballs are coming for you. Even if I don't get to kill you, they'll turn you into an abomination and do the job for me!"

Flum struggled to break loose. Dein held fast; his grip was too strong to overcome from her position.

She let out a deep breath, which elicited a crazed smile from Dein. He took it as a sign of her surrender.

"Reversion."

As soon as she whispered the spell, Dein's face changed instantly. A moment later, there was a loud snap as Dein's wrists reversed in an impossible direction.

"Gaaaaaaaaaaaauuuugh!!"

He tumbled to the side, screaming in agony. Once Flum was free of his grip, she rolled out from under him, kicked him solidly in the stomach, and jumped to her feet. She brought her sword down on him, catching him square in the shoulder.

"Nnng...graaaaaaw!!! You stupid, ugly, little wench...!" His anger dulled his pain; he didn't slow down at all, in spite of his injuries.

"Gyaaaaaaaauuuugh!!" He pressed his wrist up against the wall to hold it in place before twisting his entire arm, setting his wrist bones back in place.

He may have lost much of his grip, but he was still strong enough to hold the knife he kept at his waist.

"Haah... Flum...haah... Flum!!!"

He dropped into a low crouch and dove straight at Flum. She was ready to take him head on, when she noticed an eye creeping in close at the last second and leapt clear.

"Those eyes are getting faster?!"

Dein took advantage of the diversion to further close the distance. Flum hurried to ready the Souleater, but he was running like a bat out of hell.

"Raaaaaaaaaaaaaaagh!!!"

SQUOOSH!

The knife plunged deep into Flum's stomach. He gave the handle a twist, tearing up her organs even further. Flum gasped.

"Fluuuuuuuuum!!!" With nothing else to live for and nothing to lose, Dein's entire world now revolved around the simple concept of killing Flum.

Flum let go of the Souleater and shoved him away with both hands. The silver blade in his hand was drenched red.

Dein still wasn't finished.

"Gyaaaaaaaaaaaaaaah!!!" He lunged back at her, though she was able to deliver a swift kick to his stomach this time.

"Hnngh!" Dein doubled over and clutched his guts, giving Flum an opportunity to get in close, grab him by the hair, and knee his face into hamburger before letting him drop to the floor.

His arms shook as he fought to push himself back up. Flum kicked him in the face again.

Dein's movement slowed. Flum decided now was the time to draw her Souleater again.

"Hyaaaaaaaaaaaah!!" Somehow Dein found his second wind and charged into her like a crazed animal, swinging his knife wildly and slicing open Flum's shirt, exposing her underwear for all to see.

He lunged in for another stab, but Flum caught it with her forearm. She winced, first at the sound of the blade scraping bone and then the sensation of her flesh shearing away.

She noticed an eyeball once again creeping close to her feet.

Flum started to panic. The longer the fight dragged on, the worse her situation got.

She ignored the knife embedded in her left arm for the moment and nailed Dein with a right hook to the face that would knock a normal person out cold.

Dein had already pushed himself beyond all physical and mental limits; he hardly noticed. He glared back at Flum, yanked the knife out of her arm, and lunged again—this time for her heart. "You're done, Fluuuuuuum!!"

In Dein's mind, his victory was all but assured. He was far too close for her to use the Souleater at this range. Making matters worse, there were too many eyes around for her to escape. The deck was stacked against her.

What happened next was something neither Dein nor Flum could have predicted.

An eyeball tumbled down, landing on a bare shoulder before rolling down to a juicy-looking bicep.

"Huh?" Dein looked down at his arm and froze.

Why did it attack him? The eyes were on his side; they were only supposed to target Flum...

"I can't believe..."

He was beside himself.

"Oh, I get it..."

It all made sense to Flum, though. The eyeballs were created by the power of Origin, but in the end, they were still Ink's.

While she was scuffling with Dein's men, she noticed that some of the eyes were watching her. Had she attacked them, she probably never would have been saved by Gadhio, Eterna, or Ottilie. She'd probably be done for.

In other words, the eyes chose to help her, and Flum knew instantly who was responsible.

Whose will was so strong it could stand in the face of the gods? Ink had subconsciously fought against God to protect Flum... No, that wasn't right. She was fighting to protect her home.

"Dammit!!" A new arm sprouted. Dein's mind was starting to split; he lost control over the hand he used to stab Flum moments ago.

"Hn!!"

Flum shoved him hard, sending Dein teetering. She drew her Souleater and raised it high. She could barely hold it up. Her grip on the handle was shaky at best.

She put everything she had into keeping the blade steady and true. Just as she'd done when she destroyed the Origin core, Flum put every last ounce of her energy into this final swing.

"Hyaaaaaaah!!"

The black blade cut right into Dein's center mass, though she just wasn't strong enough to make the bone-shattering cut that would split him in two. Her slash wasn't even fatal. It was little more than a flesh wound.

"H...huh?"

But she still had magic at her disposal.

"N-no...s-ss-stop...b-b-b-brat...gaaaauh!!"

The skin where she cut him began to peel away, revealing white bones underneath before they, too, began to turn in on themselves, pressing his organs out.

"Kill...just kill...me...hngaaauh!!"

If she were to name this technique, she'd call it the Resolute Cavalier Arts Expansion: Prana Shaker Reversal. This sword technique literally turned a person inside out, though she suspected it only worked this well given Dein's weakened state.

Dein's groans ceased as the skin tore away from his neck. She could see his larynx tremble.

Flum took a few steps away.

"I hope you suffer, Dein." She made her way to the back room, making sure to step around the eyes as she did.

She left the everted jumble of loosely connected organs out in the main hall of the church. She suspected he'd live a while longer; his heart still pumped, and his lungs rose and fell.

After the hell he put her through, she wasn't about to give Dein an easy death.

**ROLL
OVER
AND
DIE**

Dawn

FLUM MADE HER WAY out of the nave and down a hallway.

Though she was relieved to have finally killed Dein, she found that she had to prop herself against the wall. Just dragging her feet along the ground was a Herculean effort.

Behind her, the eyeballs continued their pursuit. Even with the battle over, she still wasn't completely out of danger yet.

She finally arrived at a door at the far end of the hall. On the other side, she found a large reception area where Milkit and Ink sat together side by side.

"Milkit! In...k?"

Her excited shout was cut short when she noticed a massive figure, around 180 centimeters tall, standing next to them. The person wore a dress with a wide-brimmed hat and had red shoulder-length hair. They had broad shoulders and impressively muscular arms and legs. Something about them struck Flum as...off, somehow.

"Flum, is that you??"

"Master!"

"Aaah, looks like you took that guy out without much trouble. You know, with how he was boasting about killing you, I'm surprised to see you here so soon."

The voice was deep and husky. Who was this figure standing before her?

"I take it you're Flum Apricot, then. I'm Mother, the one who bestows such warm and caring love on our Spiral Children —the ideal mother."

"Step away from them!" Flum drew her sword and pointed it at Mother. So this was the person Ink had been talking about.

"And why should a mother have to step back from their own child? Wasn't it you who called my little Ink such awful names? I doubt Ink here even wants to go back, isn't that right?"

"Well, I..."

Ink's face skewed in a complicated expression as Mother stroked her cheek. She looked glad yet not exactly happy. Her expression told the whole story of what was going on in her head.

Milkit, on the other hand, was scooting away from Mother bit by bit, hoping her movements went unnoticed.

Mother didn't seem to take issue with this. Maybe what Nekt said earlier was true: they had no interest in Milkit.

Once she got far enough away, Milkit sprinted for Flum, throwing herself into her Master's arms.

Though she understood it wasn't the best time or place, Flum couldn't stop herself from scooping Milkit up into a deep embrace.

"Milkit!"

"Master, I'm so glad you came! I thought I'd never see you again."

"I wanted to see you, too, Milkit. I'm so, so glad that you're okay."

She could feel Milkit's warmth, smell her delicate scent.

Certain this wasn't just a figment of their imagination now, they finally let their happiness at being reunited take over.

"Have you been hurt?"

"No, not really. I was just left alone here."

"I see. You just disappeared all of a sudden, I didn't even know what to do..."

Even if Milkit survived, there was still the possibility that she suffered heinous injuries. But here she was, completely unharmed. Flum's greatest concern was behind her. All that remained was to settle the issue of Mother.

"My, you two sure are such good friends. If only I could have passed along some of that warmth and affection to Ink."

Flum stepped away from Milkit for the moment and faced Mother. Her face instantly grew serious.

"You're the one they call Mother? I assume that means you must know about the power Ink possesses. Correct?"

Mother responded simply. "So you're just going to ignore me? Well, fine then. Anyway, yes, I do. I was the one who replaced her heart, after all."

Flum figured "Mother" had to be the leader of the church's research team; here was confirmation.

Mother continued unprompted.

"That was her second birth. They were born of their original mother's womb, and then I performed the ritual to make them my children. I am, in every sense, the mother to Ink and the others."

Flum didn't get the sense that these were the rantings of a zealot, exactly. Like Dein, Mother wanted an empathetic audience.

"But I'd rather just be a normal human," Ink said.

"A human? But why? I mean, sure, you're one of the defective first generation, but you're still better in many ways than a lot of other children. You can create children and become a mother. Just look."

Mother pointed to the open door, where the sea of eyes gathered. Something kept them from entering the room—Ink's presence?

"Your adorable little babies are watching us, Ink."

"Babies..."

"That which you lost and long for most." Mother placed a muscular hand over Ink's eyelids.

"Origin has answered your desires and used his powers to create them from your own body. All your little babies possess the power of Origin and follow your will, Ink, in order to protect us."

"No, this isn't what I want!"

"There's no need to be ashamed; it's quite honorable of you. You're a great mother, Ink. I'm just thrilled that my own beloved child could become a mother herself. It's beautiful, really." Mother pulled Ink into a strong embrace.

This somehow made Origin's power even more terrifying than it already was. Flum doubted love had anything to do with this.

"Listen, Mother, I know this is the first time we've met and all, but..."

"Yeeeees?"

"I really don't think you're fit to be a mother."

A look of annoyance came to Mother's face. Who was Flum to speak like she knew more about these kinds of things?

"And what makes you say that? You don't know anything at all, and yet you speak with such conviction."

"You're not paying attention to the children. All you're doing is pushing your own wants and desires on them and doing whatever's most convenient for you. That's not love at all!"

"That's not up to you or me to decide. Isn't that right, Ink? You can tell that I love you, can't you darling?" Mother pulled Ink even closer until their cheeks were touching, beginning to breathe heavily through the nose.

Ink looked like she was quite used to this type of interaction and didn't seem to be particularly bothered, though she didn't look pleased with it either.

She spoke up hesitantly, her voice faint. "Well, I..."

"You like it how things are, don't you? You want to stay with Mother forever, don't you?"

"Ink!!"

"I don't think you're in any place to talk, not after all the cruel things you said to this poor child."

"I admit that I went too far with what I said to her. But that's something completely different from you trying to force her to meet your needs! Ink has wants, needs, and dreams of her own!"

Her feelings toward Ink were complex, but Flum cared deeply for the girl.

Siding with Mother would be the easy choice. But in that case, all that awaited her was life as one of the Children—a creature.

"I... I want to be a human. I don't want to turn into something that hurts people!"

This was probably the first time Ink had ever stood up to Mother. Normal children go through rebellious phases; they are, after all, humans with their own wills and desires, and won't always do as they're told. Both parents and children usually work past such phases. But...

The smile disappeared from Mother's face upon hearing Ink's words.

"I see." They stood and drew up to Ink.

"In that case, you're useless to me." Mother kicked Ink in the face.

"Yeaaaugh?!"

383

"Hey!"

"Ink??"

This sudden change in demeanor took Flum and Milkit completely by surprise.

"A disobedient child is little better than trash. You could be thrown out, for all I care. What a good-for-nothing ingrate you are, taking for granted all that love I gave you in spite of how useless you were."

Flum ran to Ink's side and pulled her close.

"Are you okay?"

"Flum..." Though her voice was faint, she mustered a weak smile, putting Flum at ease.

Flum turned back to glare at the figure walking away from her. Her anger was readily apparent in her voice. "What the hell do you think you're doing, Mother?!"

Mother turned, looking more annoyed than anything else.

"My, my, aren't you a scary one. I guess I really am the only one who can take care of these children."

Four other children appeared instantly behind Mother.

"That's...!"

She instantly recognized Luke, Fwiss, and Nekt. The fourth one, a white-haired girl, must have been Mute, the one who made the gestalts of the church knight's and Dein's men..

"Oh, what happened to you, Nekt?"

"That...that bastard hurt me when I was trying to stop him! I'm gonna kill him for real next time!"

He had a nasty gash running down the side of his face. Judging by the explosions Flum heard during their earlier battle, he must have proved a formidable opponent. Luke and Fwiss, on the other hand, only suffered minor wounds from their own battles with Eterna and Ottilie.

With arms spread out, Mother smiled broadly. "Ah, that's right. Allow me to introduce my adorable little children, Flum. These are the Spiral..."

Flum cut in before they could finish. "Your Spiral Children, I know. Luke, Fwiss, Nekt, and Mute right? Ink told me about them."

Mother was clearly annoyed at this. "What a useless piece of garbage you are, you ingrate."

Ink trembled in Flum's arms. Flum shot a glare Mother's way. Mother didn't seem to take notice.

I'm in a pretty bad spot right now...

She was now faced with four creatures able to stand toe to toe against legendary heroes and a lieutenant general.

This doesn't look good.

The power differential alone was overwhelming.

What's worse, Flum was the only one on her side in fighting shape. If Mother decided to fight, the three of them could easily be wiped out.

Fortunately, Mother didn't seem interested.

"You don't need to look so concerned. According to my Children, Origin has yet to reach consensus about what to do with you."

"Origin...reach consensus?"

Mother offered up a knowing smile in response to Flum's unspoken concerns. "Oh, you'll find out soon enough. Basically, a decision still needs to be made on whether we're best off using you or killing you. We can't kill you yet."

Fwiss tugged on Mother's sleeve. "C'mon, Mother, let's goooo."

"Fwiss is right, there's no reason for us to waste any more of our time on Ink and these other jerks. We should jus' decide now."

"Now, now, you know I intend to provide all my children with a fair chance, Luke."

Luke tsk'd in annoyance at Mother's gentle scolding.

"Mother, I've gotta pee."

"Oh, well then, we'd best do something about that in a hurry, Mute. Nekt, could you be a dear?"

"Of course, Mother."

Nekt stuck his hands out into the air, palms up. A moment later, Flum saw energy begin to swirl in the air.

"Ah, right, one last thing I need to take care of." Mother turned to Flum before Nekt finished casting his Connection spell.

"To be completely honest, those eyes are a real hassle. If you could just use Reversal on her core and take care of her for me, that'd be great."

"What's wrong with you?!"

"I'm just being logical, is all. In fact, I'd say you're the one losing your cool here. Ah well, I didn't actually think you'd help me anyway. Not like it's even that simple. It just seems like a waste to let a blind, weak, useless girl live."

There was no getting through to anyone this selfish and unreasonable.

Flum's teeth creaked as she clenched her jaw. "And you have the gall to call yourself a mother?!"

"She's a stranger to me now. Besides, Ink kicked me to the curb, remember? There's no reason for you to be mad. But whatever, I'd best be going. See you later, Flum."

Nekt closed his hands into fists, summoning forth his power.

"I'm not letting you get away that easily!!"

Flum drew her Souleater and let out a Prana Shaker, but they were gone before it had a chance to make contact.

With no targets left to take out her anger on, she felt... empty. Flum balled her hands up in frustration.

Ink turned to Flum, a look of concern etched on her face, as Milkit stood by and watched over the two. "Sorry, Flum..."

"What're you apologizing for, Ink? I'm the one who should be sorry for all the awful things I said to you."

"But it's true, you're not wrong. I do turn into some kind of creature at night and spit out those awful things... Just being alive causes so much trouble to all of you."

"That's...!"

She couldn't bring herself to say that it wasn't true. As long as Ink lived in this form, more and more lives would be lost. Flum and her friends could never stop running. It'd be hard to ever get a restful night's sleep with Ink around.

She might be able to deal with a few sleepless nights, but to do so for the rest of her life felt like a death sentence.

"It's fine."

"What do you mean? What's fine?"

"I'm just glad that I got to experience you saving me one last time and be able to talk with you and Milkit here at my side. I'm... I'm happy. You all said such kind things to me, and that's all I can ask for. So let's just end this here, okay?"

"Don't just give up like that!!"

"I'm not giving up! I'm making a choice. I'd rather die a human than live as a monster."

"That's not what I came here for."

"Then what do you plan on doing? As long as I'm alive, I'm going to keep hurting people. You, Milkit, Eterna...even Sara! If the only way I can live is by making others suffer, then I'd rather just die right here and now."

Flum wanted to shout at Ink and tell her that she was wrong, that she would do something about it. Yet she also knew just how powerless she was. She was just starting to get a handle on the fact that there were things out there that she could do nothing about.

There were some times when just giving up was the right option.

Ink kneeled and spread out her hands. She was smiling.

"All right, please do it." She spoke in such a sweet tone.

Flum's lips quivered. She choked back her sobs, but the tears stubbornly began to flow.

Was there really nothing she could do? Was the only option left to destroy Ink's core?

If she did, Ink would die.

There had to be another way, but even then, could Flum pull it off?

All she had at her disposal were the Souleater, her freezing enchantment, Reversal, and her prana. No matter which way she tried to fit the pieces together, she couldn't come up with a way to save Ink.

"Besides, I'd be happiest if it was you who killed me, Flum. I mean, y'know, it feels more like I can die as a human that way." Her voice was startlingly cheerful. It was clearly more to make her own peace with it than for Flum's benefit.

Flum really didn't want to kill her, but doing nothing would also be grossly irresponsible. She escaped the clutches of death at Dein's hands just to make it to Ink. She fought this hard because she wanted to make the decision over whether Ink would live or die.

And she'd already chosen.

It was what Ink wanted, too.

In that case, there wasn't anything left to do...but... kill her.

Flum's shoulders heaved, and she sobbed openly as she walked slowly toward Ink. Ink blurred in her vision through all the tears, looking almost like a ghost. Her smile managed to shine through. Somehow seeing that forced smile hurt all the more. Flum's cheek twitched as big, fat tears poured down them.

She still had a job to do.

Each step became harder and harder, as if she had to force her legs to obey her will. Every time her foot touched the floor, she felt another lead weight pile on her.

"Haah..."

She tensed her muscles, let out a breath, and took one step. The Souleater clattered and clanked as it dragged across the floor. A cold sweat covered her body, leaving her shirt damp and clammy.

She let out another choked sob as she arrived in front of Ink.

Flum clasped her hands tightly around the hilt and lifted the sword until the tip wavered over Ink's heart. Ink tensed up at the touch of the cold metal against her skin.

"That's right. Please make it quick, okay? I really don't like pain..." She was still trying to sound strong.

Flum understood, though she didn't want to think about it. No one really wanted to die. At the end of the day, everyone just wanted to be happy if they could. Ink had to be thinking the same thing. She was just a ten-year-old girl, after all. Flum wanted to deny that Ink's desire to live on was untenable.

She didn't want to admit it, but there was no other choice available to her.

"M-master!" Milkit ran to Ink's side and clutched the younger girl tightly.

"I know it's not a slave's place to express their opinion to their master, but I believe that Ink is not too different from you and me! She's in her own dark place, feeling lost and alone, and given up on everything. Even her own hopes and dreams. Somewhere deep in her heart, she's still crying out for help, I know it! Master, you took my hand and pulled me out of such depths too. I know it must be difficult, but please, do the same for Ink as well. I... I..."

"Milkit..."

"It's no use, Milkit. If we stop now, then I'm just gonna be too scared to die later. Look, there's really no other way, Flum, so please just get it over with and stab me." Ink's voice was still upbeat, though it began to waver the longer she spoke.

If she could open her eyes, they would undoubtedly be filled with tears.

"You...you're just putting up a front, aren't you?"

"...Am not."

"Of course you are! I mean, it'd be strange if you weren't! You're going to die, ya know, and just a few days after you finally made it out into the real world! There's still so much you don't know—so much you must want to know out there! Don't lie to me, Ink. Please, tell me what you're really thinking!"

"What good would that do? Is there any reason to tell you how I really feel other than to make everyone in this room all the more miserable?"

But that wasn't it at all. If Ink was being stubborn in her pretending to be strong, then so was Flum in her insistence on Ink telling her the truth.

"Even if there isn't a good reason, I still want to know."

Flum didn't want Ink to die under false pretenses. At the very least, she wanted her to be herself in her last minutes of life. It was a cruel request, perhaps, but it came out of a nice place.

Ink struggled to get her reply out. "Don't confuse wanting the truth with wanting to be kind."

"But you understand, don't you? Anyone... Everyone would want to live on in a warm, comfortable place. It's only natural."

Ink's whole body began to tremble as the weakness she tried so hard to hide started to show. "I... I... of course I want to live!!"

Ink was still young, not quite mature enough to hide her true feelings 'til the bitter end. Now that her facade came crumbling down, there was no way she could build it back up. She started letting out all her hopes, dreams, every little selfish desire she ever had.

"I... I'm only ten years old! I've only lived ten whole years on this planet. How could it all just end so soon??"

"That's right, you're absolutely right."

"Why do I have to die? Why do I become such an abominable creature? Why...why can't I just live an ordinary life like everyone else?! I don't want Origin's power! All I ever wanted was to just be normal!"

"Ink..."

"B-but...none of that changes anything. I know that. That's why I didn't want to tell you. Dying is the only option left to me, so I figured I'd just keep quiet and accept my fate."

"...Right."

"You're a jerk, Flum."

"Sorry."

"And you too, Milkit."

"I'm sorry, Ink."

They both knew she was right. All they could do was apologize.

Ink laughed in spite of herself at how quickly Milkit responded. It was an honest laugh, right from the heart.

"Thanks, you two. I feel a little better now."

Getting all that off her chest at least lightened some of her emotional burden—a burden that Flum would now have to bear. But that was as it should be.

"But that's all there is to say. I feel a bit better about things, but that doesn't change the situation one little bit. So are you satisfied that you got to hear what I really think? Now you can just get on with it, please."

Flum let her eyelids fall closed and took a deep breath. No matter how much she thought it over, there was no other choice. She just needed to work up the courage. All she had to do was run the blade through Ink's body and destroy her core. Then it would all be over.

No matter how long she might live, or how many trials she would have to face and overcome, she knew she would have to carry the burden of taking Ink's life for the rest of her days.

Flum swore to herself that she would never do something like this again. She would let it drive her in her future battles with the church. At some point, Ink's death would be glorified as a tale that brought people to tears.

"You're...not really going to do it, are you, Master?"

She had no choice. What other option was there?

Ink hadn't been a human from the moment they first met. The Origin core pulsating where her heart should have been made her one of the inhuman Spiral Children capable of wielding extraordinary power.

Shy of going back in time, there was nothing that Flum could do to save her. The discussion was no longer one of saving her or not, but rather who would be at Ink's side when she died.

Logically speaking, there was no reason for Flum to feel so guilty about this. It was just as Ink said: the faster she killed the young girl, the sooner she would be relieved from this living hell. She needed to move on.

"...Move...on."

Once she killed Ink, she would move forward with her life.

...What was forward, anyway? What proof did she have that the direction she intended to move was even forward to begin with? Sure, killing this girl with the power of Origin and using that as inspiration to carry on her fight was probably the righteous path.

"Master..."

But was that really the "forward" Flum was hoping for? Wasn't it possible she was mistaken, as Milkit pointed out? She had no idea what the world at large thought about these things. Nor did she care. At the very least, she knew that this was far removed from what she, Flum Apricot, felt was right.

It'd only been a few days since they first met. It wasn't much different with Milkit, either. How short their time together was didn't matter. Flum wanted to save Ink. That would be her "forward."

Who cared what common sense or the logical point of view had to say? Progress was about moving in the direction that you felt was right to go.

"No... I can't."

It was stupid to think it would all be over just by killing someone you wanted to protect. Would Flum turn her back on Milkit if she fell into such dire straits?

Of course not. If she did, she would never forgive herself. Just how long could she really go on living viewing herself as the worst of all evils? Such a decision would be her own form of retreat. It would be braver to choose to die.

Would that be the right thing to do, then? Is that what should be done?

Is that...even right?

"No, that's not the right thing to do. I..." The sword dropped from Flum's hand with a heavy thud.

"Master...!" A look of relief washed across Milkit's face, though her expression hinted that she knew this would be Flum's decision all along.

The Souleater faded into a burst of light the moment it hit the ground.

"C'mon, Flum, it's fine."

"No, it isn't fine. You want to live, don't you? Aren't there things you still want to do?"

"Then what do we do? Don't just fiddle around like this and spout pretty words if you don't have any ideas!"

The two girl's rising voices echoed throughout the room.

"How...how...wait!"

She needed some way to save Ink. If she could just destroy the core, get something to replace it, and transplant that into her body, then she would be all right. Destroying the core would be no problem—at least for Flum. The real problem was finding and transplanting a substitute.

"There's just gotta be something out there somewhere. Something that could be used as a substitute for the core..."

But how convenient would it be to have something so near at hand that could function in its place?

"We need to look for something that can keep Ink alive instead of the core..."

"There's nothing like that out there."

"Umm, Master...do you think we could just use someone else's heart and transplant that into her instead?"

Ink laughed.

"Milkit, that's crazy talk. And who would do that for us? Do you think Flum could actually carry out that kind of operation??"

"I'm certain Eterna could."

"Right, Eterna!!"

"C'mon, get serious! Even Eterna couldn't do something like that. I know I'm a kid, but that doesn't mean I'm stupid, okay?! There's no way that's possible."

"You don't know that for sure, not until we have a chance to ask her."

"And even assuming it was, what about the heart? Where would we find a living, beating heart? Killing someone for theirs defeats the whole purpose."

A living, beating heart belonging to someone who she didn't care if they lived or died...

Flum knew exactly where to find one of those.

"I'm sure Dein's heart is still beating right now."

They could transplant that into Ink. Said aloud, the whole idea sounded almost comical. Even if all of these things were doable, then how would they keep Ink alive between destroying the core and completing the transplant?

They would need something other than a heart to keep her alive temporarily.

Did something like that even exist...?

Flum let out a light chuckle as a possible solution came to mind.

"C'mon and just kill me! Please, don't drag out my suffering anymore!!"

Ink turned in desperation in Flum's direction while the older girl watched the door, awaiting Eterna's entrance. Just then, a powerful blast of air blew through the door, destroying all the eyes in its path. Gadhio, Eterna, and Ottilie walked calmly through the now cleared pathway.

"Flum, I see you made it!"

"Looks like we're finally together again. Glad to see you're still alive, kid."

"Those little punks got away. They're even more impressive than Werner!"

"You guys made it!"

A confident grin spread on Gadhio's face. "I'd hardly be able to call myself a hero if that was all it took to beat me."

"So that's Ink, one of the Spiral Children?"

"I'm glad to see you're okay, kid."

"I sense that this isn't quite the happy reunion it could be, though."

The look of concern on Milkit's face and the tears drenching Flum and Ink's cheeks probably gave away that there was something wrong. Eterna approached Ink and knelt until she was at face level with Ink. She used her finger to wipe away her tears, though they were quickly replaced with new ones.

Even though she couldn't see, Ink knew who was touching her cheek.

"Eternaaaa..." Ink sounded lonely and needy.

"What happened?"

"Th-those eyes that've been chasing you guys around... well...I made 'em. I'm some kind of living weapon."

Ottilie seemed to be the only one taken by surprise at this revelation. "She's the one behind those eyeballs?"

Apparently Eterna, after all the time she spent with Ink, had already considered this possibility.

"I'm sorry for lying to you, Eterna..."

"Aww, I know that you weren't even aware yourself, Ink. Don't worry about it."

"But...I can't control this power. No one can. I asked Flum to put an end to it all and just kill me, but..."

Eterna already knew how this story ended.

"She couldn't kill you. I know Flum."

"There must be some way we can save you."

"There isn't!!"

"Of course I want to help Ink any way I can. But first off, I'd like you to tell me why you think she can't be helped. I know there's something strange about her heart, but that's about it."

"Exactly, the problem is with her heart," Gadhio chimed in.

"Shortly after she and the other Children were born, the church performed an operation to replace their hearts with these things called cores: crystals that contain the power of Origin."

"Thank you, Gadhio. So if we destroy the core, Ink will die as well. I guess that neatly sums up why there's no obvious way to help her."

"Right, so Milkit and I..." Flum half-expected to be laughed at due to the sheer impracticality of it all but decided to tell the rest of the group her plan anyway. "Well, we were thinking maybe we could use Dein's heart as a transplant. He's still in the chapel right now."

"That's a pretty crazy plan you two worked up."

"Like I said, that's impossible! So please, just hurry up and kill me!"

"That was Ink's take on it...but I thought that maybe you might have some insight, Eterna."

"It's no use! Even Eterna can't pull off something that crazy, and..."

Eterna cut her off there. "Yes, I can."

The room went silent. For a moment, everyone thought Eterna might be joking. The idea of taking a heart from one body and putting it into another was unheard of.

Realizing that the rest of the group was still filled with doubt, Eterna went on to explain. "There are ancient procedures that were used to transplant hearts. I could do it if I wanted."

With that explanation out of the way, it seemed much less likely to have just been a mistimed joke. So it was true. She could do it. But...would they do it?

"R-really? Y-you could save her life, Eterna?"

"Well, it's not impossible."

"Hear that, Ink? She can do it! There is a way for you to live a normal, human life!"

"...No way..."

Ink was the only one still in complete disbelief. She just couldn't believe this was anything more than a cruel joke someone was trying to play on her.

Eterna turned her attention back to the young girl and spoke to her in the softest, sweetest voice she could. "I wouldn't lie to you, Ink. You should know that."

"So...you mean...you really can do it? You can save me?"

"Well, I'll certainly do everything I can for you. But we'll need the stars to align in order for this to be a success."

It was a far cry from a sure thing, but Eterna was confident that she could pull it off if they could make all of the proper arrangements.

"Flum, I'm guessing that nasty sack of meat and bones out in the chapel is Dein?"

"Right! I was thinking we could use that."

"Well, I know I saw it moving, but there are several problems with it. There's the size difference for starters, then whether or not it's the right blood type, to say nothing of if Ink's body will reject it...but all we can do is hope and pray about that. Then there's also the problem of what to do for the period in which the core is broken but the heart hasn't been transplanted yet."

"You know, I was thinking...just hear me out before you call it stupid..."

There just might have been a way to get it done, and Flum had one idea that might help.

"Gadhio, you said that prana is kinda like life energy, didn't you?"

"You could think of it that way, sure."

"In that case, then, would it be possible to keep someone alive using prana?"

Assuming that prana would be enough to sustain Ink for just a few hours, or even just a few minutes, then Eterna should be able to perform the operation.

Gadhio thought it over for a minute. "There are several techniques under the Cavalier Arts that allow you to surpass your human limits. I suppose I could probably do it."

"So then...!"

"But whether my energy alone would be enough to sustain her is a serious concern, since there will be a great deal of energy lost with her body opened up like that. I don't know if it would last through the whole operation."

"Then I'll join you."

Ottilie stepped forward. "At its core, the Genocide Arts restrict the functions of your opponent's body. In battle it binds an enemy's limbs, but used properly, it can also be used to staunch blood loss or serve as an anesthetic. We actually do it a lot in the military."

"So do you think if you and Gadhio worked together, you might be able to sustain Ink's life?"

"I think so," said Gadhio. "You don't think Henriette would get mad at you for bringing the Cavalier Arts and Genocide Arts together?"

"Aww, my sister isn't that petty."

After his many years as an adventurer in the capital, Gadhio was well known among the upper brass of the army.

There were many similarities between the Cavalier and Genocide Arts. Henriette considered Gadhio something of a rival.

"But I have to admit, I've never heard of a heart

transplant before. Was this some kind of technique from before recovery magic developed far enough to properly heal people?"

"You could think of it as a kind of ancient healing technique, though there are likely still a few people within the capital who could still perform it."

"Is it allowed by the church? I know they tend to have a monopoly on almost all medical procedures."

It was the church, after all, that forbade almost all mundane healing, including the medicinal herbs once commonly used among the people. It seemed likely that the church would be quick to stomp out things like heart transplant surgeries if they ever caught wind of it.

"Well, when you think about it, Ink's heart was transplanted with a core. So that means it has to be possible to do the opposite."

"Now that you mention it, it seems like the church still gladly uses what they bar everyone else from."

"The church is crooked in all kinds of ways."

"I guess that's true, but...it just seems like so many lives could've been saved if these things were allowed."

"The church doesn't care about the lives of your average person."

Of course the low-level nuns and priests worked fervently day after day to help their patients, but they were also quick to cut people off the moment it was clear they were no longer profitable.

Finally Milkit spoke up to Eterna, wearing a frown on her face.

"Umm... I'm not really sure if this is the best thing to ask, but..."

"What is it?"

"You seem to know an awful lot about these things, Eterna. Do you have some kind of connection with the church?"

Even Ottilie, a lieutenant general of the royal army, didn't know about this. Eterna gave a gentle snort. It only made sense that people would have their suspicions.

"No, I've nothing to do with the church. I learned about these things long, long ago, from somewhere else."

"Aah, I see. Sorry for sounding like I doubted you, Eterna. I was simply curious."

"No worries. I would've asked the same, really. I figured I'd have to mention it someday."

There were still many things they didn't know about Eterna, but the group knew they could trust her. No one else opted to ask any further questions on the subject. The successful transplant of Ink's heart was the most important thing at the moment.

"Listen, Ink, since you're going to be entrusting me with

your life, I'm not going to sugarcoat anything. I intend to tell you everything exactly as it is, and as I'm sure you've gathered, there's still a lot we don't know. I can't promise we'll be successful, and there's still a possibility you'll die."

None of this was intended to be a threat. It was simply the truth. Ink didn't look afraid.

"Just a little while ago, I was pretty much condemned to death. I don't think of this as a possibility to die but a possibility to live."

Between Eterna, Gadhio, and Ottilie's nearly limitless strength, and Flum and Milkit's sheer refusal to give up, this gave Ink a first, and final, chance at a normal life.

"Do you think I'd really say anything other than yes?"

A bright smile sprung to Ink's face. It was hard to believe she was moments away from a life-threatening procedure.

Eterna smiled and brushed a hand gently through Ink's hair.

◇◇◇

From there, it was a battle against time.

Eterna hurried back to the chapel and used her water magic to encapsulate Dein's body and bring it back to the room.

Milkit brought her hand to her mouth at the sight of the grotesque mass of flesh, muscles, and organs.

It was still twitching. It really said a lot of Dein's refusal to die.

Flum and Gadhio waited at Ink's side, watching the nervous young girl as they waited for the time when they would need to perform their respective tasks.

"On your mark, Flum. Whenever you're ready."

"Got it!"

Flum held Dein's dagger. It would cut just deep enough for her to make contact with the core and destroy it, while keeping the injury to Ink as small as possible.

She pressed the small silver blade against Ink's chest.

"I know it hurts, but just hang in there."

Anesthetic wasn't an option. Though Ottilie's Genocide Arts reduced the pain, Ink could still feel what was going on.

"...Hey, Flum."

Ink called out to her just as she was about to plunge the knife in.

"Yes?"

"I just wanted to say sorry for being so difficult. I know you and Milkit were doing everything in your power to find a way to save my life."

"No worries. After all, I was the one insisting there was a way to save you when I had no idea what I was talking about."

"No, really, it's all on me. If I live through this, and we go home together, I promise to pay it back to you."

"Sounds good. I'm counting on it." Flum closed her eyes, took a deep breath, and began to summon up all of her magic, picturing it as a sphere building up within her body. She let that energy flow down her arms, through the palms of her hands, down the hilt, and into the blade of the knife.

She was looking for the core and Origin's power locked within it.

The Reversal magic would travel through the blade until it made contact with the crystal and destroyed it.

Once she had the image firmly in mind, she locked it in place. Now she just had to carry out the actions exactly as planned.

She pushed down on the hilt and felt the knife slide into Ink.

"Hnng..."

"Reversion!"

SNAP!

The magic ran down the blade and began to turn the core inside out, creating a negative energy loop. Unable to cope with the power running through it, the crystal snapped cleanly in two inside her body.

Ink felt like she just lost something incredibly important.

"The eyes...they're drying up..."

The church was strewn with drifts of withered eyeballs.

"Haah!"

Ottilie lunged into a saber-thrust, releasing her sanguine energy into Ink's body.

The Genocide Arts-infused blood began to slow her bodily functions and reduce the extent of her injury.

Ink's face took on a distant, glazed-over look. She was still conscious but barely.

"Hnph!" Gadhio acted in near perfect unison with Ottilie. He placed his hands on Ink and began transferring his prana into her body to replenish her rapidly dwindling life energy.

Ink's body started to go cold the moment the core was taken. Her body twitched and grew warm again as soon as the prana flowed into her.

"Aaah...ah...auauh..."

Her mouth hung slack as her limbs started to twitch. The prana would sustain her life for now, but it wouldn't last long: the needs of her body were too great.

"Hang in there, Ink," Flum whispered under her breath as she stepped back to let Gadhio and Ottilie do their work.

It was Eterna's turn.

"All right, this is about to hurt. A lot. But I'll do my best to keep it to a minimum." With a wave of her hands, an array of water scalpels and other cutting implements appeared before her. A moment later, water tendrils appeared behind her and grabbed the blades.

The speed and precision at which she worked was absolutely stunning. Even from where Flum stood, she could hardly keep track of what was happening.

The tendrils were far more precise than any hand could ever be, and the water scalpels made quick work of opening Ink up.

In short order they had Ink's chest open, the core removed from all the surrounding arteries, her new heart connected to all the surrounding valves, her wounds sutured. Eterna somehow managed to perform the work of a whole surgical team all by herself.

"Nnnggggaaaaaaaa..." Ink groaned from the pain, a low thrum from the back of her throat.

Despite all their efforts, it was still an exquisitely painful procedure. Few people could endure such an exercise. The only thing that kept her going was the image of finally being able to live a normal life with Eterna, Flum, and Milkit.

After getting permission from Eterna, Flum and Milkit stepped forward and each took one of Ink's hands into their own as they whispered reassurances to the young girl.

"Haaaah..." Eterna let out a heavy sigh and leaned back as a water tendril wiped the sweat from her forehead. The exhaustion was clear on her face. Even after spending all night running from the eyes, she was still able to stay completely focused on the delicate task at hand.

Over the days they spent together, Eterna grew quite fond of Ink. She, too, wanted the young girl to live a normal life.

Dein's heart began to pump inside Ink's chest, and Eterna finished sealing the incision.

The operation finished, Eterna wiped her brow with her wrist.

"Well, we did everything we could." She slumped back into a sitting position on the floor.

Ink winced in pain and lost consciousness. The young girl was completely spent. Her chest rose and fell in a slow rhythm, and her new heart was pumping blood throughout her body.

"I think we...did it?"

"Yes, I'm sure we did. The eyes have all stopped moving, even though she's still alive."

"Well, I really hope that's the case."

Gadhio's face was ashen as he turned to look out toward the hallway. "Now we just have to wait and see if it takes."

Flum bowed sincerely to Eterna, Gadhio, and Ottilie. "Thank you, everyone."

"No need to thank me. Being able to help Ink is thanks enough for me."

"Same. I may have never met her before, but I want to spare any life I can. I'm just happy to have been of assistance."

"I didn't do that much, but I'm glad I was able to be a part of this."

They looked absolutely exhausted, though they also seemed relieved. Everyone was smiling.

Milkit looked glum, however.

"I guess… I was the only one who couldn't do anything…"

She had desperately wanted to save her young friend and that made her own powerlessness all the more difficult.

Eterna turned to Milkit and smiled. "If you weren't here, Flum would never have worked up the strength to come this far. You were perhaps most important of all."

This caught Milkit off guard.

Flum's face flushed red at this sudden accusation. "Wait, what?? So you're saying I don't have any drive of my own??"

"That's true, she does look quite a bit different from when she was back in the party."

"You too, Gadhio?"

Flum looked dejected, eliciting a round of laughter from Eterna, Gadhio, and even Ottilie. Milkit burnt red in embarrassment.

Flum scowled and hugged herself as she withdrew from the crowd.

"Eek! Master??"

"It's fine, it's all totally fine. After all, if it weren't for Milkit here I'd be tooooootally useless anyway!"

The words got to her more than they should have. That was probably because they hit too close to home. If not for Milkit, she wouldn't be standing there.

Milkit pulled Flum into a tender embrace and whispered lightly into her ear. "But, you know, I need you too, Master."

Being apart, even by the shortest of distances, tore at Milkit's sanity. Anxiety took root deep within her, and she felt short of breath. She hugged Flum tightly, wishing deep in her heart that the two would never be apart again.

Flum's cheeks burnt bright red as she held Milkit close.

Eterna broke out into a Cheshire grin, and Ottilie looked at the two in envy. If only she and her sister could be so close.

Gadhio smiled warmly as he watched the two in silence, though this only added fuel to the fire of embarrassment.

"H-hey, it's not like that!!"

Even she didn't know what that meant, but she felt compelled to say something. The more she tried to explain, the larger Eterna's grin grew.

They weren't entirely wrong. Day by day, Milkit became all the more important to Flum. This became all the more apparent by the fear and pain of loss that gripped her heart when she lost Milkit, if only temporarily.

Though she ultimately got Milkit back safe and sound, she felt that the pain she briefly experienced brought the two even closer. The sense of ease and comfort that enveloped her holding Milkit in her arms again was proof enough of that.

Even as her face flushed pink, Flum reached down and placed her own hand over Milkit's.

"Oooh..." Eterna caught sight of this movement and chuckled.

Fine, let them watch, then. Flum didn't care.

The warmth of Flum's hand instantly took Milkit by surprise, though a smile slowly crept to her cheeks as she closed her eyes and relished the warmth.

"I hope Ink wakes up soon."

"Me too."

The two looked down at the sleeping girl. Everyone in the room was convinced the operation was a success. The possibility that she wouldn't awaken was the furthest thing from their minds.

Outside the church, the sun slowly began to breach the horizon and chase away the darkness, casting a bright orange glow across the city.

The long night was finally over, and the group was reunited for a brand-new day.

ROLL
OVER
AND
DIE

An Uncomfortable Truth

FLUM COULD HEAR a bird's call off in the distance.

Her eyelids opened to reveal a familiar wooden ceiling. The light coming in through the gap in the curtain was so bright she had to bring her hand up to block it.

"It's morning...I think."

Her throat was dry.

She propped herself up on an elbow, ran a hand through her unkempt hair, and looked around the room.

There was a dresser, a desk, another bed... All of the furniture was exactly where it should be. She was in her own bedroom.

"I...think I came home yesterday and just fell into bed..."

That was the extent of Flum's memory after returning home. But they'd returned home just after sunrise, and now it was morning. Which could only mean...

"Did I sleep for an entire day?"

That was definitely a lot longer than she intended to sleep, but she clearly used up a lot of her energy reserves after an entire night running around and fighting well into the morning. Even with all her endurance-boosting equipment, her body had limits.

She felt sore all over from having spent so much time in bed.

"Aaaaaaaahh." Flum let out a massive yawn and stretched as she stared blankly around the room. She still wasn't entirely awake.

She shook her head to make herself focus, only for her eyes to stop on one particular point right next to her. There lay Milkit, dressed in her pajamas, sleeping fitfully at Flum's side. Her perfectly pale skin practically shone in the morning sun.

On a second look, she noticed Milkit's bed was empty.

Perhaps she'd just been lonely, or maybe she was worried about Flum and didn't want to be apart.

In any case, for some reason or another, Milkit crawled into Flum's bed while she was sleeping.

"Gah, she's so cute even when she's asleep..."

A silly grin came to Flum's lips as she reached to stroke Milkit's cheek and run a hand through her hair.

The fact that she was wearing pajamas at least told her Milkit had been awake long enough to change and get ready for bed after they returned home, unlike herself.

Whatever became of Gadhio, Eterna...and Ink?

Flum knew she could probably find the answer if she just got out of bed and went downstairs, but she shook her head. She'd wait until she had a chance to wake up a bit more.

She continued to run her hand through Milkit's hair and across her cheek, then gently tickled at her ears.

It wasn't like she was interfering with her sleep or anything. Judging by the height of the sun outside, it was already well past time to wake up anyway. She might as well wake her up.

"Nnmm... Mashteer..."

"Oh, are you awake?"

Milkit's eyes were still closed. Flum giggled to herself.

"Or did I suddenly appear in your dreams?"

"Master...don't go..."

Those words pulled at Flum's heartstrings. She felt hot all over all of a sudden. Considering everything Milkit went through, she could understand the sense of anxiety she must be feeling.

"You can't just play with my heart like that. That's not fair, y'know..." Flum countered by prodding Milkit's soft cheek with her finger and tracing patterns on it.

Milkit's eyes fluttered upon to look up at Flum. "Master?"

Flum beamed down at the younger girl. "G'mornin', Milkit."

Milkit didn't have to try to make Flum feel special. Just being there, the sound of her voice, seeing her there in front of her was enough.

"Ah, good morning, Master."

The mere sight of Flum was enough to bring a warm smile to Milkit's face.

The two had long since evolved past the relationship of a mere master and slave, that much they knew.

"You surprised me, appearing in my bed all of a sudden like that."

"I'm sorry, Master. You wouldn't wake up, and I began to worry that you never would."

"Sorry to make you worry, Milkit. I guess I was pretty exhausted."

"I'm sure you were. You had a pretty tough time."

"So did you."

"I was just captured, is all. You did quite a lot, Master, and it's only thanks to you that Ink and I made it home okay."

"I never could have done it alone."

"Maybe so, but even Eterna and Gadhio mentioned that your presence was vital."

Flum was filled with a mix of embarrassment and happiness at receiving praise from her companions on the great journey.

There was nothing better than for someone as useless and pointless as herself to earn praise from the people she admired.

"Oh, speaking of which, did Ink wake up? Is she doing okay?"

"Yes, she's resting in Eterna's room now. The most difficult time has passed, but it will take at least six months until she's totally in the clear."

"Six months? Wow, that's quite a while. I guess that's really not too bad, considering we put a completely different person's heart inside her."

Eterna probably hadn't mentioned that earlier to avoid dampening everyone's mood.

"We should probably stay away until her wounds have fully healed, at least. Eterna mentioned something about a risk of...infection, I think she said."

"Aww, I really want to see her, but I'm just glad that she's still alive. That's enough for me."

As long as she knew that, she could wait patiently.

Now that she knew Ink was doing well, Flum finally got out of bed together with Milkit, and the two got dressed for the day.

Her clothes were absolutely trashed during the previous night's battles; Flum had to completely change out of everything. However, due to all the fights she'd been in lately, her wardrobe had grown quite small. She'd need to buy more clothes, and soon.

She just grabbed the first thing she found in the closet before sitting down in front of the mirror to do her hair.

Milkit wrapped her face and dressed herself. She watched Flum intently, looking concerned.

"What is it?"

Milkit was even more dressed up than usual today; she wore a traditional navy maid uniform with a white apron. It suited her perfectly.

"Well, there's something I need to give you, Master." Milkit grabbed something from a dresser drawer. She stood still for a moment, her eyes shut with indecision.

Flum watched Milkit in the mirror, uncertain of what she wanted to give her. Finally, she turned to face Milkit directly.

Milkit held the item to her chest for a few more moments before making up her mind and turning to Flum.

"H-here it is." She held a hairpin with a light blue,

semi-transparent flower on the end. It sparkled magnificently under the light shining through the window.

"Oh, my! It's so pretty, Milkit. Is this...is this a present for me?"

"Y-yes. I know it hardly compares to the wonderful gifts you've given me, but...well, I planned on giving it to you earlier, but you were so hurt about losing Sara that I thought it wasn't the right timing. It's a bit late, I know, but..."

"Aww, I'm happy to receive anything at all from you, Milkit."

"Thank you, Master. I made it myself as a small token of my appreciation."

"You made this?? Wow! You're amazing!"

Milkit's cheeks flushed.

This was the first present Flum had ever received from Milkit, and that made it a treasure in its own right. But being handmade, too? That made it an heirloom right then and there.

It seemed almost like a shame to even wear it. But, on the other hand, she felt that she absolutely had to as a sign of appreciation for Milkit's hard work.

"Thank you, Milkit! I love, just absolutely love it! I'm never going to let it out of my sight."

"It's really nothing special..."

"No, really, it is! Do you mind if I use it now?"

"Of course not!"

Flum lifted up her bangs and slid the hairpin in to hold them in place. After gazing at her new hairstyle in the mirror for a moment, she grinned brightly. Milkit beamed at the sight of her master proudly displaying her handmade hairpin. Their eyes met in the mirror, causing them to blush.

◇◇◇

Flum and Milkit found Gadhio, dressed in a simple housecoat, sitting downstairs and looking out the window.

This was the first time Flum had seen him out of his armor.

He struck an impressive pose just sitting there gazing out the window, like the scene was taken straight out of a painting.

"Good morning, Gadhio."

"Ah, Flum... Milkit."

Milkit hurriedly bowed her head upon being addressed. Despite the time they spent together the day before, she still wasn't quite used to his overpowering presence.

"I'm impressed that you're up after just a day of rest, burning through all the prana you did."

"Is a whole day of sleeping actually fast?"

Hearing her concerns confirmed was a bit of a shock. She'd need to be more careful with her energy use going forward.

"So is this how you usually dress, Gadhio?"

"Aah, right. You've never seen me like this."

None of his massive black armor, which currently sat in another room of the house, was even Epic class, as far as she could tell. For someone of his skill and rank, it would almost be a given that he would be sporting Epic gear, but there was something about the black armor that he preferred.

While Flum and Gadhio sat at the table together and got caught up, Milkit jogged into the kitchen to begin preparing breakfast.

"I know it's a bit late to mention this, but I was honestly surprised to see you show up to come save me."

"Same here. I hadn't expected to find you out there slinging around a broadsword in a pitched battle, Flum. With the mark of a slave on your cheek, no less. Whatever happened to you after leaving the party?"

Even though he was smiling, there was still something slightly scary about Gadhio's expression. He must have been able to infer *something* from the mark.

"Well, starting from the very beginning..." Flum went on to give him a brief overview of everything that happened to her: how Jean sold her as a slave, how she met Milkit and gained her fighting abilities thanks to the cursed sword, and about her encounter hunting for medicinal herbs in Anichidey.

Gadhio listened intently, nodding along the whole while.

Finally, Flum reached the end of her saga.

"And that brings us to where we are now."

Gadhio crossed his arms in thought. "So it was Jean, huh? I always knew he was petty and selfish, but I never figured he'd do something like that. He sounds unwell."

"I don't think I'd ever really forgive him, but I guess things did kind of turn out all right for me."

"Because you met her?" Gadhio shot a glance in Milkit's direction as she hustled to prepare breakfast.

"Among other things."

"Other things? Such as?"

"I've come to realize that the reason I was put in the party to take down the Demon Lord at the hands of the church, and by extension, by Origin. I suspect they had something prepared for us if I arrived at the Demon Lord's castle as planned."

"So Jean's egomania spoiled the church's plot?"

"I hate to say it, but it sure looks that way."

Though that didn't mean Flum had any intention of forgiving him. If they ever met again, she'd beat seven shades of it out of him.

"Speaking of which, I guess you were also investigating the church?"

"Aah, yes. Shortly before I left the party, I began to sense there was something going on behind the scenes. I reached out to an acquaintance to gain access to the main cathedral."

"That's pretty impressive."

"I guess you could say it was a bit much."

It must have been an ordeal for a brave and proven warrior like Gadhio to laugh at his own plan like that.

"But you know, that was the fastest way to find out what I wanted to know. In the end, I learned about the history of the Spiral Children and what the church was hiding about them."

"So that's why the eyes were chasing you."

"It must've been from when I uncovered the information about the Children."

"Is the church keeping the stories about the human-demon war under wraps?"

"That, and some things about the demon attacks that happened eight and ten years ago."

"Those were the attacks on Maria and Sara's home-towns."

This reminded Flum that she hadn't asked Gadhio yet about Sara's whereabouts. She desperately wanted to, but she didn't want to interrupt his story.

"I assume you're referring to Sara Anvilen? In which case, yes. I don't know about her situation, but I know Maria despises demons with her heart and soul."

"But if the church was involved...does that mean the demons are innocent?"

"The whole situation was just too convenient for the church. In both cases, the only ones who lived were young children with impressive healing abilities."

"So the church knights were behind it?"

"Obviously there's no record of an attack, but I don't think it would be beneath them."

"So they just faked the whole thing."

"That's one possibility. But Maria was eight years old at the time; she would've been able to differentiate humans from demons."

"That's true. So maybe the demons really were behind it?"

"Or the humans disguised themselves as demons. Regardless of who was the real culprit, I'm certain the church was involved somehow."

"What makes you say that?"

"Maria and Sara weren't the only survivors."

"There were others?"

This was the first Flum had heard of that. In fact, Sara and even Gadhio himself said they were the only survivors.

"The remaining survivors were all pregnant. Across the two incidents, five pregnant women were taken in by the church."

"Pregnant women...?"

"Have you figured it out? The attacks were eight and ten years ago. Which means that the children from these pregnant women would be eight and ten years old."

Children...who were currently eight and ten years old. That left only one option.

"The Spiral Children?"

"Bingo. The church attacked the villages and took pregnant women to use in their experiments, along with the magically inclined children.."

"Was that their goal the whole time, then?"

"Not exactly. Both of the places that were attacked were condemned for heresy by the church."

"So they could achieve three different goals in one fell swoop."

There was still one major sticking point in all this for Flum.

"But why blame it on the demons, then? Couldn't they have just said a giant monster laid waste to the villages or something?"

Large monsters destroying entire villages was hardly common, but it wasn't rare either.

Were they just trying to build up the people's hatred for the demons by pinning the blame on them? Anti-demon rhetoric wasn't hard to come by in the church.

"I dug up a little on that during my visit."

Flum couldn't help but wonder just how deep he went to get his hands on such detailed records. Whatever he found, it was probably so secret that he would have been killed on sight had he been discovered.

As she listened to his story, Flum was once again impressed by just how immensely talented he was, to say nothing of Eterna and her ability to step in and save Ink's life. She hardly felt worthy of the title of "hero."

"Around fifty years or so ago, the previous king became an ardent follower of the church of Origin. Right around that time, we started to see stories of all these evil acts carried out by demons appear in the capital and its surrounds."

"Stories? You mean like fairy tales and plays? Why would they do something like that?"

"I don't know why, but in any case, the image of demons being equated with all that was evil spread among the populace for the next twenty years, which ultimately resulted in the human-demon war. In fact, the current king may be plotting a second war as we speak."

"So that's why they made the demons the scapegoats for those attacks. But wouldn't that mean the human-demon war was some plot cooked up by the church as well? I remember being taught that it was the demons who attacked us first."

"You'd be correct."

Flum's cheek twitched slightly at this. "I guess it's pretty easy to twist history to your will then, isn't it?"

"The church couldn't do it on their own. The kingdom helps to manipulate information for them. It's far from easy but certainly not impossible. Ultimately, the humans were in the wrong, and the demons were right. What's worse, we lost and came running back home. Alas, that story didn't fit their narrative, so obviously the people in power wanted to wipe it from history."

She suddenly recalled what Neigass, one of the Demon Chiefs, told her back in the cave outside Anichidey.

When referring to the human-demon war, she specifically mentioned that humans invaded their lands. Assuming that was true, then her statement that demons never killed any humans may very well also be true.

It was almost mind-blowing to consider that the demons were more trustworthy than the church.

She let out a sigh.

"There's something else that they were hiding about the war as well."

"There's more?"

"Oh, there's so much more. But with regard to the human-demon war, I learned that the demons placed one condition on humans after their loss. Do you know what that was?"

"I know it wasn't land...so money or resources, maybe?"

"In most normal wars that would be the answer. But that wasn't the case with the demons. All they asked was that neither side ever raise arms against the other again. Essentially, they wanted a peace treaty."

The gap between the war-like demons she was raised to believe in and the people suing for nothing but peace was so great that Flum almost felt as if the world were spinning.

The humans really were the villains then, weren't they? That was the only explanation the facts supported. They brought war against a neighboring nation, refused to accept they were wrong even after losing, and then went so far as to hide the truth.

"Is that treaty still in effect?"

"It should be."

"So that means Cyrill...well, not just her, but the whole party was violating that treaty?"

It was the obvious question.

Gadhio let out a cynical laugh. "The rest of this is just my own thoughts, so I can't say for sure whether or not there's any truth behind it or not."

"That's fine by me. I want to hear what you think."

"The party was made up of civilians—hence why we were able to just give up on the journey at will."

"That's true."

They all came from different backgrounds and social classes, with little that actually tied them all together. Gadhio and Linus were both S-Rank adventurers, Jean was a renowned genius, and Eterna was a magician they'd turned up in the sticks.

"Which means they were likely plotting to set us up as a private organization operating out of a sense of righteous indignation. The kingdom would bear no blame for the actions of a band of random civilians."

"That's...that's stupid!"

"Obviously the demons weren't so easily fooled, either. However, the government continued to insist that they had nothing to do with this group of people and that it wasn't in violation of their promise to the demons.

I believe this is what gave rise to the creation of the Demon Chiefs. They were created as a sort of counter to the hero party."

Flum was at a complete loss for words.

That would mean that the humans were entirely to blame for the demons' recent attacks. In fact, the demons were still being incredibly kind, between the mercy they'd shown in their skirmishes with humanity and their restraint in not wiping the kingdom from the map.

What's more, what the demons lacked in sheer population, they more than made up for it in their impressive strength. Were they so inclined, they could easily lay waste to the kingdom.

Yet they chose not to. In fact, they avoided killing or even harming any humans.

Even in the face of the fact that the humans had dispatched a party to slay the Demon Lord, they still only fought back to the minimum extent possible. All the while, humanity took advantage of their goodwill and set their own plots into motion.

It was absolutely wretched.

"Why do they hate the demons so much?"

"The simplest explanation is that they just want their land, though that doesn't really fly considering the risk involved. The real question is, what happened fifty years ago that turned the previous king to Origin's teachings and his campaign against demonkind, and why is the current king sustaining that? The only way we'll ever get answers to these questions is by cutting the church open and looking inside."

So this was all the church's scheme the whole time. If they wanted to know the truth, Flum would have to risk not only the past and future of her own kingdom, but her own life itself in order to dig deep into this mystery.

Even with Eterna and Gadhio at her side, the challenge was immense, but she couldn't just stand idly by and not do everything in her power to blow this conspiracy out into the open.

"There's no sense in thinking too hard about it at the moment. For now, all we can do is gather what information about the church we can."

"It's all so frustrating."

"Hold on to that feeling. Let it drive you forward."

Just as the conversation was winding down, Milkit started setting the table. She set up four places at the table, with Ink's food put aside for her in the kitchen.

"Well, why don't we leave it there for now and get down to breakfast?"

"Wait, there's still one thing I forgot to ask you about!"

"What's that?"

Now that Gadhio's story was tentatively finished, Flum finally had a chance to ask something that'd been nagging at her the whole time.

"Where's Sara?"

"Aah...that girl?" Gadhio scowled slightly.

It was a strange response, especially considering that he said she was fine earlier. A feeling of uncertainty began to well up inside her heart.

"Is she with someone?"

"Yes."

"An acquaintance of yours?"

"Not exactly, no. Though I have spoken with them before."

He was being uncharacteristically vague about all this. Who could Sara be with that he'd be so hesitant to discuss it with her? Flum decided to press one more time.

"No matter what's happened to Sara, I promise you that I'll be able to come to terms with it. Please, Gadhio, just tell me what you know."

"She's fine, really. She's not hurt or sick, and she's in safe keeping. The thing is, the person she's with is..."

"Who?"

Gadhio crossed his arms and paused. After a moment of silence, he finally let out a sigh.

"Neigass, the Demon Chief."

It was the last name Flum ever expected to hear.

"Whaaaaat?!"

Milkit immediately tensed up at Flum's unexpected outburst, and the plate in her hand dropped with a loud clatter, sending a lone sausage rolling across the table.

Eterna Is as Eterna Does

FLUM SLOWLY REMOVED Milkit's bandages and praised her young companion's beauty, causing Milkit to break out into a deep blush yet again.

They put on their pajamas, picked a bed to curl up in, and cheerfully chatted away well into the night.

This was their nightly ritual. Though it carried no special meaning in particular, it was still a high point of their day.

From time to time, however, there was a brief break in their routine.

"You know, I found this in the dresser the other day." Milkit picked a wooden stick up off the desk. It was curved slightly on one end and had a soft cotton ball on the other—an ear pick.

"Now that you mention it, I totally forgot to buy one of those."

"I'm always trying to think of ways about how I can be a good slave to you, Master, and make sure you're as content as you can be."

"I'd say things are just about perfect as is, Milkit."

"No, not at all, Master. It's a slave's job to make sure their master is as happy as possible."

"I dunno, Milkit. I'm pretty happy, y'know."

Flum propped herself up on an elbow and reached out to Milkit's place at the edge of the bed to stroke her cheek. Milkit's expression softened ever so slightly at her master's touch.

"You're too kind, Master."

"That's what Eterna says, too. But honestly, I'd love to spoil you even more, Milkit."

"I think I feel much the same, Master. I wish that there was more that I could do for you. So...so I was thinking this might help."

"An ear pick?"

"Right, I was thinking that cleaning your ears is an appropriate way to serve one's master."

"And where'd you hear something like that?"

"It's just my own impression, really." Milkit looked down, an embarrassed expression on her face.

As far as Flum could figure, Milkit was just looking for an in to clean her ears.

"I can't remember the last time I've had someone clean my ears for me."

"You've had it done before?"

"By my mom, when I was a really little kid. Y'know, now that I think about it, you have to rest your head in someone's lap when you get your ears cleaned, yeah?"

"That's right. Any time you're ready, Master." Milkit gently patted her lap.

Flum slowly laid down on her side and rested her head in Milkit's lap. It was about as embarrassing as she thought it would be.

I can feel my cheeks burning...

Were Eterna to see them now, she'd no doubt make some flippant remark about how they were usually doing much more than this.

This was the first time that Flum actually used someone's thighs for a pillow. There was just no way she could do this and not be embarrassed.

Milkit seemed to be feeling much the same way.

There was a fine distinction between their ideas of a slave's duty to their master. All the same, it was only a minor problem for Milkit: she enjoyed the feeling of Flum's head on her lap and the ability to tilt her face around and inspect her master from every angle.

"Can you see anything?"

"Yes, I can. Your ears are quite clean already, Master."

"Oh yeah? It's been quite a while since I actually paid them any attention..."

"No need to worry, I'll take care of the rest."

Flum laughed. "Well, I guess I'm lucky to see what you're really made of, Milkit."

Milkit gently slid the tip of the ear pick into Flum's ear. "Nng..."

"Did I hurt you, Mas..."

SLAM!

"...ter?"

Milkit was interrupted by a loud crash coming from the other room.

"That was pretty loud. I wonder if Eterna dropped something."

"I suppose so."

"Anyway, I was just surprised by the sound, Milkit. You can get back to it."

"I've never done this before, though. I'm not sure how deep to go..."

"You can keep going deeper."

"All right then, I'll go a little further."

Milkit was still being far too cautious. It felt a lot more like she was tickling Flum's inner ear than doing any form of cleaning.

Milkit giggled lightly to herself. "This is actually pretty fun."

"I'm enjoying it, too, but you could be a little rougher, ya know? It just kinda tickles, really."

"Are you sure? I'm a little scared..."

"I know, but we won't get anywhere like that."

"Hmm, it's hard to make sure I'm using the right amount of pressure..."

Slowly but surely, Milkit seemed to get the technique down and started to scrape away all the wax from Flum's ear.

Flum narrowed her eyes and smiled. "Mmm, that feels great."

"Am I doing all right? It's hard for me to tell how it feels for you, Master."

"Oh, yeah, it feels really good. But I think it'd be even better if you'd just go a little deeper..."

SLAM!

There was another loud bang from Eterna's room.

Flum and Milkit both tensed up immediately. It was a miracle that Flum's ear wasn't hurt from the sudden movement.

"Whoa, that was close!"

"Are you okay, Master??"

"Yeah, I'm fine. I just wonder what's going on with Eterna."

"Should we go check on her?"

"Nah, she'd let us know if she needed any help. She's probably just carrying out an experiment."

"At such a late hour, while Ink's sleeping nearby?"

"Hmm, let's give it a bit longer and see if anything else happens."

The two put aside Eterna's odd noises for the moment and went back to the ear cleaning.

Milkit turned the ear pick in her hand and brought the fluffy cotton ball near Flum's ear. "All right now, time to clean it out."

Flum tried to stifle her giggles. "Th-that...hee...that tickles. Especially when someone else is doing it."

"It seems like your ears are a bit of a weak point for you, Master."

"Yeah, my friends always used to tease me by playing with them."

"I think I can see where they were coming from."

"Now don't tell me that you're coming to find your naughty side, Milkit..."

"I-I don't mean to tease you, of course."

"You're a good kid, Milkit. It couldn't hurt to tease people a bit. I'd let you do it, at least."

"Well, I won't."

Flum instantly broke out in a fit of laughter as Milkit

started to delicately rotate the cotton ball against her inner ear. "C-cut it out! Th-that tickles!!"

Milkit's skillful attack reduced her to a fit of giggles. She could barely get a word out between her laughs.

"Hey! Hehee... Y-you're...hee...you're doing this on... tee hee...purpose!"

"Of course not. This is just what I have to do in order to properly clean your ears, Master. I'm absolutely not enjoying the sight of you..." Milkit's cheeks were a bright pink and her breathing ragged.

There was something impish about the look in her eyes as she lost herself in relentlessly teasing her master.

THUD!

More clamor from elsewhere in the house finally brought her back to reality.

"Gaaah...!"

Flum sat up in an instant. Obviously they couldn't ignore the commotion any more.

The two sat tensely on the bed for a moment as they stared at the door. They turned to exchange a curious glance.

"That was Eterna just now, right?"

"I believe so, yes."

"It sounded like she dropped something and then cried out in pain."

"That's what I heard, too. Maybe we should go check it out."

"I think that might be best."

"I'll be right back."

"I'll go with you!"

"You can't leave the room without your bandages, though, remember? I know Eterna's seen you before, but... well, I don't want other people to see you."

"Master..." Milkit clenched her hands tightly in front of her chest. The feeling rushing through her was beyond anything she'd ever felt before, something that couldn't fit into her familiar slave-and-master framework.

"Understood. I'll wait here, then."

Flum shot a smile Milkit's way before going to check in on Eterna.

She stood outside the door for a moment to listen for any other noises but heard nothing from inside. It was almost too quiet.

Putting her ear up against the door, she listened closely for the sound of Ink snoring, or Eterna flipping the pages of one of her books, but all she was met with was silence.

Which could only mean one thing: that they were being intentionally quiet.

"What kind of stupid games are they up to..." She figured it'd be faster to just ask and knocked.

"Eternaaaa!"

No reply. But no matter, she already knew they were awake.

"I'm coming in!" She didn't bother to wait for a reply before stepping inside.

Inside, she found Eterna with a pained expression on her face and her hand clasped tightly over Ink's mouth.

"Just what are you up to, Eterna?"

"Funny, I was going to ask you the same thing." Eterna's face was flushed. "Listen, I knew you two were way too close at times, and I'm not going to say there's anything wrong with what you were doing, but you really should think twice about being so loud when Ink's still awake."

"Mmph! Mmmmphmmm!"

Ink's response was unintelligible. Finally Eterna took her hand away, realizing just how tightly it was clasped over Ink's mouth.

"Haaaaah! Finally, free. Why'd you do that? You scared me! 'Sides, I was still asleep until you dropped your book."

"That's...well, that's irrelevant right now. In any case, I really don't want to hear that kinda thing."

"What are you going on about, Eterna?"

"You know...that! The things that slaves do with their masters! That stuff!"

"That stuff...?" Milkit had been cleaning Flum's ears.

It seemed a bit odd for that to be what people thought slaves and masters did together. Flum thought it over but kept coming up blank. "I'm sorry, Eterna, but I have absolutely no clue what you're going on about. Could you just tell me?"

"Tell you?! Right here, in front of Ink? I can't do that! And I figured you'd at least know that, Flum!"

"Is it so bad you can't say it in front of Ink?"

"She's a ten-year-old girl! It's a tad early for that kinda thing!"

"Really? I think it's a pretty common thing to do with kids. My mom and I used to do it all the time."

"Your mother??!"

"What's so surprising?"

"Ohmygod... Well, I guess that explains how your morals ended up so out of whack."

"Look, this has nothing to do with morals. Milkit and I were just..."

Eterna quickly slapped her hands over Ink's ears before Flum could finish her sentence.

"I can't heeeear agaaaaain." Ink looked surprised but didn't object.

"Listen, I get that Milkit has a slightly...skewed outlook on the world—that's just because of the environment she grew up in—but I figured you'd have a little common sense, Flum. Was that some sort of custom back in your village?"

"No, I think that's pretty normal for most people, to be honest."

"Of course someone who was raised in an environment like that would feel that way."

"I think you're blowing this just a tad out of proportion, no?"

"You need to show some self-control, Flum. I mean, I guess I get it at your age, but Milkit's so young."

"I don't think age has anything to do with it, really. Besides, it wasn't me doing it, it was Milkit."

"You mean Milkit was the one being assertive here? And you were taking it?"

"Well, she found this item in the closet and suggested we try it out."

"And now you guys are using items, too? And you found it right here in this house, no less!"

"Are you serious right now? I have no idea what you're even talking about!" The more Flum tried to explain, the more bent out of shape Eterna seemed to get. "I think you're misunderstanding something here."

"Me? Misunderstanding? Oh no, I heard it all, Flum."

"I guess the conversation carried down the hall. But I still think you misunderstood what we were talking about."

Flum quickly ran over what she and Milkit discussed in her mind, but nothing seemed to stand out. She had absolutely no idea what bizarre story Eterna was making up in her head.

"Well, first Milkit took a look at your...well, you know, and said how pretty it was," Eterna said.

"I think she was just being polite. Besides, I haven't really been paying much attention to it lately. I really should do these things regularly."

"Regularly??"

"Is it really that surprising? I mean, I guess you could just do it from time to time, too."

"It's like we're from different worlds here, Flum! But I guess you did say something about it being awhile. I don't remember anything about you not doing it often, though."

"You don't do it at all, Eterna?"

"I, well... I've no one to do it with."

"Can't you do it alone?"

"W-well, of course you can."

"I mean, why don't you help Ink out and do it for her?"

"Are you trying to get me arrested, Flum??"

"Why would they do that?!"

For the first time since they met, Eterna felt honestly afraid of Flum. She could only imagine the bizarre, twisted rituals conducted in her small village of Patolia, off to the south of the capital.

"Well, after that, Milkit was worried about not having any experience and I heard you telling her to put it in deeper."

"I mean, it's tough to do it for someone else. You don't really know where's the right spot or how much pressure to use. Everyone's different, y'know."

"How should I know? I don't have any experience with stuff like that!"

"Well then, why don't you try it on me sometime?"

"Whoa, hey, now that's a pretty sudden offer."

"With how skillful you are with magic, I'm sure you'd be good at it."

"I don't know how you got that impression."

"With your water magic, you could probably finish pretty quick, too."

"I don't *want* to know where that idea came from." Eterna gave Flum a long look, halfway between astonishment and horror.

As far as Flum was concerned, she was having a completely normal conversation. She couldn't figure out why Eterna was looking at her like that.

"Hmm, it might be a bit hard to do anything for you this late in the game, but as the only resident adult here,

I can't just turn my back on you, Flum. With the right medicine and some light counseling, I might be able to set you on the right path..."

"Just what're you talking about, Eterna?? You've been going on like this for a while now!"

"I'd like to say the same, I'd think! I don't know what kind of environment you grew up in, Flum, but none of this is right. You've gotta show a little bit of moderation—the tiniest sense of virtue—here, ya know."

"Sense of virtue?" Flum cocked her head to the side at the sudden change in topic. Where did that come from?

Finally Ink butted in. Even with her ears covered, she was still able to pick out what everyone had been talking about. "Don't you think you're overreacting to ear cleaning just a bit, Eterna?"

"Ear...cleaning?"

"Yup. I have no idea why you're going on about virtue and all that, but I don't think it has anything to do with ears, at least not last I checked."

"Oh...oh! Ears, right." Eterna mumbled the words over and over to herself as she tried to put the whole conversation back into perspective. "Cleaning ears...yeah...I guess if you put it that way it makes sense...but still, it seems off... Nah, must've been. They had to've been talking about that...and yet I took it differently..."

She continued to mutter for some time, trying to convince herself. In time, her expression once again went blank, and her gaze fixed on something in the distance. Eterna let go of Ink and walked uneasily past Flum before diving into her bed and curling up.

In a matter of seconds, she was apparently asleep.

"Eterna?"

Eterna only replied with a loud, exaggerated snore. Flum wasn't about to give up that easily. She leaned in close and called her name several times. "Eteeeeeerna?"

Eterna kept up her dramatic snoring.

"Listen, I don't know what you thought was going on, but I promise I'm just going to let it drop and pretend nothing happened, okay?" Flum's face flushed red as it finally dawned on her what Eterna had been thinking. "Milkit and I haven't done anything like *that* yet, okay?!"

Her face covered in a mix of embarrassment and indignation, Flum stepped angrily out of the room.

Ink still wasn't exactly sure what happened. With a loud yawn, she crawled into bed next to Eterna. This was the first time they'd shared a bed in quite some time.

"Hey, Eterna..."

Eterna had given up on pretending to be asleep by now. "Yes?"

"I don't really know what Flum meant by 'haven't done anything like *that*,' but what do you think the 'yet' part meant? Do you think they plan to?"

It was an innocent, and yet very perceptive, question.

"I don't know if they realize it or not, but I think it's just a matter of time."

"Huh. Well, I guess I'll figure out what it means eventually, then."

Eterna slowly closed her eyes again. Perhaps it was best that Ink not figure it out for some time.

Afterword

HELLO, THIS IS KIKI, the author of *Roll Over and Die: I Will Fight for an Ordinary Life with My Love and Cursed Sword*. Thanks for picking up the second volume in the series.

In this second volume, I was hoping to tell a full-throttle story full of lesbian romance with just a hint of horror right from the cover. I hope it worked out that way.

There is one thing I'd like to say, though: the slow life is all over now.

I'm sure even those of you who were expecting the change of pace may have found yourselves in for a shock at some of the pictures in the middle of the book. Don't worry—I felt exactly the same way. I've been referring to this volume as "Ink's story" in my own head, but what do you think? Does it fit?

I made a lot of revisions and additions to the version of Chapter 003 that appeared online, which has led to the final version you see here. The web version ended at Chapter 010, but in addition to all the little sentence tweaks and the major revision to Chapter 003, I'm pretty sure even those who read all the way through the online version of the story will still have a few surprises waiting for them. Just know that I'm working hard to make sure *Roll Over and Die* will be an exciting new experience for all readers—both those who've never experienced the series before and those who already read through it online.

By the time this book hits the book shelves, I believe the manga adaptation will have already been announced. Sunao Minakata, the author in charge of the manga, has done an absolutely stunning job blending cuteness with action in the art. I've actually known of Sunao's work for several years now after a friend introduced me to a manga being serialized in a popular lesbian romance manga magazine. It's an absolute shock to me that they would be in charge of turning my story into a manga. I guess you just really don't know where life will take you, huh?

To be honest, I still don't really believe that this is all happening. Between the volume of the manga I'm looking at, right here in my hand, and Kinta's excellent character designs...it's all too much. My mind is a whirl-wind of thoughts lately: "Is this really my book?" "I wonder if this is all really okay..." "Am I going to die to-morrow??" "...Wait, am I already dead?" "Did I die and go to a land of lesbian fantasy romance?"

Sorry, that last one's not true. Men aren't allowed in these mythical lands of lesbian romance, and I suspect I'd be decontaminated right at the entrance.

Once again, it's really, really hard to write an after-word. For some reason, it takes a lot longer than writing chapters of an equivalent length. After looking around online to see what other authors write in these things, I'm at least relieved to see I'm not the only one struggling.

I guess my only real option is to go with the tried-and-true approach of letting the characters talk for themselves and throw myself into the conversation.

ETERNA: "Hi, I'm Eterna Rinebow. I was rudely called in here on short notice."

INK: "I dunno, this seems kinda fun! Nice to meet ya, I'm Ink Wreathcraft!"

AUTHOR: "And it's me, ki..."

Okay, never mind, that was awful. Just writing these three lines was painful enough. I can only imagine the amount of mental fortitude it must take for an author to carry on conversations with their characters.

Maybe someday I'll get good enough to do that. Like in my next life, maybe.

Lastly, I'd like to take an opportunity to thank those who helped bring this book together.

Kinta, you truly are amazing, and your work on all the additional character designs is greatly appreciated. I always found myself completely blown away by each new character design or book insert. Thank you for your excellent work.

To my editor—thank you for your immense patience with all the annoying little problems I caused and the massive increase in word count over volume one. You've been an immense help, and I don't think I could have done it without you.

And of course, there are the many other people working in publishing and you, my dear readers, who also deserve a lot of credit for making this book a reality. I truly am in your debt.

I hope you stick around for the continuation of Flum's exciting adventure!